A PIECE OF THE SKY IS MISSING

David Nobbs was born in Orpington and educated at Marlborough, Cambridge and in the Royal Corps of Signals. His first job was as a reporter on the *Sheffield Star*, and his first break as a comedy writer came on the iconic satire show *That Was The Week, That Was*, hosted by David Frost. Later he wrote for *The Frost Report* and *The Two Ronnies* and provided material for many top comedians including Les Dawson, Ken Dodd, Tommy Cooper, Frankie Howerd and Dick Emery. David is best known for his two TV hit series *A Bit of a Do* and for *The Fall and Rise of Reginald Perrin*, now revived in a contemporary version, starring Martin Clunes. He lives in North Yorkshire with his second wife, Susan. He has four stepchildren, eight grand-stepchildren and one great-grand-stepchild.

Praise for David Nobbs's novels:

'Painfully hilarious, wonderfully observed and slight sour at the same time'   *Guardian*

'Thank goodness for David Nobbs! He carries on the comic tradition of P G Wodehouse with this marvellous new book; a sweet and touching love story written with his trademark sly and subversive humour. A perfect antidote to these dark times'   JOANNE HARRIS

'Probably our finest post-war comic novelist'   JONATHAN COE

'A marvellously comic novel'   *Sunday Times*

'One of the most noisily funny books I have ever read' MICHAEL PALIN

'Very funny sketches of provincial newspaper life'   SUE TOWNSEND

'The most satisfying novel I have read in years'   *Express*

Also by David Nobbs

Obstacles to Young Love
The Itinerant Lodger
Ostrich Country

DAVID NOBBS

A Piece of the Sky is Missing

HARPER

Harper
An imprint of HarperCollins*Publishers*
77–85 Fulham Palace Road,
Hammersmith, London w6 8jb

www.harpercollins.co.uk

This paperback edition 2010

First published in Great Britain by
Methuen & Co Ltd 1969

The Author and the Publishers are committed to respecting the intellectual property rights of others
and have made all reasonable efforts to trace the copyright owners of the text, artwork and other
copyright materials reproduced, and to provide an appropriate acknowledgement in the book.

In the event that any of the untraceable copyright owners come forward after the publication of this
book, the Author and the Publishers will use all reasonable endeavours to rectify the position accordingly.

David Nobbs asserts the moral right to
be identified as the author of this work

A catalogue record for this book is
available from the British Library

ISBN: 978 0 00 742784 0

Typeset in Garamond by Palimpsest Book Production Limited,
Falkirk, Stirlingshire

Find out more about HarperCollins and the environment at
www.harpercollins.co.uk/green

Contents

1 A Joke Misfires

The caricature began to take shape. He drew with confident if unprofessional strokes. The forehead, redolent of drab efficiency and solemnity. The long nose, absurdly elongated. The concavity of the chin, grotesquely exaggerated. The humourless weakness of the mouth, cruelly exposed. The hint of underlying effeminacy, broadened into a positively offensive suggestion. Here was an executive with a role to play in an expanding Britain. Here was a bachelor over-fond of his mother. Here, on the rough gravelly wall, was Tadman-Evans.

Robert was pleased with his work. He added Tadman-Evans's telephone number, pulled the chain, and left the non-executive gents.

On his way out into the corridor he met Martin Edwards, a non-executive. Martin Edwards smiled at him and said: 'Been demoted, have you?'

'Ours are full,' said Robert.

Later that Friday morning he met Tadman-Evans in the executive gents and found that the caricature had drained him of dislike. The man's combination of efficiency and effeminacy no longer got him on the raw. Tadman-Evans smiled, not yet having heard about the caricature. Robert felt ashamed.

The executive gents, like the non-executive gents, had a blue ceiling and blue doors. But here there were individual bars of soap, not a swivelling bulbous container jammed solid with yellow goo. And here the wall was smooth, and somehow less inviting to caricature.

In both the executive and the non-executive ladies the ceilings and doors were pink. Robert knew this, having been in them several times, by mistake and out of bravado. Once, for a bet, he had used the ladies for a week. That hadn't gone down too well at Cadman and Bentwhistle Ltd. Nor would his caricature.

He thought: 'I'll wash it off.' But Herr Muller was waiting, to eat lunch and talk pumping equipment, and he didn't wash it off.

As he passed the end of the typing pool that evening Rosie giggled. It's got around, he thought.

On Monday morning up-and-coming £2,500-a-year thirty-two-year-old executive Robert Bellamy arrived at Cadman and Bentwhistle Ltd. promptly at nine o'clock. Five foot eleven, beginning to look prosperous and well-fed, handsome, with red hair, blue eyes, a straight slender nose, delicate well-shaped lips, light skin, freckled in summer. An unusual combination of masculinity and softness in his face. Popular with the girls of the typing pool. But nervous now. Caught in the same lift as Tadman-Evans. Avoiding his eye.

The lift smelt of damp coats this wet November morning. They were crowded into it, fifteen of them, the maximum permitted by Messrs Melrose and Oxley of Middlesbrough. He must show that he wasn't cowed by the situation.

'Second floor. Accounts, vouchers, canteen and lingerie,' he said. Rosie giggled. No-one else smiled. Couldn't expect them to. It wasn't worth it.

He left the lift at the third floor. As he walked past the end of the typing pool he said: ''Morning, girls.'

''Morning, Mr Bellamy', in tones that intimated: 'Oh, you are a one'. Robert felt himself to be on their side in an endless, unacknowledged battle. He spoke clearly into the dictaphone, didn't demand the impossible, bought them chocolates after he had lost his temper, and always kissed them at the Christmas party, not lecherously, like Wallis, or jocularly, like Perrin, or officially, like Tadman-Evans, but affectionately, because he liked them and wished life held more for them.

At the last Christmas party he had given Wallis a black eye. Things had been rather fraught in 'Europe' after that.

He entered 'Europe'. In the outer office sat Julie.

''Morning, Julie,' he said.

''Morning, Mr Bellamy,' said Julie.

Every day he worked on her, so that by five-thirty she was calling him Robert. But every morning she called him Mr Bellamy again.

'Sir John wants to see you at ten,' said Julie.

Damn. No chance of pretending it wasn't his work. His style was well-known, his doodles notorious. Sir John himself had never quite forgiven a portrait that had appeared five years ago on an official report about circular saws.

Robert gazed out over the friendly inelegant skyline. He could just see St Paul's among the office blocks. It was still almost dark, as if the weekend was reluctant to let go. The next reorganization was just beginning. Soon he'd get a new office, his sixth in eight years. The moment one reorganization ended, the next began. There were people whose only job it was to plan them. Soon all the internal walls would be knocked down, new internal walls would be knocked up, and everything would go on exactly as before. And once again the typing pool wouldn't get a room. They'd get the bit in the middle that was left over when all the rooms had been planned. And there they would sit, like a cargo of rotting bananas in the stuffy, airless hold.

Tadman-Evans didn't call them reorganizations. He called them rationalizations.

Punctually at ten Senior European Sales Officer Robert Bellamy, thirty-two, presented himself at Sir John's office. With each reorganization his title changed. He had been European Sales Liaison Officer, European Area Demonstration Consultant, European Technical Sales Adviser. The job always remained the same. He sent technical information to European agents and firms. He made visits to demonstrate and sell their machines. His judgement might be instrumental in fixing a new price for a machine, or in deciding how many of a certain line

3

they should make. It was a responsible job. He did it, he thought, quite well.

'Sit down, Robert,' said Sir John Barker.

He sat down.

'Well, how's tricks?' said Sir John genially.

'Not bad, thank you.'

Sir John's cordiality alarmed him.

'Still not – you know – thought of taking the plunge?' said Sir John.

Impertinent bastard. Absolute knighthood corrupts absolutely.

'No.'

'Nice girl, Stella.'

Sir John had met Sonia twice, once by chance in a pub near the Hog's Back and once at a party given to drink away the profits of Europe's bumper sales year in 1962. Suddenly it came to Robert that he ought to marry Sonia. Desire for her flooded over him, taking him by surprise. Help. Press the legs inward. Ouch. Hope he hasn't noticed. Pretty hard to fool Sir John, from all accounts, where genitalia are concerned.

'I believe you're having a course of – er – er —'

'Analysis. Yes, sir.'

Sir John wanted to say 'Why?' but was too much of a gentleman to do so. He tried so hard to be ruthless, but his manners were too good for him. He'd been to Winchester.

'I hope nothing's – er – er —' said Sir John.

'Wrong. No, nothing's wrong. In fact, I'm intending to give it up,' said Robert.

'Good. Glad to hear it. As you know, Robert, I've always been a bit worried about your – shall we say your – er —'

'Quick temper.'

'Exactly. You're high spirited. Emotional. Say what you think. Good thing, too. Far too little straightforwardness around, I often think.' Sir John leant forward very seriously. 'You've done some excellent work for us, Robert. Excellent.

4

And that's a quality we value very highly at C and B. But, Robert. But . . .' and Sir John paused.

'Well, thank you,' said Robert.

'I'd be the first to admit that you have great charm. Great charm, Robert. First to admit it. I like you very much as a . . . a chap. Which, heaven knows, you are. And a jolly good one. But in a big, highly competitive organization like ours there have to be certain ways of doing things, certain ways in which certain things for certain reasons always have been done and always will be done and always should be done. You do at times tend to be slightly – shall we say – er —'

'Unconventional.'

'Exactly. A fine quality, mind you. A fine quality. And you get on jolly well with those Europeans. I appreciate that. Some of our chaps are so insular, so narrow. They haven't your culture, your flair, your vision. They're at a premium, Robert, qualities like that. At a premium. And you have them.'

It was going to be the sack. Robert knew it.

'God dammit, I don't want everybody to be conformists. Far too many conformists about. But the fact remains, Robert. The fact remains.' Sir John let out a deep sigh, forcing himself to be more ruthless still. 'You may not see a good reason why there should be a distinction between the executive and non-executive – er – er —'

'Loo.'

'Exactly. Washroom. Nevertheless, that is the C and B system. Everyone's happier that way. And we're a team here, Robert. We must all pull together.'

'And I pulled the wrong chain.'

'Exactly. You pulled . . . oh, I see.'

'I suppose the executives might get V.D. if they used the non-executive bogs.'

'Really, Robert, there's no need to be so – er —'

'Vulgar.'

5

'Exactly. You do have a way of picking the – er —'

'*Mot juste.*'

'Exactly. But, Robert, there is a time and a place for everything. And the time for talking about – er —'

'Bogs and V.D. is not in your office.'

'Exactly. I'm glad you understand it so well. Not that I thought you wouldn't. You're highly intelligent. Highly. And you have a sense of humour, too. A quality sadly lacking at C and B. Mind you, you have – er —'

'Gone a bit far on occasions.'

'Exactly. Exactly. Can't overlook the odd managerial black eye entirely. Failing in my duty if I did. But to turn to this – er – caricature in the non-executive – er – washroom. Quite amusing, in its way, I grant you that. I inspected it and I must admit I had a little chuckle. Quite the talk of the – er – non-executive canteen. But, Robert. But . . .'

'Yes, sir.'

'I understand why you did this. Not as unimaginative as I look. I understand that there was genuine irritation behind this, genuine dislike of the – er —'

'Petty class distinctions.'

'Of industrial life. Exactly. I'm aware that you aren't just striving for cheap popularity on the shop floor. But nevertheless, nevertheless, Robert, that is the effect. To make you popular – though not necessarily respected – and to make Tadman-Evans look ridiculous. And you know it was somewhat gratuitous to use his real telephone number. He had fourteen calls over the weekend.'

'I'm sorry, sir.'

'So under the circumstances I really feel that I have no – er – er —'

'Alternative.'

'Exactly. No hard feelings, eh?'

'Well, sir, no.'

Sir John stood up. The interview was over.

'Glad you're taking it like this. I quite thought I might end up with a black eye. Amuse Lady Barker no end. Huh.'

Sir John extended his hand. Robert took it.

'Well, Robert, there it is.'

'Yes, sir.'

'There it is.'

'Yes, sir.'

Sir John let go of Robert's hand.

'There it is.'

'Yes, sir.'

Robert made his way to the door.

'Good luck,' said Sir John Barker.

He walked slowly back to his office. Oh, well, what did it matter? It was time he left anyway. Twelve years was too long with one firm. This was an opportunity, not a setback.

'Nothing wrong, Mr Bellamy, is there?' said Julie.

'No, Julie. Nothing wrong.'

'Oh, it wasn't . . .'

'The sack. Yes, I rather think it must have been.'

'Oh, Robert.'

2 A London Night

Robert had first met Sonia twelve years previously, in the early December of 1955, at a party given by a friend of a friend of Doreen's. Doreen shared with Brenda the room above Robert's, at number 38. They were Yorkshire girls, from Dewsbury. They knew of every party within a six-mile radius of Kentish Town. They were waiting for the arrival of Mr Right. They liked Robert, and often dragged him off to parties, even though he wasn't Mr Right.

Shortly after their arrival at the party, Robert found himself all alone. He took a second glass of the punch and drank it rapidly. He was twenty. He had just started at Cadman and Bentwhistle. He had never had a girl, and believed that this fact was written on his face. All the girls in the typing pool knew, and he hated it when he had to walk through the typing pool.

The room was dimly-lit, red, stripped for action, crowded. God, I hate parties, he thought.

A girl came in, apparently on her own. He made to move towards her, decided against it, decided in favour of it, did so, said: 'Can I get you something to drink?'

'Thank you,' she said, in a confident upper-class voice.

He fished two butt ends out of the punchbowl and poured out two glasses.

'What is it?' she said.

'Revolting,' he said. 'What's your name?'

'Polly.'

'I'm the Maharajah of Inverness.' She laughed, embarrassingly loudly. 'My real name's Robert,' he said.

'What do you do?'

'I work in a firm that makes instruments.'

'What sort of instruments?'

8

'All sorts. Just instruments.'

'Why aren't you at the university? You aren't thick, are you?'

'No. I didn't fancy it. I wanted to get out into the real world, and do some work.' How incredibly pompous. Any minute now she would go. He didn't want her to go. She was attractive. Dumpy, half-way towards being fat, with big breasts. Her nose was squashed, her mouth big and lazy. She was sexy in the way that Christmas pudding was appetizing. 'I'm sorry. That sounds rather pompous,' he said.

'Not particularly.'

'I've been in the army. National Service.' How utterly boring. 'One day, when we're married, I shall tell you my amusing experiences.' How ludicrously twittish and coy.

'Were you an officer?'

'God, no,' he said, making a face – rather an effective face, he thought. He had been to a public school. His parents had been well off. He hated privilege and rank.

'Daddy's an admiral,' she said.

'Oh, really?'

'Yes.'

She still hadn't gone.

'What do you do?'

'I paint.'

'I'd love to come and see your pictures.'

She chortled, embarrassingly loudly for a chortle, though not as loudly as her laugh.

'I've heard that before,' she said. 'You want to get me alone in my room.'

'Can't anyone be interested in you and your work without being accused of being a sex maniac?' he said. She would like that. She would begin to realize that he wasn't just like all the others, that he had finer feelings.

'Excuse me, there's Bernie,' she said.

He wandered into the kitchen, slowly, trying to look both

9

calm and purposeful. There was still a little punch left. He fished out a cigar and poured two glasses. A very drunk man asked him if he was of Rumanian extraction. He said he wasn't. The drunk accused him of being a liar. He pushed the drunk against the wall, and went back into the main room. Doreen gave him a cheerful hullo. He scowled back. The room smelt of cigarette smoke and sweat. A nervous young man with glasses was describing the sexual habits of an African tribe to five girls. Over by the mantelpiece stood a tall girl, unattractive but alone. He leapt across at her.

'Ah, there you are,' he said.

'Yes, I am. Who are you?'

'The Maharajah of Inverness.'

She recognized this as a piece of invention and accepted it with a lack of amusement so deep and unpretentious that he vowed never to invent a false name again.

'Robert.'

'Sonia.'

'Hullo.'

'Hullo.'

He must make some brilliant remark, to capture her interest.

'What do you do?' he said.

'I work for a publisher. And you?'

'I make China models of the leaning tower of Pisa.'

'Is there much future in that?'

'Possibly. At the moment they're a failure. They keep falling over. But I'm working on it.' He sipped his drink, tasting it carefully. 'A cross between Spanish Burgundy, Merrydown cider and a rather immature Friars Balsam. Have some,' he said.

'Well, the thing is, I'm with someone. He's getting me one. Give me a ring. Bayswater 27663.'

What use was that? He was alone again, drowning. Nobody here knew that a woman had given him her phone number.

'Hullo, love,' said Brenda. 'Enjoying yourself?'

'No.'

'Dance with me.'

'No.'

'Come on.'

She dragged him into the middle of the room. It was packed solid. People weren't dancing, they were just marking time sexily.

'No luck?' she said.

'No.'

He resisted telling her about the phone number. Sonia seemed too mature to be boasted about.

'And you?'

'No.'

He pressed his body against her, but felt no thrill. In any case she lived in the same house. Mr Mendel had said: 'Why don't you make for our Brenda? She's a nice girl.' 'Too close,' he had said.

'Excuse me, will you, love? There's a feller over there I want to work on,' she said now.

He went into the kitchen. The punchbowl was a mass of leaves and red silt and sodden butt ends. He opened a bottle of light ale.

'Oh, there you are. Sorry about that,' said Polly.

He gave her his glass of light ale and opened another bottle. The drink would be running out soon.

'He's someone I know from art school. I want him to do something for me. Carry some heavy paintings.'

'What's wrong with me?'

'Nothing, but I *like* you.'

He must say something amusing. But nothing came. He fell back upon his memory.

'This man was carrying a grandfather clock down the street,' he said. 'And he knocked over this man with it. The man got up, looked at him very crossly, and said: "Why can't you wear a watch like everyone else?"'

'We've got rather a super grandfather clock at home,' said Polly.

'Have you?'

'Daddy would die if he could see me here. He's an admiral.'

'What attitude does he take to your being a painter?'

Polly did a loud and for all Robert knew wickedly accurate impersonation of her father. A group of people, entering the kitchen, were amazed to hear her say, in a gruff naval roar: 'Well, it's your choice, little Polly Perkins. All I'll say is this. Make a success of it. Be a good painter, and we'll be damned proud of you, the bosun and I.'

He smiled, not without a nervous glance at the new arrivals. He put a hand on her muscular arm and steered her back into the main room. Her flesh was cold and flaccid.

They began to mark time.

'Will you be a good painter?' he said.

'Extremely,' she said.

He flung his mouth on hers, too violently. She shook it off.

'We're supposed to be dancing,' she said.

'There isn't room.'

'Then we'd better talk. Ask me about my grisly family.'

'Tell me about your grisly family.'

'They think art is un-English. Unless it's ducks and sunsets, of course. We live near Haslemere. It's grisly.'

Up and down, up and down, marking time, a great mass of drunken people, much to the annoyance of Muswell Hill.

'Do you really want to stay at this party, Polly?'

'Not particularly. Why?'

'Come home and have a drink.'

'No.'

'Don't you trust me?'

'It isn't that.'

'Well let me come and look at your pictures.'

'There's only coffee.'

'That's all right.'

'Well all right then.'

'Come on,' he said. 'We'd better say good-bye.'

'It doesn't matter.'

'Yes, it does.'

They said good-bye to Doreen and Brenda, and their host. He wanted them all to see that he was going off with a girl.

The night was cold. 'That's better. It was so unreal in there,' he said.

'I hate parties,' said Polly.

He offered her a taxi, but she said she'd prefer to walk. 'It's only just round the corner,' she said.

They walked for ninety minutes. On Hampstead Heath he held her tight against a beech tree and squeezed two fingers down as far as they would go between her breasts. Then they walked in silence. He was frozen. An owl hooted. A goods train answered. The owl hooted again.

'Aren't you cold?' he said.

'I don't feel the cold,' she said. 'We admirals' daughters are tough.'

At last they arrived. Polly lived on the top storey of a grey nineteenth-century terrace behind Swiss Cottage. Her room was quite large. It was full of dirty things, cups, knickers, brushes, overalls, paintings. The bed wasn't made. There was a smell of cat. All three bars of the electric fire were on. It was stifling.

She began to make two very disorganized cups of coffee.

'I'm warning you. You're not making love to me,' she said.

'Well?'

'I just don't want you to get the wrong idea, that's all. I've decided to be a virgin until I fall in love. And I hope I never do. Men want you to give yourself to them. I want to be me. I'm an individualist. I believe people should be conventional in unimportant matters like sex. I reserve my rebellion for my work.'

'Are these your pictures?'

'Yes.'

13

They were all purple. He hated them.

'I like them,' he said.

'They're pretty good. But my next ones'll be much better.'

'Will they be purple too?'

'I don't know. Why, don't you like purple?'

'Yes, I do. I love purple. Polly, would you mind if we opened the window?'

'Sorry, it doesn't. Why, are you too hot?'

'It is rather.'

'I don't feel the heat.'

'Could we switch one of the bars off?'

'Sorry, they don't. It's all or nothing. The switch has gone.'

He took a sip of his coffee. He was beginning to sweat.

'Do you think this milk's all right?' he said.

'Oh, God, isn't it?'

'No.'

'I'll make you a black one.'

'Thanks. Do you have a cat?'

'No. Why?'

'I just wondered.'

He hated to admit to himself his delicacy over smells, and sweating, and sour milk.

'It's funny you should say that. People often ask me that,' she said.

'Perhaps you strike them as the sort of person who'd like cats.'

'I don't. I hate them.'

The sweat was pouring off him. His skin was prickling all over. How loathsome it all was, parties and sex and purple paintings and sour milk and unmade beds.

Over their coffee Polly amused him with further mimicry, imitating to perfection such well-known characters as her mother, sister, brother and headmistress. He felt too tired to do more than laugh in the right places, and as soon as he could he took his leave.

'Thanks, Polly. It's been lovely. See you,' he said.

As he went down the stairs his pants and vest stuck to his body. He opened the door and breathed a great gulp of air. He was feeling sick. He was a lump in the sore throat of night. He felt messy and miserable. He wanted to play Scrabble and read books and improve his mind and work hard and help British exports and raise a family. His own children, loved and loving.

He picked up a milk bottle and hurled it viciously at the railings. Nothing stirred in the Swiss Cottage night.

It was 2.45 a.m. Perhaps Brenda or Doreen would be there and they could have a cup of coffee, delaying the moment when he'd be alone again, alone in bed. But perhaps they wouldn't.

Bayswater 27663. Probably she'd be in bed, or still at the party, or with someone. It was absurd to ring her up at 2.45 a.m.

The tone of her telephone was French and encouraging. He whistled to keep up his worldliness.

'Hullo.'

'Hullo. Robert here.'

'Who?'

'Robert. I met you at the party.'

'Oh, yes. Hullo.'

'I hope I haven't disturbed you.'

'No. I was just having a coffee before going to bed.'

'It's just that I've sort of found myself in your area and . . .' And what?

'Twenty-three, Leominster Crescent. Top bell.'

He took a taxi. She lived between Bayswater and Notting Hill, also in a nineteenth-century terrace, but this one was cream. She had a glorious Persian carpet – a family heirloom – and a great number of books. She had a record player but no television. She was tall, slim, angular, with rather a large nose and a voice that sounded as if she had a perpetual cold caught at a very good school. When she was old there would be a permanent dewdrop on the end of her nose. She wasn't his cup of tea, unlike her coffee, which was superb.

She represented good coffee and elegant maturity. She had bags under her eyes, and looked tired, but made no effort to get rid of him. She was 23. He couldn't kiss her, couldn't rouse himself to anything like that, and she seemed to understand this. She told him how much she hated parties. She didn't mention the man she'd been with. They played a desultory but enjoyable game of Scrabble and she gave him a pile of books which she thought he'd enjoy. She asked him why he tried so hard to be amusing. Did he think himself dull? She didn't think he was dull, except perhaps when he tried to be amusing.

They had further cups of coffee and he began to tell her the story of his life. At last the grey nicotine-stained thumbs of a London dawn began to squeeze the darkness out of the sky. Sonia drew back the curtains and made breakfast, and then he went home to bed.

'I'm sorry I told you the story of my life,' he said.

'Not at all. I enjoyed it,' she said.

3 Early Days

Our story begins in the early hours of a fresh May morning in West London – in Richmond, to be precise – in the front second floor bedroom of number 10, River View West, to be still more precise. At 4.14 a.m. on that day in 1935 there was born to Emma Jane Bellamy, frail young wife of Thomas Robert Cunard Eddison Bellamy, a son. It was a surprisingly normal and easy birth. The boy weighed eight pounds, five ounces, had a hearty pair of lungs, sought more of his mother's milk than his mother's frail health permitted him, and was christened Robert Thomas Cunard Eddison Bellamy.

The prosperity of the Bellamy family had been founded in the eighteenth century by one Thomas Robert Bellamy who invented new ways of curing warts and herrings. Bellamy's Bloater Paste and Bellamy's Herbal Bunion Remover have a modest reputation even today in some of the more outlandish corners of Eastern England. But the family did not remain for long in these traditional pursuits. They turned their backs on the vulgarities of industry and became farmers and lawyers. Thomas Bellamy was already, at the time of his son's birth, making a considerable name for himself in the harsh discipline of the bar. On the night of the happy event his attention was in fact divided between the bawling but as yet uninteresting infant and the preparation of what was perhaps to be his greatest case – the prosecution of the notorious Butcher of Wentworth, also known as the Stiletto Niblick Murderer, who lured his innocent victims into a bunker on the dog-leg seventeenth, always a treacherous hole. Thomas Bellamy was a staunch Conservative and a stern though humane disciplinarian. He loved his country, his wife and his only child – in that order.

Emma Bellamy's flawless beauty revealed little of her physical frailty. Only her intimate friends knew how much suffering her asthma, anaemia, weak heart, gall-stones, ostler's ankle, Higson's disease and nervous headaches cost her. After Robert's birth her husband did not permit her to rise until twelve-thirty or to remain up after nine-thirty. She spent most of the day reclining on a sofa reading books about art and architecture. Young Robert adored her from afar. He respected his father from afar and adored his mother, while his practical wants were taken care of by his nanny.

'Ah!' said Dr Schmuck.

The Bellamy household was, as households go, a happy one. The young child, too, seemed happy. Perhaps he had to be rather more quiet than he would have wished, because of his mother's health. Perhaps his contacts with the other young children of the neighbourhood were not quite as frequent as he would have liked. Perhaps his social life was unduly restricted by his family's fear that he would fall into the Thames. But there was a reason for this. He was the only male Bellamy of his generation. On his well-being depended the continuation of the family name. He must have mumps as early as possible, and no other serious diseases at all.

Grandfather Bellamy, the only man among five sisters, and now dead, had three children – Robert's father, and his aunts Margaret and Hetty. Grandfather Bellamy's cousin, Thomas Bellamy, never married and Thomas's brother Robert had two children – Phyllis, who became a nun, and Thomas, who was struck by lightning at the age of twenty. Robert's Great Uncle Thomas, a keen ornithologist, spotted a new kind of warbler near Wootton Bassett, and for a few glorious years it was accepted as a sub-species and known as Bellamy's Warbler. But it was struck off the list in 1928, having proved to be only a slightly albino Dusky Warbler, and it now lay in Robert's power, and his alone – for his mother was too frail to have further children – to save the family name from being associated solely with bloaters and bunions.

One Sunday afternoon in early 1938, Nanny and Robert were brought downstairs to have tea with his parents. In the street could be heard the merry pre-war street cries of the muffin man, the crumpet man, the ice-cream man and the itinerant furniture remover. But already the clouds of war were beginning to gather. At lunch Aunt Margaret had commented: 'There'll be war, you mark my words. That Hitler – he's a bad lot.' His mother had said: 'I'm not so sure. I think Herr Hitler has been misjudged.' Now at tea, Nanny struck a more domestic note.

'Which little boy doesn't like potty?' she said.

Robert threw a buttered muffin at her and was taken upstairs, screaming and kicking, to bed. Such scenes were surprisingly common, did the parents but know it.

When they were alone Emma said to her husband: 'Will there really be a war?'

'Probably.'

'Poor Robert. What sort of a world have we brought him into?'

'A man's world,' said his father.

'I don't think a child ought actually to like potty,' said Emma. 'He should endure it as a necessary evil.'

'Yes. Quite right,' said his father.

'Thomas?'

'Yes?'

'It isn't true, is it?'

'What isn't true?'

'That you – what people are saying, Thomas. That you keep me in poor health because – because you have – another woman. Oh, Thomas, I know it isn't true.'

'Of course it isn't true, my dear.' He kissed her gently, so as not to hurt her. 'How could I keep you in poor health? Your poor health is your own.'

'I know. It's ridiculous. People are wicked to say such things. I could believe them of some men, but not of you. You're such an idealist.'

'I've tried to be,' said Thomas.

'I only hope Robert grows up to be like you, Thomas.'

'It won't be our fault if he doesn't.'

And then the war came.

4 War

When he was young they had a war. They lived in a house in the country then. It was a small house. Mummy and Nanny and Robert lived in it. His daddy was in the war. His daddy had gone a long way to the war, because it was very important, and his daddy was brave. You had to be brave to go to the war, because it was such a long way away.

Mummy wasn't well. She spent a lot of the time in bed. Daddy sent her dispatches, in which he was mentioned. Nanny did the cooking. Soggy pudding. Soggy Nanny pudding. Once his daddy came home. Everything was different from before. Nobody enjoyed it. His daddy was very quiet. He smelt of war. Mummy smelt of bedrooms and Nanny smelt of soggy Nanny pudding. Robert went to school. He fell in love with Cerise. He had tempers. You mustn't show your temper. Cerise doesn't show her temper. But Cerise doesn't show her temper because she hasn't got one, Nanny. Then you shouldn't have one. But I have. It's so unfair. Who ever said life was fair, said bitter jilted long ago dealt with unfairly always unlucky Nanny. I did, said Robert. And God. We did. I wonder where he gets it from, said his mummy. It's his red hair, said his nanny. Yes, but I have red hair too, said his mummy.

One snowy evening his friends Trevor and Cerise and Helen and Simon came to tea. The world was white. The light faded. The logs crackled. Helen was a fat person. Cerise was a thin person. Nanny was a Nanny pudding. Mummy was upstairs.

After tea Cerise built a hospital with some bricks. He tried to help and knocked the bricks down. Cerise howled and said: 'You've spoilt my hospital.'

'I didn't know it was a hospital.'

Cerise built the hospital again. The others played other games, but Robert had eyes only for Cerise.

'It's finished,' she said. 'This is where I work and this is where you eat and this is where people who are ill go and this is where you put all the broken legs and this is for dead people and this is outpatients and this is babies and this is the annexe.'

'What's an annexe for?'

'I don't know.'

'Then why do you have one?'

She stuck her square little jaw out and said: 'All hospitals have one.'

'Will I go there when I die?'

'Yes.'

'Hard luck, I won't, because I've decided not to die.'

'Everybody dies, silly.'

'No, they don't. They get better, because it's a hospital.'

'A hospital is where you die.'

'Won't you make them better, then?'

'If I made them better, I'd be God.'

But that's just what she was.

She left the hospital and joined in the game with the others. He kicked the hospital and it fell down. She didn't care. He couldn't hurt her that way. So he bashed her face in. She cried. She had a nose-bleed and a black eye. Simon bashed his face in. They fought bitterly. Nanny rushed in, flailing and shouting. Order was restored. Cerise held her head back and still the blood came. He wanted to say sorry and he wanted to taste the blood. Cerise was taken home by her big sister Jessica.

The next day they heard that his daddy had been killed. The snow was white, and the sun shone. His mummy cried, and his nanny was very quiet. That night Mummy didn't go to bed so early. She read a book until very late, and during the next few days people came, and his mummy was up and about, and his

mummy did some of the cooking, and Nanny was ill, and
Cerise never mentioned it, and the snow melted, and they had a
war, when he was young.

'How do you know Nanny'd been jilted?' said Dr Schmuck.
'I don't,' said Robert.

5 Above the Sex Emporium

Promptly at five-thirty the long six-storey chalky grey concrete slab began to regurgitate its half-digested human pellets. Wives and husbands, boy friends and girl friends waited outside, watching people putting on their coats in six symmetrical rows of windows. These were all offices. The actual making of instruments was done in two long low blocks, tacked on behind the main building.

The crowds began to pour out through the glass doors, between the huge Ionic columns which were just façades. The bonds of Cadman and Bentwhistle Ltd were loosened, its employees disappeared into their own private darknesses. Some of them would find the evening harder to endure than the day.

Robert looked back at the massive building almost lovingly. He sometimes claimed that he worked in the ugliest building in London. In four weeks' time he would work there no longer, and he would miss it.

He walked slowly through the drizzle, conscious of the Georgian houses at the far side of the square, their proportions mocked by Messrs Cadman and Bentwhistle, conscious too of the 1930 pub on the north side of the square, looking like a Moorish public convenience. Beside the pub was a 1960 garage, a cheap garish toy blown up to life size. He really hated that garage tonight, and gave its wall a savage kick as he passed.

He took his annoyance out on the newspaper seller. The poster read: 'Mystery Murder Sensation'. Everyone else's front page lead announced: 'Knifed diplomat – Commons told of "Mystery Parcel"'. But his paper had 'Premier orders big union probe'. It was an early edition. He demanded his money back. The man argued. He told the man he only wanted the paper because of the knifed diplomat. He got his money back and immediately felt ashamed.

He went on to the platform and waited for the little Broad Street line train. It was too pathetic, taking it out on the paper seller, too pathetic even to tell Dr Schmuck. And that was another thing. He must break with Dr Schmuck. It was doing him no good at all.

The train arrived. He stared at the lights of London, wishing he had a paper. They rattled across the Caledonian Road, past decaying residential areas and railway sidings. He could do with a drink. He didn't fancy a quiet evening at home. He didn't fancy cooking or eating alone at the Blessington Café.

He got out at Kentish Town West, an intimate crumbling little wooden station. He would ring Sonia. Tall, long-faced, fractionally-equine, comfortable sexy Sonia. It was sad that she hadn't married, she was eager enough. She never would now. She'd have her moments, but they'd be sad and snatched. Sonia, uninhibited, perhaps too uninhibited, knitting sexual balaclavas for the neurotic troops of London. Why haven't we got married? Thus mused Robert Bellamy, noted Kentish Town raconteur and gourmet, as he made his way through the damp streets.

Number 38, Blessington Road, was the end house in a row of three-storey late Georgian houses set far back behind the shop fronts that disfigured their ground floors. Number 38, like Number 12, at the other end, had an extra storey, an attic. They were small eccentric shops, the shops in Blessington Road. They sold tropical fish, gentles, hamsters, dustbins and scarlet watering cans. Numbers 38, 32 and 26 were owned by Mr Mendel, a big untidy Austrian Jew who walked like a woman. He leased out the shops.

The shop at Number 38 was the North London Surgical and Medical Supply Centre. It was run by a wizened hypochondriac cockney who lived in a council flat in Bethnal Green and was never seen in Kentish Town outside shop hours. Robert called his shop the sex emporium.

The row of houses opposite Number 38 was unoccupied, waiting for demolition.

He let himself in without so much as a glance at the trusses and dirty books. They bored him, but it amused him to live above them.

He entered his room with a little shock of pleasure and dismay. He had gradually replaced all Mr Mendel's furniture with his own, and now the room was exactly as he wanted it. Wood was its major material. The stained floorboards were bare save for two small rugs. By the window, looking out over the great expanse of the sex emporium roof, was his dining suite – a simple wooden table and four wooden chairs. Robert dumped his rain coat on one of these chairs, went into the little kitchenette and put the kettle on a low gas. Then he went to the communal phone in the corridor and rang Sonia's number. She was thirty-five, a bit old to start having children, but it still wasn't too late. The phone still had its sexy French tone. He breathed harder.

No reply. He dialled again, just in case there had been a mistake. But there had been no mistake.

He went back into his room, switched on the television with his remote-control switch, drew the wine-red curtains, and made his pot of tea. As he did so he was conscious that something in the room irritated him intensely.

He let the tea stand for a couple of minutes and examined the room. It wasn't the dining suite. Nor was it the wine-red Finnish sofa, matching the curtains, or the high-backed wooden chairs that stood at each side of the electric fire. Perhaps it was his divan, behind the door at the end of the room farthest from the window. An uninteresting piece of furniture, the divan.

He poured himself a cup of tea, sat on the sofa, watched 30 seconds of Quiz Ball, Kilmarnock *v* Arsenal, pressed his hand switch, watched 20 seconds of the BBC 2 Test Card, pressed his hand switch, watched 15 seconds of 'Voyage To The Bottom Of The Sea' and switched the television off.

It wasn't the divan. The wicker waste paper basket? The cheap ash-trays? The Dutch cigar box? The heavy wardrobe? The solid chest of drawers? The streamlined radio? The home-made wooden bookshelves? The three modern paintings, carefully yet in the last resort arbitrarily chosen? The electric fire and its surrounds, painted blue to contrast with the shining whiteness of the walls?

He sighed – and wondered whether the time had come to leave Number 38. Dr Schmuck had said it would be a great help. You paid £4 a session for analysis and that was the kind of deep advice you got – move from Number 38.

He poured himself a second cup. His mouth thirsted for something stronger. He picked up a book, one of Sonia's, like almost all his books, she dispensed books as she dispensed her affections, with no real expectation of their return. But tonight he couldn't concentrate on a book.

The wardrobe. Suddenly he knew it was the wardrobe. He must get rid of it. It was manic-depressive.

He drank his tea slowly. Number 38, he thought, isn't what it used to be. The sociability has gone. For too long I have refused to admit it. He hardly knew the present incumbents at all. O'Connor and Tooley, the young Irish lads, he met oc-casionally in the Blessington Arms. He liked Mrs Palmer, who never had any letters or visitors but insisted that she had once been Europe's foremost female unicyclist. It was, however, rather a one-way relationship. Miss Flodden and Mr Marshall left insulting notes about tidiness and unlocked doors, and, rumour had it, bathed together. He never saw them and didn't like them. Dr Strickman was inaccessible, with his shifty eyes, his strange-shaped parcels from Munich and his cryptic telephone calls. And he didn't really know Mr Pardoe, who ran three launderettes, one of which, near Westminster Bridge, was named 'The Diplomat'.

He went to the phone and rang Sonia again. Still no reply.

He met Mrs Palmer, going upstairs.

'Hullo. How are you?' he said.

'Lübeck,' said Mrs Palmer.

'I'm sorry. I don't understand.'

'Lübeck,' she said again, more slowly. 'I was telling you about the time I had to step in and do the high wire act, due to the indisposition of the Amazing Esperanto. I couldn't remember where it was. Well, I have done. It was Lübeck.'

It was at least six months ago, that conversation.

'It must have been a great thrill,' he said, knowing that this meant ten minutes' more reminiscence, but not minding in the least.

Then he rang Sonia again. Still no reply. He felt vaguely ridiculous, ringing her again and again, as if she knew and was laughing at him for his persistence.

There were various people he could ring, various friends. But he wasn't going to plead for company.

On Saturday he was going down to Cambridge to see Elizabeth. He'd met her at a party over the weekend. They seemed to hit it off, but what chance did he stand alongside all those undergraduates?

He switched the television on, but didn't see it. He was thinking about Frances now. That, he still thought, had been love.

Things hadn't worked out. He'd had bad luck. Somebody up there didn't like him. Too many jokes, perhaps. He saw God for a moment as a stern face, listening patiently to all his jokes, then saying 'Heard it'. Not much future in telling jokes to the omniscient.

He smiled, then the smile died. He switched the television off. His thirst was becoming stronger. He would go round the corner to the Blessington Arms.

The phone rang. Please let it be for me and let it change my luck and my whole life.

Dr Strickman wasn't in. He took a message. 'Eliminate Rathbone.'

28

He rang Sonia. No reply.

He went down the stairs and met Dr Strickman.

'There's a message for you. Eliminate Rathbone,' he said.

'Thank you,' said Dr Strickman calmly.

He went out, past the trusses and ointments, and headed towards the pub.

All the regulars would be standing by the bar. Sometimes he went to the pub frequently and sometimes he didn't go there for weeks. He was familiar there, he was known, but he wasn't a regular. Being a regular was incredibly boring, and yet he resented not being one.

Perhaps Kevin, the actor, would be there, or John, the West Indian bus conductor who wrote poetry and had a university degree, or O'Connor and Tooley, or Bert, the confectioner with a fund of reminiscences about East Africa. More probably there would be no-one, just a few silent regulars, one on every other bar stool, watching the television.

But he didn't feel sad. Everything was going to be all right. He would get a new and better job, move into a new and more cheerful house, and marry Sonia.

He had had his joys and his sorrows, and he would have his joys and his sorrows again.

He ordered a pint of bitter and a straight malt whisky, to celebrate the fact that there was nothing to be sad about.

6 Joys

November, 1953. Robert is up before the War Office Selection Board. Deep in the sodden Hampshire downs he has undergone a series of illuminating tests. He has climbed ropes, swung from trees, erected flagpoles, outlined briefly the history of the British Empire, and planned the urgent evacuation of the small resort of Seatown (pop. 10,000). He has also attempted, unsuccessfully, to organize the passing of a large oil drum across a very wide ditch with three very short planks. Clearly passing large oil drums across wide ditches with short planks is his Achilles Heel.

Robert feels that on the whole he hasn't done too badly. He hasn't distinguished himself, but he has passed muster. Yesterday at breakfast he told a colleague that if he passed muster he was going on to take advanced muster. The colleague hasn't sat next to him at any meals since then.

During all these tests Robert has asked himself why he is here, trying to become an officer. And he has been unable to think of any answer, except that it was expected of him, and that his basic training unit at Catterick was so awful that he leapt at any chance of getting away from it.

Now, at his final interview in that gloomy country house, surrounded by bare wet trees, he thinks of another answer.

'What's your father do?'

'He's dead, sir. He was a lawyer.'

'Oh, I'm sorry.' Sorry he's dead, or sorry he was a lawyer? 'Did he die in the war?'

'Yes, sir.'

They seem pleased at that.

'Why do you want to become an officer?'

'I want to order the lower classes around, sir.'

They take this seriously, and seem surprised, but not displeased.

'What qualities do you think are needed by a successful officer?'

'Loyalty, cruelty, insensitivity, stupidity and courage, sir.'

January, 1955. The snow is thick in B.A.O.R. In Munster, Westphalia, the wind is bitter cold. The wind howls through the B Block ablutions, whistling round Robert's legs.

He was drunk last night. He went out with Stephen. They met Scouse Edwards, Taffy Lewis and Geordie Wilkinson. They all got drunk. Robert picked a fight with Connolly, a driver. He was lucky the M.P.s didn't pick him up. He had terrible hiccups when he signed in at the guard room, but Sgt Clarke just smiled. Not a bad chap, Nobby.

He works a shift system, and although today is Thursday it is his day off. But Thursday is also C.O.'s inspection. He has to get up early and make a tidy bed-pack. He has to square off his large pack, small pack and basic pouches. And then he has to go out, because the living quarters are out of bounds for C.O.'s inspection.

But he can't go out. He is too ill. He goes to the lavatory and is sick. He sits there, hunched up, shuddering gently in the wind.

He hears footsteps. The C.O.'s inspection.

The lavatory door does not extend to the ground, and he raises his feet so that they are not visible beneath the door. He jams his feet against the far wall and remains seated.

He hears the little procession enter the ablutions.

'Smell of sick,' says the C.O. 'What was for breakfast?'

'Poached eggs, sir,' says the orderly officer.

'Treacherous chaps, poached eggs,' says the C.O.

He hears the grunts and exclamations of keen inspection. Then his doorknob rattles.

'This door won't open,' says the C.O.

His doorknob rattles again.

'This door won't open, sarn't major,' says the orderly officer.

'Saaarrrrhh.'

The knob rattles again, more violently this time.

'This door won't open, saarn't,' says the sergeant major.

'Sarn't major,' says the sergeant.

The knob rattles again.

'Corporal Higgins, this door won't open,' says the sergeant.

The knob rattles again. Robert wants to be sick again, and all the blood is running from his legs.

'Jammed, sarn't,' says Corporal Higgins.

'Jammed, sarn't major,' says the sergeant.

'Jammed, saaaarrrrhh,' says the sergeant major.

'Jammed, sir,' says the orderly officer.

'Get the carpenter, sarn't major,' says the orderly officer.

'Saaaaarrrrhh. Get the carpenter, saaaarn't,' says the sergeant major.

'Sarn't major. Get the carpenter, Higgins,' says the sergeant.

'Sarn't,' says Higgins.

He hears Higgins depart.

The knob rattles again.

'Funny thing, door jamming like that,' says the C.O. He sniffs loudly. 'No more poached eggs,' he says.

The party moves off. No-one has suspected that there might be someone in the lavatory, because no-one is allowed in the lavatory during the C.O.'s inspection.

As soon as he dares, Robert hurries over to A Block ablutions, and is violently sick. But he doesn't mind. It was worth it.

May, 1956. The first really good time with Sonia. Early evening on a spring day. The sexuality in him all day, warmed by the spring sun. He walked slowly down from Cadman and

32

Bentwhistle, making crablike progress down the hill towards the Caledonian Road. He felt romantic. The tenements in Laycock Street were liners trapped in concrete, the tired housewives leaning over the rail, hoping to see some foreign port beyond the lines of washing. He admired the Georgian and Victorian houses of Barnsbury. He walked past Belitha Villas and Thornhill Square, some streets going up in the world, others down, but all warmed equally by the sun. He went down Caledonian Road, up Copenhagen Street, through the jungle of railway bridges behind King's Cross and St Pancras. In Euston Station he rang Sonia. He had never doubted that she'd be in. It was an evening when things must go right. He heard her deep French telephone and her nasal English voice. No, she wasn't doing anything. Yes, she would like to see him.

He walked on down the Euston Road and entered a public convenience. The attendant was cleaning it, at this hour on this lovely evening his world was a lavatory. Robert smiled at him as he peed, and hoped it helped. The man smiled back. Half the lavatory was roped off, and the wet floor that he had washed was protected by cardboard. As he went out Robert noticed the words 'Sell your eggs in rotation' on one of the pieces.

'I will,' he said cheerfully.

The man smiled again.

He was impatient now and caught the 27 bus. Sonia was wearing a simple summer dress. Her thin white arms were bare and the hair under her armpits was newly cut. He wondered how he could ever have thought she wasn't attractive. She had bought a bottle of sherry, an extravagance on publisher's pay, to drink to the summer. They drank to it.

'Surprised?' he said.

'Perhaps I'm rather surprised every time I see you again.'

So was he. But she was nice and peaceful to be with, and this time she was beautiful and it would be all right. They had only made love once and her ardency had taken him aback and afterwards he had wished that they hadn't. It was messy and grotesque. He had left her at ten-twenty and drunk five whiskies rapidly in a pub round the corner. On the tube he had been rude to an Italian tourist, who had shrugged benevolently. He had picked up a milk bottle and lobbed it through the window of the Blessington Pet Shop. Fined £5. Luckily no mention of it in the papers. He had gone up to Doreen and Brenda's. Michael had been there, and a boy friend of Brenda's. They had all drunk cocoa, and he had been very rude to Michael.

He sat on the floor and kissed her knees. There was a ladder in the right stocking. He put his little finger in and ran it along her flesh.

'This is excellent sherry,' he said.

He could feel her gritting her teeth with desire. He unrolled the stockings and began to kiss her legs and feet. Her legs had blue veins in them but the skin was smooth. He said nothing. He could feel the tension even in her feet. On the sofa was an author's manuscript. The window was open. She bent down and kissed the top of his head.

He stood up and looked down at her in her chair. She also stood up. She was almost as tall as he was, and her slight smooth lips were wet.

'I love you,' he said.

She shook her head ever so slightly. He kissed her for a long time, and then he undressed her and carried her into the tiny bedroom. When he touched her breasts she groaned as if the pleasure was too great. They made love quickly and violently, a rhythm that suited them both, and her groans were like the cries of a tortured woman. Afterwards he felt relaxed and happy and grateful. The sun fell slowly behind the curtains as they talked. She talked about her father. Her mother had died when she was two, and her father had married again, but the spark had gone out of him. He was a bank manager in Bristol. She loved him with the same compassionate love she seemed to feel for all the world.

34

He asked her why she wasn't married. She said she was much too particular, rather too cowardly, slightly too intense and not quite attractive enough. He demurred. She insisted. He changed the subject. They discussed places they would go to and things they would do – not that places and things meant much to her, except as experiences shared with loved ones.

Again he entered her and this time it was slower and gentler and more deeply satisfying. And afterwards he felt sated but contented, and he knew that her desire remained and he would never be able to satisfy her.

He was hungry. They dressed and had more sherry. She wore black trousers, and a check shirt. They ate the left-over bits of a chicken and there was a little cucumber and plenty of bread. After that there was red Cheshire and Edam and a pot of her excellent coffee. They played Scrabble and he kept making indecent words. It was his way of stimulating himself for what was to come.

He needn't have worried. His desire responded to hers and they made love again, and again it was good, but this time he felt too sleepy to say that he loved her. He just let his fingers touch her thighs as he slid into a deep and happy sleep, vaguely conscious that she was rubbing herself gently against his body and clenching her teeth in excitement.

Then it was eight thirty-five and they were both going to be late for work. The sun was shining again, thrushes were singing, he shaved with Sonia's razor, and she hardly spoke.

'See you tonight,' he said.

June, 1960. His first trip abroad for Cadman and Bentwhistle to sell a new high speed drill to a French firm. The drill was supposedly capable of distinguishing between different kinds of rock and soil. The French firm was supposedly capable of building channel tunnels and major tunnels under the Alps. Robert was supposedly capable of winning the deal in the face of

German and French opposition. It was an important transaction. Tadman-Evans wished him luck.

'We've every confidence in you, Bellamy,' he said.

'Thank you.'

'It's pity you've got to do such an important job on your first trip abroad, but there it is. There's no-one else available,' said Tadman-Evans.

Tadman-Evans warned him that the French were all extremely clever, extremely cunning and extremely arrogant. Robert's worry as the plane descended towards Orly wasn't the French, but his French. It was the schoolboy stuff, and rusty at that. He'd meant to brush it up, but somehow he hadn't got round to it.

A car was waiting for him at the airport, and this drove him to the site of a great road building scheme on the southern edge of Paris. There, at the site office, among mounds of dry earth and dust, he met M. Bonnard.

'Sir John tells me how well you speak French. That is unusual, for an Englishman,' said M. Bonnard.

'He's exaggerating,' said Robert.

'But I am afraid you will have no chance to speak it. I insist on speaking English. It is my little vanity. You aren't minding too much, I hope?'

'No. I don't mind.'

'Good. Now, we shall examine the machine at two. But first, lunch.'

They lunched in a small, unprepossessing restaurant, in an untidy, dusty suburb, all cobbled cul-de-sacs and railway embankments. The food was excellent. Robert immediately found himself much more confident, and able to work much better, away from the petty snobberies of Cadman and Bentwhistle. If there were similar petty snobberies in Europe he was insensitive to the nuances and failed to pick them up. He could function in a larger, more generous sphere here. He could be a shining example of tact and diplomacy, all the more impressive because it came from an Englishman. He treated M. Bonnard on the assumption that he was clever but neither arrogant nor cunning. They got on well. Robert expounded on the British debt to European culture, and M. Bonnard showed him photographs of his two very Americanized young boys. Robert essayed some tart criticisms of British insularity, and M. Bonnard had some scathing comments to make about the system of rubbish clearing employed in the western suburbs of Paris. Robert made a frank summary of the inferior taste of the British to the French bourgeoisie, and M. Bonnard invited him to dinner to see his house and rookery. Robert was treated to a concise history of French landscape gardening, and then they returned to the site, affability personified, and the afternoon's work began.

They made steady progress. The French were impressed by the drill and by Robert's knowledge of it. He was able to ring their agent, M. Phillipe, and tell him that things were going well. M. Phillipe apologized for having been unavailable during the day, and suggested that they met after Robert's dinner party for a little drink, to get to know each other.

In the evening Robert went back to M. Bonnard's stark, white, modern house, decorated throughout with flimsy, spiky objects which he hated. He examined, and expressed profound admiration for, the rookery, which turned out to be a very formal, very spiky, very ugly rockery.

The dinner was delicious. He got rather drunk. The two boys were incredibly polite and only spoke when spoken to. M. Bonnard asked if there were many rookeries in England. Robert replied that there were some, but not enough. The English showed a distressing preference for gardens with enormous numbers of plants grown higgledy-piggledy. M. Bonnard wrote down 'higgledy-piggledy' in a notebook. Mme Bonnard asked Robert if he had ever met Peter Townsend. He had to admit that he had never had that pleasure. We lacked the severe logic that inspired French horticulture, he added, with the relentless self-denigration of the true patriot. We were not as cultured as the French. London had nothing to compare with the elegance and unity of Paris. Mme Bonnard agreed, but pointed out that the French had nothing to compare with Marks and Spencer's. And was it true that Prince Charles was by nature artistic, poor boy? Robert confessed to a lack of intimate knowledge of the tastes and interests of the young prince, and compared the gardens of Buckingham Palace to those of Versailles, to the decided advantage of the latter.

'I have been reading some years back a very fine book about your famous landscape gardener, Herbaceous Brown. Did Herbaceous Brown not build rookeries?' said M. Bonnard.

Robert said that in England it was generally held by the gardening establishment that Herbaceous Brown had marred an otherwise brilliant, some would say meteoric, career by his failure fully to understand the charms of the rookery.

Mme Bonnard asked if it was true that Princess Margaret entertained fellow guests at parties by her brilliant mimicry. Robert conceded that he had never been to a party at which Her Royal Highness was also present, bid his hosts a cordial good night, and left. In the road he met their two sons, who were incredibly rude. Later he met M. Phillipe, who said that he would show him the Paris the tourist never sees. In the morning he could remember nothing whatsoever about the Paris the tourist never sees.

At eight-thirty M. Phillipe rang him. 'What a night,' he said. Robert was relieved. Evidently things had gone well.

Two weeks later a large order was placed. Robert suspected that the British drill was slightly superior to the French and German ones, but when he told the story of his first European success to Sonia and Bernard and Martin and Dick and Stephen, it was Herbaceous Brown and his rookeries that had tipped the scales.

. . . . .

August, 1966. A fine summer's day. Lunch in the garden of Aunt Maud's little cottage in Hartingsford Magna. Aunt Maud had planted shrubs to hide the new housing estate, the butterscotch factory and the pylons. Only to the West was there a view, over unspoilt fields and farms. In the distance, rising above the willows that fringed the canal, were the spire of Hartingsford Parva Church and the tower of Hartingsford Juxta Poulsbury. The willows hid the new estates and factories in these villages.

The sun shone fiercely and the lunch was laid in the shade. The daube was excellent, its peasant strength miraculously captured by Aunt Maud. Swifts were screeching overhead, and combine harvesters purred productively.

'This is perfection,' he said.

'Nonsense,' said Aunt Maud. 'The tower of Juxta Poulsbury should be a spire. Towers don't go with willows.'

Aunt Maud never went to church, but she was great friends with the vicar and supported all his charities. 'I don't believe a word of it, but it can't do any harm,' she used to say.

In the last five years Aunt Maud had left the village just three times. On each occasion she had been utterly miserable. She had seen the world, and liked Hartingsford Magna better. She was charming, attractive and soft-featured. No-one knew why she had never married. Perhaps she had seen men and simply liked Hartingsford Magna better. She responded warmly to company, yet seemed to prefer solitude. Every Christmas she had six invitations. Every Christmas she refused them. 'It's all a lot of nonsense,' she would explain tolerantly, to anyone who pressed for a reason.

Aunt Maud was sixty-eight now. On top of her lined yet peaceful face the hair was grey. She kept in touch by reading the newspapers. She had a clear mind, but affected to believe that nothing ever happened in Hartingsford Magna, and everything always happened in London.

'What's the news in the village?'

'News? Nothing ever happens here. The Peck has complained to the council about the new traffic sign at Parva Lower End. Nothing'll come of it. Crosby's youngest's living in sin with a butcher. Clutterby was drowned in the canal last week. Mr Sims is carrying on with Mrs Leach, and Mr Leach is carrying on with Mrs Sims. Otherwise very quiet. It's a quiet place, Robert.'

'It's certainly restful for me.'

'Oh, and Blounce is giving up the shop.'

'Good Lord. Why?'

'Going to Jamaica to die.'

Blounces had run the Hartingsford Magna shop since elms immemorial. Vicars came and went, but not Blounces. The churchyard was full of them. The window of Blounce's contained nothing but juniper back-ache pills. A perfect pyramid, since none was ever sold.

Aunt Maud cleared away the daube and brought the syllabub. It was miraculously light. He knew that she knew that he knew how excellent it was, so he didn't mention it.

'The Summer Exhibition's rotten again this year,' said Aunt Maud.

'So I gather.'

'You've not been?'

'No.'

'Too many distractions in the big city. What are people talking about in London?'

Many country people, in every other way perfectly rational, believe that the streets of London are paved with intelligent conversation. It amused Aunt Maud to share that belief.

'Oh, I don't know,' he said, with contented ineptitude.

'Have you see any Lichtenstein?'

For a moment he thought she was talking about the place. He had seen bits of it, briefly, from the Arlberg Express.

'Oh, the painter. No, I haven't.'

Aunt Maud cleared away the syllabub and brought the

coffee. The whole garden smelt of warmth, all the individual scents of flowers and crops were gathered under the wings of the sun, and reissued smelling of warmth.

They moved from the upright canvas chairs to the deck chairs. He moved his chair into the sun. Aunt Maud poured out the coffee.

'Titmus seems to be handling his bowlers quite well,' she said.

'Yes. It's the batting that's letting Middlesex down.'

'Have you been to Lord's this year?'

'No.'

'It's all underground films, these days, I suppose. Four hundred Japanese bottoms. It sounds rather monotonous to me, but I daresay it's more amusing if you see it with friends.'

Aunt Maud cleared away the coffee. He didn't help, because giving pleasure was her hobby. He lay back and closed his eyes, the lids red and transparent against the sun. By dozing he paid Aunt Maud a compliment. Then he opened one eye and peered at the sky. There must surely be something there, a spirit, an emanation of good intention? Surely there must?

The joy that Robert was feeling was pure love. He loved Aunt Maud, and Aunt Maud loved him. And neither would ever express that love, for fear that it would go away.

Hartingsford Magna was the only place in England where he didn't need to make jokes. As he entered the village he thought: Caution. You are entering a joke-free area, and that was the last resemblance to a joke he needed to make until Fangham's taxi drove him out again to Foxington Station, and he thought: Caution. You are leaving a joke-free area.

When Aunt Maud returned after doing the washing up, they came nearer than usual to expressing their love.

'Thank you. That was a lovely lunch, as always,' he said.

'Good to have someone to appreciate it, as always,' said Aunt Maud.

7 Sorrows

October, 1946. Robert was a day boy and others of the boys were boarders. Boarders were people who were better than day boys who were people whose noses ran. Boarders knew more than day boys because when the day boys went home the boarders went upstairs and had sin upstairs, whatever that was. You didn't know everything when you were young.

Robert wanted to be good and serve his God. Sometimes he would fool around and all the boys laughed but this was not what life was for. Life was for fighting against sin upstairs but it would be foolish to admit this to the boarders. Robert was quite a strange boy because he had led a sheltered life, but he thought that people jolly well ought to lead sheltered lives.

One day Big Joan was cleaning the corridor with her mops and brushes. Not only was Big Joan a bit of a tease but she was something to do with sin upstairs. Robert walked past Big Joan and she said: 'Hey, don't I get a kiss?' and he went along the corridor which smelt of rissoles and carrots, and he went through a swing door, which led to the cloakroom where the day-bugs left their coats. There was dark green paint everywhere. His childhood was inextricably bound up with dark green paint.

In the cloakroom were Stevens Major and Sewell and Waller. They were boarders.

Sewell said: 'Do you love Big Joan, Bellamy?'

Robert said: 'No,' and turned red.

'Don't you like girls?' said Stevens Major.

'No,' said Robert.

They laughed. They were enemies. Perkins and Thomas and Willoughby were friends and he wished that Bernard Howes was a friend, but these were enemies.

Waller came at him and grabbed his arm. Robert wasn't afraid of people in ones but there were three of these. There always were.

Sewell grabbed his other arm. He was ashamed of not liking girls, and besides it wasn't true.

'I like some girls,' he said.

He was angry with himself for saying this. He lashed out, but there were three of them and they pinned him against the wall. Sewell smelt of sick and Waller smelt of feet.

'Which girls do you like?' said Stevens Major.

He didn't answer. They twisted his arm. Stevens Major kicked him.

'Which girls?' said Sewell, twisting his arm some more. He wasn't going to tell them, but they kicked him and twisted his arm until he thought it was going to break, and his eyes were full of tears, and eventually he told them.

'Cerise,' he said.

They let go. The door opened and Big Joan came in. If he had hung on a bit longer they would never have known.

Big Joan looked at them suspiciously, and smiled at Robert. Her smile turned him to jelly.

The three boarders ran off down the corridor, shouting: 'Bellamy loves Cerise. Bellamy loves Cerise,' and behind them the door went boing-boing-boing.

September, 1948. Bernard Howes had come to his new school and now a year later Robert followed him. He wished he could be friends with Bernard Howes, who was superior without being snotty.

After three days of term they met. Bernard was in a different house, and a year senior, but it was all right to talk to him because they had been at the same prep school.

'Hullo, Howes,' he said.

'Hullo, Bellamy,' said Bernard.

'I say,' said Robert hurriedly, before Bernard moved on and was lost. 'Could we meet some time so that you could show me round. It'd be a terrific help.'

'I'll see you this afternoon, after early grind,' said Bernard.

'After what?'

'Early grind.'

A master passed by. They said: 'Hullo, sir.'

'That's Stinky R,' said Bernard. 'See you on the corner of Lower Broad half an hour after early grind.'

'Where's Lower Broad?'

'Go down the little lagger-bagger behind the ogglers' tonkhouse, turn right at Pot Harry's, and you can't miss it'.

Another master passed by and they said: 'Hullo, sir.'

'That was Toady J,' said Bernard. 'O.K., see you this afternoon, Bellamy. Bring your iron and we'll go for a hum.'

Robert didn't find Bernard. He didn't take his iron and they didn't go for a hum, because by the time he had found out what all the school slang meant it was two hours after early grind.

He walked away from the school, anger mingling with depression, the depression urging him to run away, the anger telling him to return and fight it out. He nodded to Clammy L, barely seeing him. Take me away from this horrible place, God, he said.

He walked up the lane towards the heath. I'll never return. Never never never, he thought. I'll die of exposure. Then they'll be sorry.

Twenty minutes later he turned round and went back to school. He got there just in time for late grind.

October, 1948. It was Sunday, he was thirteen years of age, and school wasn't quite so bad now. He had managed to find Bernard Howes again and this time Bernard had been decent and had given him some useful tips from his Olympian heights.

Lessons were quite good and chapel was the best thing of all, although of course you had to pretend that it was absolutely awful.

He went for a walk up the lane again. School wasn't so good yet that you didn't need to go off up lanes on your own sometimes.

He reached the heath, and saw one of the older boys walking towards him. He knew that the older boy was up to no good, and expected, being thirteen, that he was going to be beaten up.

'Hullo,' said the older boy.

'Hullo.'

'You're a new-bug, aren't you?'

'Yes.'

'What's your name?'

'Bellamy.'

The older boy walked along beside him. He was about eighteen and almost six foot. Perhaps nothing was wrong after all.

They were walking down a narrow path which led towards the edge of the heath, through gorse bushes. It was a lonely, windswept place. Robert wished there was someone about.

'Which house are you in, Bellamy?' The older boy seemed nervous.

'Drake.'

'That's quite a good house. Spotty D isn't a bad chap. Where do you come from?'

'Richmond, but we live in the Cotswolds just now.'

'What do your parents do?'

'My father's dead. My mother's bought a house in the Cotswolds and she's modernized it. Now she's going to sell it, and there's another place she hopes to get in Sussex.'

The older boy put his arm round him. Robert shrugged it off and began to run. The older boy caught him up and rugby-tackled him. He tried to get up but the older boy overpowered him. He lashed out and struck the older boy one or two good blows, he was the better fighter, but in the end he had to give in because he was more than four years the younger.

The older boy took Robert's trousers down. The grass was damp and repulsive.

'I can't help it, Bellamy,' said the older boy. 'I'm sorry.'

It was soon over. The older boy didn't say anything, just walked away. Robert pulled up his trousers and walked away too. When he got back to school there was bread and peanut butter. He didn't report the incident.

'We're making excellent progress,' said Dr Schmuck.

April, 1949. It was early afternoon, a traditional April day of sudden spring showers and brief bursts of warm sunshine. Outside, in the traditional churchyard, the traditional rooks were cawing. All was well with the world, except for Mr Randolph Clegg. Mr Randolph Clegg was his mother's friend, and he looked rather like Hitler.

His mother had bought the potentially charming but ruinously dilapidated Elizabethan cottage for a song – 'Pack up your troubles in your old kit bag' had been the comment of embryonic funster Robert Bellamy, thirteen, to the mild but gratifying amusement of his colleague Bernard Howes, fourteen. Now she was engaged, in company with Mr Clegg, her 'business associate', in knocking down a dividing wall.

At the end of the war his mother, her health much improved, had been kept busy looking after poor Nanny, who had retired permanently to bed, a prey to malaria, bronchitis, rheumatic fever, scurvy, Braithwaite's Disease and fear of lizards. His mother had nursed her devotedly until she died, late in 1946. His mother, who didn't need the money, had decided that she must occupy herself, and had gone into the business of renovating old houses. Robert had immediately become a boarder.

Now home for the Easter holidays Robert stood awkwardly in an obscure corner of the cottage's low-beamed living-room, hoping that his mother would notice him and that Mr Clegg wouldn't.

His mother was up the step ladder, wearing trousers. She was really rather a smasher. He didn't know what she saw in Mr Clegg. Adults fell for very peculiar people sometimes.

'If you're going to hang around here, son, fetch me some nails,' said Mr Clegg, handing Robert a box of odds and ends.

Robert hunted through the box. There were no nails. Mr Clegg would blame him, silently. Mr Clegg would take one look at the box and find nails galore. Vicious, spiteful, disappearing nails.

Robert liked to help, and at first his mother had encouraged him, but lately, seeing that he was never any help at all, she hadn't bothered. Robert knew that he wasn't by nature helpless. He was only helpless when Mr Clegg was around. Mr Clegg rendered him mute and helpless.

'What do you think this is holding up?' said Mr Clegg.

'I was wondering,' said his mother.

'Nothing, if you ask me.'

'I don't see what it can be.'

'Well, no. I mean, look, it ends there.'

'Yes.'

Mr Clegg was standing very close to his mother, just touching her back with his front. She turned and gave him a look which said: 'Careful. Not in front of the boy'. He gave her a look which said: 'Blast the interfering little brat. You think of him too much. He wouldn't notice anyway, the steaming great loon. Look at him, standing there all thumbs. Hasn't found a single nail, even. You can't spend your whole time worrying about him'. She gave him a look which said: 'Now, Randy, we've been through all that'.

Robert had once heard his mother say: 'If you'd only try to be nice to him, Randy.' Mr Clegg had said: 'But I do. I try all the time. I'm just not a child person, Emmie,' and his mother had said: 'He *is* taking to you a bit, isn't he?' and Mr Clegg had

47

said: 'I've tried to get him to call me Randolph. He won't. It's Mr Clegg this, Mr Clegg that. He does it to hurt me. I'm a sensitive man, Emmie. I'm easily hurt. You know that. I have delicate feelings. The boy knows that. Children sense these things. He calls me Mr Clegg to hurt me. He hates me.'

Robert would have been prepared to call him Randolph if he was even remotely Randolphish. That would have been only fair. But he never was. He was Mr Cleggish, and the more Randolphish he tried to be, the more Mr Cleggish he became. You will not have my mother, vowed Robert.

Mr Clegg began the simple task of removing the short length of wood which was holding nothing up. Robert felt that it might be dangerous, but they knew better than he.

Twice Mr Clegg's hands touched Robert's mother and paused momentarily before passing on. That sort of thing gave adults a big thrill. They really were the most extraordinary people. Especially since Mr Clegg's hands were like uncooked fillets of plaice.

The length of wood was so rotten it came away in their hands. Two cross beams and a whole section of the ceiling collapsed with it. One of the beams struck his mother across the head. Mr Clegg fell in a shower of plaster.

Half his mother's money went to Mr Clegg and half to Robert. Half of Robert went to Aunt Maud and half to Aunt Margaret. It was the fairest solution the family could find.

September, 1953. The first dark night at Catterick. Lectures from the hut sergeant and the two hut corporals. Practice at making bed-packs. Your bed-pack is not considered to be up to standard, probably because you have a refined voice. Out it goes on to a soaking flowerbed. Finally at 12.30 a.m. the lights are put out. You make your bed in the dark, and struggle into the damp sheets. Your bed smells of wet earth. The hut smells of huts. In the morning you are awakened at 4.14. After two and a half hours devoted to making straight lines round the barrack-room floor with boot polish you are allowed five minutes for breakfast. After two days of this sort of thing you have to wear your denims for the first time. They have been issued without buttons, and you have to sew the buttons on yourself. To you this smacks more of sheer inefficiency than of inspired character building. You begin to sew them on. Your efforts do not meet with success. You begin to master the technique, but it is too late, and you find yourself on parade with safety pins in place of fly buttons, and your trousers held up by the thread from your spare pair of green drawers cellular. As you march the safety pins stick into your genitals. This hurts. The trousers begin to slip. You look down. A voice yells out: 'You can look down when your trousers fall down, Bellamy, and not before, yunnerstand?' The voice says: 'You can look down now, Bellamy.' You pull your trousers up.

The squad halts and the corporal summons you to the front. He recognizes you as someone who makes the others laugh and is dangerous. He would like to break you. The corporal is a little tin god and a sadist. When he makes a joke, you laugh. When you make a joke, he does not laugh. He permits you to do up your trousers, commenting: 'I wouldn't have believed it. He's tying himself up with his green drawers cellular.' Obedient titters from F Squad. 'You think you're bloody funny, don't you, Bellamy?' says the corporal. 'Yes, corporal.' 'Right. Then we'll all laugh at you.' The voice is calm, spiteful, holding great power in reserve. He is not altogether an unsubtle operator. He has a sense of rhythm, and even rations his swear words. 'You will all go ha ha ha by numbers. Squad will laugh at Bellamy by numbers, squaaaaaaaaaa – wait for it – squaaaaaaaaaaaa krwghaaaarrrh. Tups three. Ha. Tups three. Ha. Tups three. Ha ha ha. Tups three. Stand at ice. Tups three. Stand easy. Are you funny, Bellamy?' 'They seem to think so.' Titters and gasps. 'Shurrup. They seem to think so what?'

'They seem to think so, corporal.' 'I suppose Mummy thinks you're very funny, Bellamy, does she? I suppose the mater thinks you fraightfully amusing.' 'My mother's dead, corporal.' 'I don't care what she is, Bellamy, you're in the army now. Any more impertinence you're on a charge, yunnerstand, yunnerstand?' 'Yes, corporal.' Your breath stinks of fascism. 'Now listen, Bellamy, I can break you, I can break you just like that, yunnerstand? Yunnerstand?' 'Yes, corporal.' 'I've broken wogs, I've broken krauts, I can fucking break you, yunnerstand?' 'Yes, corporal.' 'If I have any more trouble from you I'll shove your rifle so far up your fucking arse you'll be coughing point two two bullets. Yunnerstand? Eh? Eh? Eh?' 'Yes, corporal.' 'What's wrong? Itching, are you? Got crabs? What do you think you are, the London Zoo? Eh? Eh?' 'No, corporal.' 'God help me, he's got safety pins in his balls. What's wrong with you, Bellamy? Eh?' 'Nothing, corporal.' 'Potential bloody officer? You're not fit to be a potential bloody sanitary inspector. Now get fell in.'

When you aren't marching you're up to your elbows in cold greasy water in a cookhouse sink, and when you aren't up to your elbows in cold greasy water in a cookhouse sink you're picking the loose leaves off the trees so that passing officers won't be struck and possibly seriously injured by falling leaves. Three huts down the row there is a suicide.

January, 1956. All he remembered about Sally afterwards was that she had dark hair and a perfect physique. He met her at a party. She made a pass at him. Therefore he took her home. She was drunk, perhaps also a nymphomaniac. She kissed him with tremendous pressure and perfect teeth. She forced him back on the divan and ran her body over him as if he was a harp and she was a musician's passionate fingers. They asked no questions about each other.

It was easy. She practically did it for him. He could have stopped at any moment, but didn't. After all, he was only giving her what she wanted. It wasn't hard to imagine a society in which she would get him on the national health.

Afterwards he wondered who had been using whom the most. He felt for Sally a disagreeable mixture of disgust and pity. He felt very young and small. He felt both a sinner and a prig. He lay in bed, no longer a virgin, ready now for Sonia, and he wondered just how much he had lost. Nothing, he suspected. And that was terrifying.

November, 1966. 'She was a good woman. We shall all miss her,' said the Rev. J. W. Scott.

'I know I shall,' said Robert.

'She never came to church, but she was generous in her support of all our activities,' said the Rev. J. W. Scott.

'So I believe,' said Robert.

'She has been called to a better place,' said the Rev. J. W. Scott.

'She's dead,' said Robert.

8 Hopes

He was ninety minutes late. It had been a hard day at the office.

'I've missed you, Robert,' said his wife, a delicate warmth and charm softening her severe, almost feudal Emmentaler-Battenburg beauty. Can this superb creature really be mine, thought Robert. I, dull gross fellow that I am, can I really have won the hand of the fairest daughter of the most gifted family in all Europe?

They had met on a steamy July day in the Bavarian Alps. He had paid his 1 mark 50 pfennigs and had joined the small multi-lingual party waiting in the hall to tour that unrivalled gem of the baroque, the Schloss Hohenbattenburg, sometimes affectionately known, after a disastrous dinner party of legendary fame, as the Schwarzkartoffelnhof. Who should be his guide but the youngest daughter of the house herself? He could never remember afterwards whether he fell in love in the Festsaal, with its famous musical chandeliers, or in the Crystal Grotto, but he was certain that they became engaged in the Huntsman's Lodge. He gave her a 20 pfennig tip. That night she played all ten Beethoven symphonies exquisitely. Beethoven had bequeathed his Tenth Symphony to her family on condition that its existence was never revealed to the world. Robert was the first foreigner ever to be entrusted with the secret. They were married four days later in the family's summer chapel high in the mountains, the tiny Battenburger Maria-Kapelle, to the tinkling of mountain streams and cow-bells, and the thundering of a massive organ.

Did she really renounce all that without hesitation, and come back to Kentish Town, and so charm Mr Mendel that he gave them the whole top two floors of Number 38? Could it all be true? Yes, it's true, says her smile. Yes, echo her sweet lips. Yes indeed, whispers her slight but infinitely appealing Adam's Apple.

'I've missed you too,' he said.

'See what Kate has done,' she said, handing him a beautifully simple and wonderfully flattering portrait of himself.

'Bless her, the lamb,' he said, lighting the rough but effective pipe that Tim had made for him in woodwork.

'I've done you some Trout Battenburger Art and Emmentaler partridge with grapes,' she said. 'But first you must go upstairs and tell them a bed-time story.'

'I don't want to leave you.'

'I don't want you to go,' she said, handing him a large sherry in the rude but serviceable goblet that Michael had made for him in pottery.

'But on the other hand I want to see them,' he said.

'I want you to see them too,' she said.

He kissed her. A glazed faraway look came into his eyes. She pinched him playfully and rapped his cheek gently with the raffia Radio Times holder Jennifer had made for him in handi-crafts.

'It is true. It isn't a dream,' she said.

He went upstairs. They all looked so clean and fresh in their beds.

'Tell us a story,' said Tim.

'Yes, do,' said Michael.

'Daddy tells the best stories in the world,' said Kate, the youngest.

'Daddy's the best daddy in the world,' said Jennifer.

'Are you ready?' said Daddy.

'Yes,' chorused the children.

'Then I'll begin. Once upon a time there was a man, and he was the happiest man in all the world.'

'Why?' said Tim.

'Because one day he met a woman, and she was the happiest woman in all the world.'

'Why?' said Jennifer.

'Because one day she met a man. . . .'

9 Fears

He was ninety minutes late. It had been a heavy day at the office.

'How's your secretary?' said his wife.

'What do you mean? I'm late because I've been working.'

'Oh, yes!'

'Yes.'

Something hard hit him on the back of the head.

'Hullo, Michael,' he said.

'I told you to take your shoes off when you come in from the garden,' said his wife. 'Look at that mud all over the carpet.'

'Rules, rules, rules. It's as bad as school,' said Michael.

'Well, you'll be back there soon,' said Robert.

'These are my worst holidays ever.'

Michael slammed the door behind him and stormed upstairs.

'I'm sorry,' said his wife. 'I knew you were working really.'

'Well, why did you say that, then?'

'It's not easy not to think it when you aren't here. I keep thinking of that Norwegian dancer.'

'Oh, God, we're not back on her again, are we?'

'And that French water skier.'

'How many more times do I have to tell you? Five minutes before you got there I fell in. I got stomach cramp and almost drowned. She rescued me. What do you expect her to do?'

'It looked like it, I must say.'

'That was the kiss of life.'

'You didn't look to me as if you needed the kiss of life.'

'Not afterwards, no. It had been effective. I was just coming round as you got there.'

'I bet you enjoyed her kissing you. I bet you were glad it was her and not some policeman.'

'Oh, for God's sake.'

'And why had you got stomach cramp anyway? What had you been doing?'

'Eating too much sweet and sour pork.'

'With some Swedish *au pair* girl, I suppose.'

'Shut up. Where's the sherry?'

'We're out of it.'

'I suppose you've never heard of an off-licence.'

Two large lumps of sodden clay entered through the French windows. Stuck to them was an evil-looking little girl.

'Take your shoes off,' roared his wife.

'There's no need to shout at her,' he shouted.

'Oh. Charming. Insult me in front of my own daughter.'

His wife stormed out of the room, slamming the door. Jennifer took off her shoes, shedding clay over ten square feet of carpet. She advanced into the room.

'What's that?'

'My boomerang. Auntie Flo gave it to me.'

'She should have more sense.'

'Look. You fire it and it comes back.'

Jennifer aimed it at the French windows.

'Those Japanese toys always were unreliable,' he said.

'My boomerang's broken,' said Jennifer, bursting into tears and running from the room.

Tim entered from the garden, and took off his shoes, sullenly.

'Hullo. How's Tim today?' said Robert.

Tim walked through the room without speaking. It was four days now since he had spoken to either of them.

Civil war broke out upstairs. He trudged up the stairs angrily, wondering why his wife didn't see to it. He knocked over a large tipping lorry. It tipped largely. Its cargo, three bags of self-raising flour, rolled down the stairs and burst. There was a sharp squeak under his feet. If he'd killed the white mouse . . . but it was the life-size doll – 'She talks and wets herself'. He had knocked its left leg off. He picked it up. It wetted itself. He dropped it. The right leg fell off. They would never speak to him again.

He went into the boys' bedroom. The boys were mauling the younger girl, Kate.

'Stop that,' he shouted.

'She's my worst sister ever,' said Michael, not stopping.

He hit them both hard. All three children wailed.

'I'm not crying,' said Jennifer, looking unbearably virtuous.

'What's all this porridge on the floor?' he said. 'And what's that?'

'Treacle.'

'And that?'

'Cherry jam.'

'And that?'

'Herring roes. They're three and two a pound.'

'What on earth have you been doing?'

'Playing grocers.'

'You boys can jolly well clear out those herring roes yourselves or sleep with them.'

He went into his bedroom. His wife was putting on her boots. She was deadly white.

'Where are you going?' he asked.

'Out.'

'Why?'

'To get drunk.'

'Where's my dinner?'

'Get your own bloody dinner.'

She forced her way past him, and slammed the door. The doors were proving to be a triumph of British workmanship.

He went slowly downstairs and sank into an armchair. He stood up, scraped the squashed grapes from his trousers, and sat down carefully on the sofa.

Wearily he reached for his cigar box, and opened it.

It was full of curried beans.

10 Just Good Friends

He was determined to give good value during his last month at Cadman and Bentwhistle. He would hand over his affairs in good condition. On Tuesday, therefore, he worked hard. There was no time to think of Sonia.

At five-forty he left the office. It was a clear night, with winter in the air. He couldn't face an evening alone at Number 38, or in the Blessington Arms. He must see Sonia. He rang her, but she wasn't home yet. In his mind he planned his week, fighting against solitude. Tomorrow he was having his fortnightly session with Dr Schmuck. On Thursday he was visiting Aunt Margaret. On Saturday he was going out with Elizabeth in Cambridge. He must see Sonia tonight or on Friday. He must propose marriage.

He knew what he must do to change his luck. He must ring her from Euston Station, from his lucky phone box. He walked down Laycock Street, down Belitha Villas, through Thornhill Square, down the Caledonian Road, along Copenhagen Street, past the Lewis Carroll Library, Alice in Concreteland, through this land devoid of magic, where the bleak council flats are surrounded by strips of lifeless grass, like blades of green concrete, on which no-one will ever play, or sunbathe, or kiss. Under and over the railway lines he walked, briskly, in the cold night air. Ahead of him loomed the Post Office Tower. We have substituted greed for lust, he thought. Even our phallic symbols have revolving restaurants at the top.

Euston Station was being rebuilt, and his lucky phone box no longer existed. He had to use another booth.

Her deep French tones. Please be in, Sonia darling. No reply. He tried Dick. Again no reply. Probably out playing squash, or fives, or real tennis. Always taking exercise, Dick.

58

Next he tried Bernard, in Pinner. Jean answered.

'Hullo. I'll fetch him,' she said.

'Hullo, Jean.'

'He's upstairs. I'll . . .'

'How are the kids?'

'All right.'

'Good.'

He could think of nothing more to say.

'I'll fetch him,' she said.

A notice invited the traveller to visit the cinema coach on platform 11. 'Through Highlands and Islands', 'Castles of the Principality', 'To the Sun by Southern', and 'Midland Region Modernization – phase 12'. In front of the notice an impatient man hopped from one leg to the other as if waiting for the Gents. In the other boxes people appeared to have battened down for the night.

'Hullo, Robert,' said Bernard.

'Hullo. How's school?'

'Not bad. Pretty busy. Quite a lot of marking to do.'

'I was wondering if you'd like a drink.'

'That sounds like a good idea. When?'

'Well, what about tonight?'

'I can't really manage tonight. We're eating at eight. It's carbonnade of beef.'

Jean's carbonnades flamandes. Her speciality, a relic of her year as an *au pair* in Ghent. It was always her bloody carbonnade. She had carried the good news of her carbonnade from Ghent to Pinner.

'I can't really manage this week at all,' said Bernard. 'I've got all this marking.'

'Don't you want to see me? Is that it?'

'Of course I do. But I've got marking.'

He rang off, and tried Sonia again. The impatient man swore in vivid mime. No reply. He left the booth and apologized to the impatient man, who said: 'I do have a right, you know. Forty-two years I've lived in this bleeding country.'

He fancied a good Chinese meal. His favourite Chinese restaurant was 'The Just Good Friends', haunt of the stars of celluloid, just off Wardour Street.

It depressed him, sitting alone amid all that flock wallpaper, with his stuffed chicken wings and abalone. He no longer fancied a good Chinese meal. He fancied Sonia.

'How's Crispy Noodles?' said his regular waiter. He always called Sonia 'Crispy Noodles', following an incident involving that commodity.

'Not too bad.'

'And stuffed pancake roll?' (Dick).

'O.K.'

At the next table sat four stars of celluloid, one male lead, two character actors, and a starlet. They had all been busy signing contracts, and they laughed constantly at the top of their voices, and drank three bottles of champagne.

He tipped the waiter generously, to compensate for his conversational ineptitude.

He tried Stephen next. Stephen was working but could manage a few minutes off in his Fleet Street local.

The bill-boards announced: 'Mystery Murder Sensation Search'. He bought a paper and read it until Stephen arrived at eight-forty, accompanied by Alastair. It irritated him that Stephen wasn't alone.

'What great epics are you on tonight? Simon, three, drinks bottle of whisky – it's "on the wagon" for him from now on, vows father? Kevin, six, beats chess master? Three hundred tortoises had no lettuce in British Rail "Torture Trip"?'

'You don't have a very high opinion of us,' said Alastair with the tolerant benevolence of a reporter with a full glass.

Stephen's expression said: 'Oho. Danger signals. Robert's in one of his moods.'

60

There was a moment's silence. It's because I'm here, thought Robert.

'We have substituted greed for lust,' he said. 'Look at the Post Office Tower. Even our phallic symbols have revolving restaurants at the top.'

They laughed. He wondered if they were really amused, or if they merely felt it politic to laugh. He tried out a complicated joke that he had made up that weekend.

'Did you hear about the launch the customs picked up off Newhaven?' he said.

'No. Tell us about the launch the customs picked up off Newhaven,' said Stephen.

'Well, they were told last week by the French customs to look out for a black motor launch with two men and 10,000 cigarettes on board, and yesterday they picked up a blue motor launch with one man and 500 cigarettes on board. The man said: "I have a complete explanation. I murdered my colleague, I'm a heavy smoker, and I bought the paint in Italy".'

'Very good,' said Stephen.

'Very good,' said Alastair.

'Of course humour's a very personal thing,' said Robert.

Stephen went back to work, and Robert felt foolish, staying there with Alastair and meeting other journalists whom he didn't know. Soon Alastair went too, and he was left among total strangers. He heard about midnight NATO bathing orgies, night news editors who'd got women into trouble, famous footballers who took drugs, a TV personality said to have a plastic ear, where to get a drink after hours in Newcastle, midnight MCC bathing orgies, the foulness of public lavatories in Aden, a cricketer dropped from the England team because he'd put a selector's daughter in the pudding club, the head of a friendly government said to have a tin foot, where to get a drink after curfew in Aden. He began to feel more and more edgy and dispirited, unable to contribute, knowing no facts or rumours, useless, meek, aggressive. He willed himself to keep his temper, to control the temptation to break his glass over somebody's head.

Gradually the group broke up, and his glass was still unbroken. Shortly before closing time Stephen reappeared. It irritated him that Stephen was alone. Presumably he felt that by this time Robert might not be presentable even to reporters.

'Pissed again?' said Stephen.

'No,' lied Robert.

'We've supped some lotion in us time,' said Stephen, reverting to his native vernacular.

'Aye. We have that. I wonder what Scouse Edwards and Taffy Lewis and Geordie Wilkinson are doing now.'

'What on earth made you think of them?'

'I often wonder. I wish we hadn't lost touch.'

Inevitable. Only one thing worse than army reunions. Old school reunions. But sad. Like to see everyone again. Especially Martin. Martin was the one that really rankled. He had announced, six months ago, that he was depressed, he was giving up his job as a teacher, he'd return when he felt better. He hadn't seen Martin since, and birds crawl under hedges to die, not to recuperate.

'How's Bernard?' said Stephen.

'I wouldn't know. I never see him.'

'Poor old Bernard.'

'What do you mean?'

'Fulham. They're not doing very well.'

Robert suspected that Bernard hadn't been to a football match for years, but the myth that he was a fanatical Fulham supporter died hard.

Despite his drunkenness Robert felt a heavy pang of social conscience. He must ask Stephen about his German girl, who really was a smasher and was hotly tipped by the cognoscenti to become the second Mrs Lester in the near future.

'By the way, how's . . . your kraut bird?'

'Gertrud. Fine. Fine. I anticipate a happy announcement.'

'Congratulations.' This rather bitterly.

'Well, there's no need to sound so thrilled,' said Stephen.

Careful, Robert. Control yourself.

'Sorry.' He must tell Stephen. 'I've got the push.' He described his dismissal, trying to make it sound like a funny story.

'Never mind. You'll get something else,' said Stephen.

'Oh, yes. I've got five firms after me already. One of them's offered £50,000, plus a comptometer operator in part exchange. Oh, I'll be all right. Don't you worry.'

Stephen wouldn't. He didn't care. They were drifting apart. It was a friendship that would not survive the end of youth.

His head was swimming. He felt ill. His gut was full of indifferent beer. He was drunk in the worst way, flat and maudlin. The lights were switched off. Time was called in an offensive, aggressive manner. Alastair had joined them for a last desperate pint. Robert forced a little more beer down his throat and composed his face into what he hoped was a reasonably cheery expression. The barmaid, collecting glasses, said to him: 'Don't worry, dear. It may never happen.'

He caught the 63 bus. When he got home the phone was ringing. Sonia!

Dr Strickman was either asleep or out. Robert wrote: 'Rotterdam too hot. Try Vienna' in enormous drunken letters, and slipped the message under Dr Strickman's door.

11 Dr Schmuck

Dr Schmuck was five-foot six tall, entirely bald, and corpulent. He had enormous brown eyes, and his age could have been anything between forty-five and sixty. His right eye had a tendency to twitch, and he picked his nose with intense concentration. He had lost all traces of a foreign accent but had picked up none of the characteristics of an English one. He spoke the dialect of statelessness. Sometimes he seemed to have lost interest entirely and to be just staring out of the window at the pigeons. At other times he would fire off rapid staccato questions. He was very sparing in his use of the couch. He was an enigma, and that was how it should be, because you didn't pay £4 an hour to find out about him.

And yet surely you did? Weren't you supposed to fall in love with your analyst? Robert seemed to remember reading something of the kind, and how could you fall in love with someone you didn't know?

He had gone to Dr Schmuck in 1964, on Martin's recommendation. Martin thought him the best analyst he'd ever had. It was true that Martin didn't appear to have changed in any way, but it was possible that only Dr Schmuck had prevented him from going into the most terrible decline. Martin had arrived at Number 38 once and said: 'I'm going to insult you, but don't worry. It's only because my doctor has told me to.' Martin had left Dr Schmuck in 1965. 'I'm not saying he's no good. It's just that he and I have reached a blockage,' he said. That was when Martin had finally walked out on industry and become a teacher.

Robert had never decided whether Dr Schmuck was any good or not. Dr Schmuck arranged things so that there was no way of telling.

His first visit to Dr Schmuck had not gone very well. He'd felt a fool, sitting there in that spacious, quiet flat, with its heavy red carpets and deep brown depressing furniture. He had felt it to be sheer self-indulgence. His problems were merely the problems of being alive. There was nothing an analyst could do.

'I really don't know why I've come,' he had said. 'I'm not desperate. I wouldn't actually say there was anything wrong with me. Nothing you could label.'

'I don't like labels,' Dr Schmuck had said.

'I'm wasting your time.' How absurd to care about that. Dr Schmuck would get his fee. He'd be delighted to waste time. 'There are people far worse than me around. I'm sorry. It's been a mistake.'

'Robert – it is Robert, isn't it? – for someone to come to me at all is sufficient reason. And then to want to leave again immediately, that's even more of a reason. And to fear that you are wasting my time, that is a guarantee that you will not waste my time. So now let's start. Tell me something about yourself.'

'What do you want to know?'

'My dear chap, how can I tell until you tell me? Start at the beginning.'

'I don't believe all that nonsense about childhood.'

'You can start where you like. Start with today if you like, and work backwards.'

'I was born in Richmond in 1935. My mother died when I was thirteen, killed in an accident engineered either deliberately or through inefficiency by her lover, whom I hated. I was raped by an older boy at school. Is this the sort of thing?'

'I don't want you to tell me things simply because you think I want to hear them. These events sound interesting. We will come to them in the fullness of time.'

And they had. They had come to everything in the fullness of time, and still they continued, on and on and on. He had grown to enjoy it. Perhaps this was why he had come, because here was one place where it was one's duty to be egocentric, where one could be self-indulgent in order to please someone else. Perversely, he immediately became deeply curious about Dr. Schmuck. And then again perhaps the perversity was an essential element in the analytical process. This was his dilemma – that the whole relationship with one's analyst is by its very nature so absurd that one can never turn round and tax the analyst with its absurdity.

Sometimes he just sat there and wished he was with a girl, although on other occasions he'd been with a girl and had wished he was with Dr Schmuck.

Nevertheless the time had come to break it off. He couldn't afford it, in any case, now that he'd got the sack. He had given away most of his half of his mother's money to the poor.

As he walked towards Dr Schmuck's flat off Baker Street his main worry was that he would hurt Dr Schmuck's feelings.

He entered the room, dead on time. All he had to do was make a simple, business-like pronouncement. 'I've decided to leave, Dr Schmuck,' would do very well.

'I've discovered what's wrong with me,' he said. 'Love-hate narcissism.'

'You know how I mistrust labels,' said Dr. Schmuck. 'They have a limited value, as reference points, but one must examine each one very closely.'

'Like epigrams.'

'What do you mean?'

'By its very nature an epigram sounds meaningful. More often than not this is mere illusion. It makes obvious truths sound new and new falsehoods sound obvious.'

'Very possibly.'

Dr Schmuck stared at the curtains. Robert knew that he must break the news gently.

'Tell me. Do you think I'm getting any better?' he asked.

'Better is a relative term.'

66

'I know it is. And do you think I'm getting any better?'

'We can't achieve progress by talking about it.'

'Well, how long is all this going to go on?'

'I'm not some kind of cheap miracle worker, Robert.'

'You're certainly not cheap.'

'You resent my fees. It's a common phenomenon.'

'How can anything be a common phenomenon? And anyway I don't resent your fees, in that sense. I can't afford them, that's all.'

'I don't like to talk about my fees. It gets in the way. It's an irrelevancy.'

'Not to me, it isn't. Look, Dr Schmuck, I must have a simple answer. How long is this going to go on?'

'It's an impossible question. There is in your case no disease as such. There cannot be a cure as such.'

'So there's no end? We go on for ever?'

'We go on until we've covered all the ground. This is progress, Robert. We are making progress all the time. We are piecing together this infinitely complex jigsaw puzzle which is one man's life.'

'I only hope we don't find a piece missing. There always is, with jigsaws.'

'You find it so hard to be entirely serious. Poor Robert. Seriousness means so much to you.'

'That's very true, actually.'

'You are surprised when I speak the truth. Do you think I'm a complete idiot? Do you think I'm just floundering around, simply because I don't come up with some marvellous solution?'

'What made you take up analysis?'

'We aren't here to talk about me.'

'I thought I was supposed to fall in love with you. My mother told me never to go out with strange men. So naturally I want to get to know you.'

'You're on edge today, Robert. What has happened?'

He oughtn't to answer. It was diverting him from his line of attack. He was supposed to be leading up to the tactful announcement of his intention of leaving. But Dr Schmuck made it impossible. He blocked all lines of approach. And so Robert found himself answering. The sack. His stupid joke. His justification for his stupid joke. His feelings about Tadman-Evans and Cadman and Bentwhistle. There were red roses on the polished round tables. The curtains were brown. It was warm. Dr Schmuck was picking his nose. Outside, mesmerizing, the traffic, muffled by the curtains. It was so restful, telling your life story over and over again, getting your feelings off your chest, so restful, just like falling asleep.

Someone was tapping him on the shoulder. It was Dr Schmuck.

'Wake up, Robert. It's time to go.'

'How long have I been asleep?'

'About forty minutes.'

'You just let me sleep on, and then expect me to pay you?'

'Certainly. It was very valuable for you, falling asleep just then. We're making excellent progress.'

12 Trouble at the Mill

Next morning he felt annoyed with himself for not having broken with Dr Schmuck. Nor did the affair of the twelve missing salinity analysers FX1475 improve his humour.

He put his call through to Poole, scanning the situations vacant in *The Times* as he did so. He had already applied for five posts, and hoped to have some interviews during the following week. After talking to Poole he got on to McGregor in Dispatch and issued some urgent orders. Then he rang Jansen. Jansen was out, but his secretary took the message. Robert then switched on the dictaphone and began his letter to Jansen. He spelt out the Danish address and repeated his apologies.

'The analysers were sent to our packaging department clearly marked for dispatch to the Anglo-Danish Shipping Company, Goole,' he went on. 'Unfortunately, a new employee in our packaging department erroneously addressed them to Poole, a South Coast port. Due to a mistake in the G.P.O. sorting office they were in fact sent, ironically enough, to Goole, where the "mistake" was spotted and the consignment returned to Poole. There they were erroneously delivered to the Anglo-Spanish Shipping Company, where a junior employee mistook them for a consignment of Pere David Deer in transit for Barcelona Zoo. They were loaded on to a boat which departed last week, accompanied by a large quantity of food and an RSPCA inspector. I have spoken to an official in Barcelona, but I don't think he fully understood my questions. He said they were being well-looked after, and two of them were breeding.

'Under the circumstances I feel that we must temporarily abandon them, and as I informed you on the telephone I have ordered twelve analysers to be sent to you immediately, and these will be delivered in Goole tonight by our own transport in time to catch tomorrow's boat. I can only apologize once again for this unfortunate mix-up.

I hope that Mrs Jansen and the children are well. I still recall with pleasure our outing to the deer forest and our evening at the Tivoli, Lorry, Sexy, Blue Fang Grotto and Hans Christian Andersen Jim-Jam Bar. I fear that I shall not be visiting you again, as I am leaving the company next month. I am only sorry that our happy association should end in this way.'

The hierarchy of 'Europe' was strict and rigid. At the head of the department came Drew. His present title was Head of Department. No-one ever understood what his task was, nor apparently did he. Most of the real administration was done by his second in command, Tadman-Evans, who was currently known as Exports Manager. Drew and Tadman-Evans disliked each other, and had offices opposite each other. Robert was now the senior of the four European salesmen. He roamed over the whole of Europe, while the others each had a special area – Neaves Northern Europe, Wallis Central Europe, Perrin Southern Europe. In the old days, before the latest rationalization, the salesmen hadn't had special areas, but had specialized instead in particular instruments. Robert had inherited from those days a fairly thorough knowledge of marine instruments and metals analysers. The scientists and servicing staff had quite a good opinion of him.

Below the salesmen there were four correspondence clerks, who dealt with routine correspondence and were occasionally given some of the easier jobs that cropped up 'in the field'. They had no secretaries, and used the typing pool. Neaves, Wallis and Perrin had two secretaries between the three of them and resented the fact that Robert had a whole secretary to himself. In fact Robert rarely had Julie to himself. Tadman-Evans was always borrowing her to replace his secretary, a girl much given to minor ailments whose length she could always judge in advance with suspicious accuracy. She would ring up and say: 'I've got one of these two day stomach bugs,' and would return two days later bursting with health. She was a source of constant, rarely acknowledged irritation between Robert and Tadman-Evans.

On this occasion she had 'this three-day flu thing', and Tadman-Evans had requisitioned Julie. As so often, therefore, Robert resorted to the typing pool.

In the typing pool this November morning it was managing to be both airless and draughty. He gave his piece to Janet. All the girls were sorry he was leaving. Mrs Roberts, the supervisor, thought it a diabolical shame. Some of the others, they were pig ignorant. They might be foreigners for all the sense you could make of their English.

He rang Sonia at work and was told that she was unavailable. Mr Wilcox would be able to deal with the matter. This assumption annoyed him. He had no intention of marrying Mr Wilcox.

He wanted to fix himself a final trip to Europe. He had some unfinished business in Amsterdam and Paris. Perhaps if he made a call on Brinkmann in Dusseldorf as well Drew would agree that the trip was worthwhile. But Drew referred the matter to Tadman-Evans, and Tadman-Evans was non-committal.

Robert finished off some routine correspondence and then lunched rapidly off a Scotch Egg in a pub not frequented by C and B. The Scotch Egg spoke eloquently of the reasons for this neglect. Then he had a haircut, returned to his office, and sent off two more applications for jobs.

At half-past two there was a joint meeting of 'Europe' and 'Home Sales' in the fourth floor conference room North. The meeting was to discuss a 187-page report on the internal communications structure of Cadman and Bentwhistle.

The report had been commissioned by the big white chief, who was concerned about falling morale and rising absenteeism, and so a communications expert had spent three weeks at C and B. He arrived with such a bad cold that during his first week absenteeism rose by eleven per cent. He stated in his report that 'Vertical first and second phase communications are substantially better, both by oral media (i.e. mouth) and by non-oral media (i.e. departmental or interdepartmental memo) than horizontal communications'. He made great play with OCSPs (Optimum Communications Stress Points) and RCPs (Recurring Communications Problems). His report was almost entirely incomprehensible.

Tadman-Evans popped his long, tapering head round Robert's door and said hopefully: 'No need to come to this meeting if you don't want to.'

'I'll come,' said Robert.

Robert was determined to show himself off at his best at the meeting, to prove to them all and to himself how wrong they were to sack him.

Outside, a watery November sun was shining. Inside the conference room the atmosphere was thick with memos and individual blotting pads. A glass of water stood before each seat. Beside the door an automatic coffee dispenser was dispensing automatic coffee. Sir John was presiding. He arrived dead on time and said: 'Sorry I'm late.' Europe was represented by Drew, Tadman-Evans, Robert, Perrin and Wallis. Neaves was abroad. Home sales had six representatives – Trencher, Wells, Brewster, Newby, Meredith and Pearce.

'Perhaps you'd start the ball rolling, Drew,' said Sir John.

'Yes. Well, I must say I think the report really is rather a waste of time,' said Drew.

'I think it's brilliant,' said Tadman-Evans.

'I think it's got some very good points to make,' said Trencher.

'Lots of good things in it,' said Drew. 'But perhaps it's a little long.'

'I must say I found it a little – er – er —' said Sir John.

'Heavy going,' said Perrin.

'Very heavy going,' said Newby.

'A lot of waste matter in it,' said Drew.

'We'll have to employ another communications expert to explain it,' said Robert.

'That's not a bad idea,' said Brewster.

'It was a joke,' said Robert.

'Oughtn't we to decide on a show of hands whether we are or are not in favour of the report?' said Wells.

'Good idea,' said Sir John.

Those in favour and those against were found to be of equal number. Tadman-Evans suggested that they recommend that a committee be set up to consider the need for setting up a committee to revise the communications system. Robert felt familiar currents of annoyance welling up. The self-importance and intensity of it all annoyed him. The fact that so much was decided on a basis of personal hostility annoyed him. Tadman-Evans and Wallis annoyed him. Drew's very existence embarrassed him. It annoyed him that there were never any women at these meetings, except for one secretary from each department, seated beside the coffee dispenser, dispensing coffee and making occasional notes on their pads, for the sake of their self-respect.

Suddenly it was all too much. 'Bollocks,' he said.

'Would you care to amplify that?' said Tadman-Evans.

'What we want is action,' said Robert. 'We want to keep personal feelings out of this. The situation in this firm is terrible. We ourselves are a symptom of the malaise. There is no real communication at all. I mean, take the typing pool.'

'I thought we'd get round to them,' said Wallis.

'Take the typing pool,' repeated Robert icily.

'Thank you. I'd like to,' said Wallis.

'I don't doubt it,' said Robert.

'Please, gentlemen, let's not be so . . .' said Sir John.

'Personal,' said Tadman-Evans.

Home Sales sat back and enjoyed Europe's internal strife. Except for Wells, one of nature's negotiators.

'Isn't the point here, unless I've misunderstood this entirely, a question of whether the lower-grade staff are sufficiently integrated into the decision-making structure of the company,' said Wells.

'Exactly,' said Robert. 'Though I hate that phrase "lower-grade". It makes them sound like petrol.'

'I'm sorry, but I want to know what he thinks he means by "I don't doubt it",' said Wallis.

'I mean,' said Robert,' that your interest in the typing pool is well-known.'

All his annoyance became centred on poor Wallis, who hadn't asked to be dirty-minded and lecherous. He had had a furious drunken row with Wallis at the last Christmas party. He had discovered Wallis taking advantage of a very drunk Rosie in the broom cupboard. There had been a fight. Robert had armed himself with a stiff broom, Wallis had grabbed the Eezie-Kleen Squeezemaster. Wallis had dipped the Eezie-Kleen Squeezemaster in the wine cup and had squeezed white wine, Merry-down Cider and brandy over Robert's head. Robert had hit him with the stiff broom, causing a severe cut and a black eye. It had all been a very bad example to the non-executives, especially Rosie. They might have been sacked, if everyone else's behaviour at the Christmas party hadn't been so disgraceful. The whole evening had been a blot on the high traditions of British instrument making.

'Please, gentlemen,' said Sir John.

'I will not please,' said Wallis. 'I've had an insinuation made against me.'

'Not an insinuation. A statement of fact,' said Robert.

'You'll be sorry you said that,' said Wallis.

'Children!' said Tadman-Evans.

'I'll give you a fact,' said Robert. 'The girls in the typing pool and people like them throughout the whole firm – of both sexes, Wallis – have no idea what goes on. They've no stake in our success – or lack of it. They're just doormats to wipe our feet on. You won't decide anything today. You won't ever decide anything. You don't want to. You love all this. Nothing will ever be changed. This is England. This is Cadman and Bentwhistle. This is human nature. I've had enough of it. I'm off. Goodbye.'

He left the room with as much dignity as he could muster and then collapsed into self doubt. He sat quietly in his office, in despair, feeling that he had been utterly childish, utterly ridiculous, and utterly right – a most unpleasant combination.

He switched on the dictaphone. The routine soothed him. He dictated two letters about pumping equipment. He rang Sonia again.

'She's rather hung up at the moment. Will Mr Wilcox do?'

'No, he won't do at all. Totally inadequate.'

'Oh. Well, I'll see. What name shall I give?'

'Robert.'

'Just a moment.'

Tiredness swept over him. He didn't want to go and see Aunt Margaret this evening.

'Hullo, Robert.'

'Hullo, Sonia. I'm sorry you're rather hung up. When am I going to see you and unhang you?'

'Well, I'm off on holiday on Saturday. Father's ill.'

'Oh, I'm sorry.'

'It's nothing much.'

'Good. What about tomorrow?'

'O.K. Tomorrow.'

Ten minutes later Dick rang. There was a party at his father's tomorrow. Could Robert and Sonia come? Yes, they could. Good. How were things? Bad. Oh dear.

Robert rang Sonia again. No, Mr Wilcox wouldn't do at all. He told Sonia about the party. She wasn't pleased. She didn't like Dick or his father. Robert promised that they wouldn't stay long. Sonia had heard that before. This time Robert meant it. Sonia laughed.

Robert dictated a letter to Julie. She called him Robert. It must be almost time to go home.

Tadman-Evans entered his office. Robert avoided meeting his eye.

'Constructive meeting,' said Tadman-Evans. 'We're recommending that a committee be set up immediately.'

'Good.'

'You get a nice view from this window.'

'Yes.'

'Very constructive. I've been thinking about your Europe trip.'

'Oh, yes.'

'I think you should go.'

An air of magnanimity about Tadman-Evans, an air of virtuously ignoring personal feelings. An almost irresistible temptation to say: 'I suppose you want me safely out of the way.' But he wanted the Europe trip. He must resist the temptation.

'Oh. Good,' he said.

'Good. Yes, very constructive.'

13 In Darkest Putney

After work I have a quick lasagne in the Italian café, apologizing mentally to the tall waiter for sitting in the small waiter's half of the room. The lasagne looks as if it has been excavated rather than cooked. There is a small insistent nervous hollow in my stomach. I am going to see Aunt Margaret.

Mystery murder sensation search row. I buy a paper, walk down to the Caledonian Road, and catch a number fourteen to Putney. The bus proceeds in fits and starts through the late rush hour traffic. In the Fulham Road I look for Frances, without real hope of seeing her. Or even the children, though perhaps I wouldn't recognize them now. Just before Stamford Bridge the bus passes the end of her street. A man is walking down it. Her husband, perhaps.

Every other Christmas, I came down here, sad at heart, to spend it with you, Aunt Margaret, and not Aunt Maud. We went to church, your presents were always just wrong, we went to the Webbers for Boxing Day. You made an effort for my sake, and that effort grated on me so much that I revealed my boredom to you. You made a big Christmas dinner, specially for me, because I was a growing lad. I just couldn't eat it, because I knew that it had been cooked specially for me, because I was a growing lad. I had visited you earlier, as a small child and you had placed a wet kiss on my cheek and a florin in my hand. It is colder in your house than anywhere else in London. For the last eight years, since your sister Hetty returned to England with her husband, you have spent your Christmases at Charlscombe, because Christmas is a family time. You loathe the journey to Wiltshire. It is like crossing Africa in a dug-out canoe. But you will do your duty by your family.

We cross the Thames. On the other side of the river it is darker. In London, Paris, Dusseldorf, Cologne, Verona, Florence, it is always darker on the other side of the river. I disembus at 19.34 hours. I turn into a side road, less well-lit than the High Street. The houses are small. Nothing stirs in the eternal winter. I turn into another, even darker street. Soon I shall be at the igloo. Poor Aunt Margaret. You took the plunge and married. Your philistine heart took a husband who loved art. He vowed to open that heart of yours. You honeymooned in Tunbridge Wells, though he favoured Paris. You were married one year. Then he took you to Florence, though you favoured Llandrindod Wells. He planned to start you on the spare, classical asceticism of Florence, and reveal to you, bit by bit, like a tactful undressing, her secret voluptuous depths. He fell into the River Arno. In his bedroom nothing is changed. Did it never occur to you how terrifying that bedroom was to me, fourteen years of age, sensitive, religious?

I turn down yet another street. Your house is at the end of a maze of streets, opposite the cemetery. It stands on a corner, a square Victorian why no monkey puzzle house, a lodge on the estate of death.

I walk up the path. I cannot believe that this is me, red-haired sensitive-lipped, hairy-legged bibulous North London semolinaphobe and friend of the small shopkeeper Robert Bellamy. My life ends when I step ring the bell across this threshold and I become something here she comes divorced from myself and everything I stand for unlike she's peering out to see who it is with Aunt Maud who brought me into the she's unlocking the door full flower of love love love hullo Aunt Margaret.

'Hullo. Come in.'

I recognize that, as usual, I have been unfair to Aunt Margaret. She is sweet and kind, although her kiss is wet and cold, and she smells of absence.

I enter her small living room. It is cold. She has been reading a biography.

'I'll put the kettle on,' she says.

'I'll do it,' I say.

'No, I'd better.'

She doesn't trust me. I use the new-fangled automatic gas lighter. Aunt Margaret uses matches. She has a revolving spit on her new stove – a present from Aunt Hetty. This too she never uses.

She returns. She is walking a little slower these days. Dante is still meeting Beatrice on the bridge. It is a deliberate gesture, keeping a Florentine picture in the living room.

'You look well,' she says. 'You've put on weight.'

She always says this. She is always surprised that I am no longer the skinny youth she remembers, little Belsen boy in the changing rooms of yesteryear.

'It's good of you to come all this way,' she says.

In her eyes it is a tremendous journey, a victory over almost insuperable odds, this trip from Islington to Putney. She has no idea of the extent to which it can be eased by the simple ruse of walking 500 yards, catching a number 14 bus, and walking another 500 yards at the other end.

I feel pleased about my haircut. I always have one before visiting Aunt Margaret. Oh, don't mistake me, I wouldn't have haircuts just for her. My argument is this – I must have haircuts some time, therefore why not have them just before visiting Aunt Margaret?

'How are things in London?' she asks.

'Oh, not too bad.'

'I'll make the tea,' she says. 'Are you hungry at all?'

'No, thanks, Aunt Margaret.'

'There's some cold tapioca. You could have it with some prunes.'

'No, really, Aunt Margaret, I'm not at all hungry.'

She goes to make the tea. Five minutes of my visit have

passed already. I gaze at the Putney, Fulham, Mortlake and Barnes Argus. She has marked several of the items in her tiny handwriting. She has some obscure form of classification. I am discovering anew what I discover anew each time I visit Aunt Margaret. I like her. I did not like having her as half a mother and I do not now like having her as a whole mother, but objectively I like her very much, this Queen Victoria of darkest Putney.

She returns with the tea and a seed cake.

'You can manage a piece of seed cake,' she says.

It is a command.

She sees that I have been looking at the paper.

'Old Turton the greengrocer is dead,' she says. 'Enlarged heart. He came to our church. I used to wonder how he could come to church and then rob us all like that, all the good sprouts on top and the rotten ones underneath. Now I wish I hadn't thought such a thing.'

Silence falls. I can't tell her what books I've read or what films and plays I've seen because to her they would all be works of wickedness.

'My Hubert would have been seventy-two yesterday,' she says.

I make a kind of noise. What else can you do?

'You still have no plans to get a television?' I ask, trying to change the subject, feeling inept tonight.

'I still have a mind of my own. Have another cup of tea.'

'Thank you.'

'It saddens me to see the young people these days. Amusement, amusement, amusement. We made our own amusements. Two spoons. That's right, isn't it?'

'No. I don't take sugar.'

It was Hubert who took two spoons. Perhaps she is failing.

'I'll go and wash the cup out,' she says, for she has put in the sugar.

'It's all right. I can drink it.'

'No. You come all this way and you can have your tea the way you like it.'

I sigh, expelling nervous tensions. When I was younger I used to take issue with Aunt Margaret. I have learnt better now, but this means that a nervous tension builds up inside me. Sometimes I use Aunt Margaret as a kind of yardstick. I see a new film, I like it, I look at it through Aunt Margaret's disapproving eyes, and if I still like it in spite of her then it is good.

She returns, pours me another cup. Dear Aunt Margaret, how Hubert would have softened you, over the years, Hubert whom I never knew, or would you have hardened him?

She welcomes loneliness. She has often told me so. She welcomes suffering. These things are sent to try us. I once said that if you welcomed suffering it couldn't really be suffering. She was furious. I was younger then. I thought it such a shame that she should live like this, with Hubert's room untouched, and Dante always meeting Beatrice on the bridge.

'You don't know how much it means to me, seeing you like this,' said Aunt Margaret. 'It's a pity Hubert isn't alive, to be some male company for you.' She sighed. 'I never wanted to go to Florence, you know. I favoured Llandrindod Wells. But Hubert was adamant.'

'Let me help you clear away,' I say, trying to keep her off it, ostensibly because I don't believe it does her any good.

'No, Robert. You sit there. You've done quite enough, coming all this way to see your poor old aunt.'

I read the paper. Putney shopkeeper jailed. Putney man in Turkish earthquake. Councillor accuses Putney of parochialism.

Aunt Margaret returns.

'Adamant, he was,' she says. 'He was going to open my eyes to the beauty of art. We were going to start with Florence and Siena. A lot of the paintings were religious. I suppose he thought that would appeal to me, and I daresay in their day they did serve some purpose. But those Madonnas. I daresay ordinary girls sat for those, girls who were no better than you or I.'

Don't put your daughter on a triptych, Mrs Worthington.

'Hubert couldn't see enough. He had to lean over the parapet to see the Ponte Vecchio better. He slipped. There were all those horrible carabinieri diving for my Hubert. He was punished for his greed. And say what you like, Robert, that sort of thing can't happen at Llandrindod Wells. And then there was your mother. So frail and lovely she was, like an angel. Your father was a gentleman. Then that wretched Hitler came along and killed your father, and your poor dear mother was led astray. Not that I blame her. I blame Hitler. He was the one who started it all. Invading the Sudetenland, indeed, and your mother so frail. I shall never forget the shock I had when I saw her wearing trousers, up to her knees in plaster. Dear Emma, whom we all loved, dressed like an actress. Dabbling with all those houses. I shouldn't be surprised if there was a bad influence at work there somewhere.' Aunt Margaret had never knowingly met Mr Clegg. 'Material beauty. Your family's associations with art have not been happy.'

She pauses. I wish to change the subject. I make a remark of which I am not particularly proud. 'The street lighting is terrible round here,' I say.

We discuss street lighting, the crime wave, the reasons for this, the vicar, the butcher, and our Christmas arrangements. I do not tell Aunt Margaret that I have been sacked.

Finally I leave.

'I'll try and come again before Christmas,' I say.

'There's no need,' says Aunt Margaret. 'It's a difficult journey, all the way from London. I shall understand it if you can't come. But I know you'll try. You're a good boy to me.'

14 Mixed Company

Robert and Sonia arrived at Dick's father's party shortly after nine. Robert hadn't yet proposed to Sonia. He felt very little doubt that they would be happy as man and wife, but he didn't want to have to announce the fact at Dick's party. It wasn't the right day for popping the question.

Dick's father was a Labour M.P., newly appointed a minister, and he lived in a vast, neo-Georgian house surrounded by high hedges of some vaguely repulsive evergreen.

'I hope you won't be bored,' Dick said. 'But I felt I needed a little moral support from my own generation. Lovely to see you again, Sonia.'

Sonia didn't reciprocate the compliment. She wasn't given to reciprocation, where Dick was concerned.

Robert hadn't liked Dick either when he first met him. Bernard introduced them, when Robert and Dick were both seventeen. Dick had been playing tennis. He had white hairy legs, and smelt ever so slightly of rubber. And he moved fast, and never lost his resilience, as if he was actually made of rubber. He was small and compact and full of energy. He got his smallness from his mother and his energy from his father. In their last school holidays they had become friends. When he finished his National Service in August, 1955 Dick took a room above the sex emporium, to see a bit of real life before he went to Oxford. Robert took over his room in October. Dick already knew that he was going to be a barrister. He had decided when he was eight.

During his first long vac Dick worked in a factory making lavatory seats, because it was time he did something truly socialist. The Queen Mother toured the area, and they all had to pretend to be making plastic life-belts. She came nowhere near the factory.

Shortly after this incident Dick took Robert home for the first time, to Sunday lunch.

'You'll hate father,' he said. 'He's the worst kind of socialist. Satisfies his snobbery and his greed by drinking enormous quantities of the best wine, and satisfies his socialist conscience by calling it "plonk". He's terribly left-wing.'

Robert expected to meet a monster, but he met instead a large attractive man, with a rich voice, grotesquely untidy off-duty clothes, and a passionately committed handshake.

'Gather you're politically mature,' he said, pumping a sense of purpose into Robert's right hand. 'Good lad. Some Spanish plonk?'

Robert drank his Tio Pepe, and listened to a lecture on the merits of the English test team. Dick's mother entered, pale and drab, and he tried to be polite to her without being rude to the father. Then they had lunch.

'I hope you like plonk,' said Dick's father.

'Yes, thank you,' said Robert.

'No reason why we shouldn't enjoy ourselves just because we're socialists.'

Dick said: 'This isn't plonk. It's Château Mouton Rothschild.'

'Is it? I never know what we get. Like a child in these matters,' said his father, tasting a mouthful as carefully as if it was power itself.

Later, in the garden, Dick said: 'Well, what do you think of him?'

'Rather nice, in a rather nasty way, which I suspect is the impression he likes to give.'

'You're new to him, so he treats you as if you were a floating voter.'

Now that he was a cabinet minister Dick's father had changed. There was no more sherry in the household, the cabinet having decided that there was no country left in the world which combined acceptable politics with tolerable sherry. And at the party there was no foreign drink at all. A large banner in front of the house announced: 'I'm Backing Britain'.

'Hullo, Robert,' said Dick's father, pumping a brief sense of dynamism into him with a handshake that managed subtly to suggest that he was no longer as left-wing as before. 'Lovely to see you. Must rush. Sorry. Bloody bigwigs everywhere.'

Robert toyed with one or two British wines, consumed one or two British cheeses, looked at one or two Turners and Gainsboroughs hired for the occasion, talked to a few British bores, and spent most of the time drinking whisky with Sonia and Dick. Dick introduced him to a tall, well-spoken, cleanly attractive girl who said: 'Are you one of them too?'

'I beg your pardon?'

'Labour.'

'Oh. Yes. Aren't you?'

'Heavens, no. I'm a Tory. I think I must be the only one here. It's rather exciting.'

Robert said: 'Be discreet. The house is bugged by the CIA.'

'Honestly?'

'Yes.'

Robert rescued Sonia from Dick and said: 'I can't stand much more of this.'

Sonia said: 'Dick suggests we all go on to a night club.'

'All?'

'The four of us. Dick has some girl.'

'Do you want to?'

'I wouldn't mind.'

The low roar of human chatter droned on. Sonia got out a packet of Gauloises and they ostentatiously blew French fumes. It became clear that Dick's girl and the tall Tory were one and the same person. Robert had forgotten how pleasant it was to start smoking and how horrible it became after about three minutes. At last Dick felt able to leave.

They drove to the West End in Dick's car. Dick's girl was

formally introduced. She was called Joanna. Dick was hopeless at people, especially women. He never seemed to get anywhere. In the Finchley Road people were driving like spoilt children, lots of dark-jowled men with blondes in sports cars, Latin waiters and *au pair* girls standing outside tatty clubs. Rain now, hard and vigorous. Thickening traffic. 'Mystery murder sensation search row inquiry' announced abandoned sodden bill-boards. Robert's hand on Sonia's bony knee, Sonia's hand on Robert's crutch, why aren't we going home, feeling definitely rather drunk, and utterly unhungry. Out of car, heavy rain, bright entrance, off with coats, Sonia's armpits, crowded room, table next to group of international philatelists.

Over the unwanted dinner the conversation turned to Dick's father, as it almost always did.

'How's your father liking being in office?' said Sonia.

'He doesn't like it. He's never really quite decided whether to be the *enfant grise* or the *eminence terrible* of the Labour party. Now he's got to make his mind up.'

'I always thought it was *enfant terrible* and *eminence grise*,' said Joanna. There was a silence. Snatches of smut and international philately drifted towards them. Presently Joanna spoke again. Her words were stones hurled into still waters. 'I suppose you'll think this pretty incredible, but I think this is the first time I've ever been out with a socialist,' she said.

'They're human underneath,' said Robert, and he was the recipient of two mild warning kicks under the table. Sonia had managed to whisper: 'You're drunk. Don't be rude to Joanna,' before they sat down.

'I've begun to see why you don't get on with your father,' said Sonia.

'It's impossible, because he has power and I don't.'

'Absence of power corrupts absolutely,' said Robert.

'I say, rather good,' said Joanna.

'Not one of my best,' said Robert.

'But then I always love champers,' said Joanna. 'It makes me

86

go all tingly. I know you shouldn't really drink it with steak, but honestly I could drink it with anything. But go on about your father. I find him frightfully interesting, having his house bugged by the CIA and all that.'

'What?'

'It was a joke,' said Robert.

'Oh, sorry. I'm not always awfully bright with jokes. Go on, Dick.'

'He treats mother abominably. He's had all sorts of affairs – all with socialists. While this Back Britain thing still breathes they'll all be British socialists. I'm sure he thinks that adultery is a purely political offence. And he encourages mother to be utterly drab and dowdy, because that sort of thing goes down so well in the constituency.'

'I suppose that's true,' said Joanna.

'Well, surely most Labour women are dowdy because they aren't well off, and it costs a woman so much more than a man to be well-dressed?' said Sonia.

'I suppose it does,' said Joanna. 'I've never thought.'

'You've never had to,' said Robert.

'Ow,' said Joanna.

'What's wrong?' said Dick.

'Somebody kicked me,' said Joanna.

'It's very crowded in here,' said Sonia.

'Are you all right?' said Dick.

'Gosh, yes. I'm used to being bashed about. Arthur threw me into the mill stream on Tuesday.'

'Who's Arthur?'

'My horse, of course.'

The cabaret was about to begin. The philatelists waited expectantly. The waiters sweated and smiled, and served as much as they could before it began. The lights were dimmed. Dick talked about his father intently, deaf to the world.

'I'm very rude about my father, but I've always admitted that he's a personality. Well, just you watch him now he's got a ministry. He'll get drabber and drabber. He's developing a constant political tone in his voice. He even snores persuasively.'

'How tinglifying.'

'When he makes a joke he's coming down from his Olympian heights and letting his carefully calculated hair down. We have carefully calculated family horseplay and he's carefully calculatedly cuddly. A political teddy-bear, over-anxious not to offend the golliwogs. He behaves as if there's a permanent colour supplement photographer perched on the chandelier.'

'Perhaps there is,' said Robert.

'I suppose I'm lucky,' said Joanna. 'I get on so well with Daddy. He's frightfully easy-going.'

'He can afford to be,' said Robert.

'Ow,' said Dick.

Then there was the cabaret, and afterwards Joanna said: 'Jolly clever. I don't know how they think of these things. And he really did look just like a woman. But I must say if I was Margot Fonteyn I'd be furious. But then I suppose I'm not.'

Robert danced with Joanna. He couldn't resist pressing himself against her. It was like dancing with a piece of the English countryside, a beautiful, green, luscious piece of fertile countryside. She made no reaction to his advances, but just tried to dance divinely, despite the crowd. Robert was glad when it was over, because poor Sonia wouldn't enjoy being landed with Dick.

Afterwards Sonia said: 'I must say I thought Dick handled Joanna very well. He must have realized how awful she was, but he never even gave a hint.'

'He may not have noticed.'

'I'm surprised he doesn't do better for women. He's not unattractive.'

'I love you, Sonia.'

15 Light Blue Interlude

Robert sat in the buffet car of the Cambridge train, nursing his hangover with five cups of coffee. He had met Elizabeth at a crowded party two weeks ago, and as an excuse for seeing her again he had told her that he'd never visited Cambridge, although he knew it quite well, having often visited Bernard. So now he would have to admire King's College Chapel, and the Backs, and profess astonishment when told that there was no high ground between Cambridge and the Urals, and show interest in its unique railway platform. He felt exhausted and sick. The spacious chalk fields were sodden, the villages and towns lifeless. He regretted now that he hadn't got engaged to Sonia. The train slid in gently across miles of deserted playing fields.

He hardly recognized her. She had a small face, with a tiny bunched-up nose and an assertive lower lip, and her body curved and thrusted with a youthful and commendable enthusiasm which might, one felt, turn suddenly to fat at the drop of a careless meringue. She would probably get a second in history, go to the cinema once a week, play hockey but not to excess, go to parties whenever asked and attend union debates without speaking.

'Hullo,' she said.

'Hullo. It's cold.'

'It always is in Cambridge. It's because there's no high ground between here and the Urals.'

'Really? None at all? That's astonishing.'

He expressed the requisite admiration for King's College Chapel and the Backs.

'You should see it when the tulips are out,' she said.

He had, five times. He remembered someone saying:

89

'You must come when the tulips are out. Terrible people, the tulips.'

'Which college is that?' he said, as they passed the University Press.

Elizabeth nodded to three men, wearing hideous scarves and inflated sweaters. 'Hullo, Liz,' they said. It was unpleasant to witness her acquaintanceship with all this latent virility.

'What would you like to do?' he said.

'It's for you to say, really. You're the visitor.'

'I don't know what there is to do. You do.'

'Yes, I suppose I do.'

These were perhaps the most banal lines spoken that day, in the great seat of learning beside the Fens. But there would be, Robert felt, others.

He knew three excellent pubs and two reasonably good restaurants. But he wasn't supposed to know them, so he had to accept Elizabeth's recommendations. Over a greasy kebab they discussed the afternoon's programme. It boiled down to a choice between an Ingmar Bergman film at one cinema and two Ingmar Bergman films at another. They chose the double bill.

'I hope you like Ingmar Bergman,' she said.

'I don't, actually. Wild Strawberries wouldn't drag me to see him.'

'Oh, Lord. You should have said.'

'No, I do like him. It was a joke. Wild horses, wild strawberries. Wild strawberries is one of his films.'

'Oh, Lord. Sorry. It's the cold. Hullo, Mike.'

'Hullo, Liz.'

Once one has started telling lies there is no reason to stop, so he concealed from Elizabeth that he had seen both films twice, at the Hampstead Everyman.

At least it was warm in the cinema, there being a thick cinema wall between the seven and sixes and the Urals. He held her hand, and she responded automatically to his massage. He held

90

her knees, and moved his hand slowly up her leg and held it there, four inches above the knee, until his arm went dead. The film ended. Someone in the row behind said: 'Hullo, Liz,' and she said: 'Hullo, Adam' and then the lights went down and they saw trailers for next week's Ingmar Bergman films, and then they saw the second film, and then they went out into the cold steel of early evening, and had tea and crumpets.

'I enjoyed that,' she said. 'Thank you.'

'I did my best,' he said. 'I thought. Elizabeth, now, unless I'm very much mistaken she'd like idyllic summer-houses and boats and ill-fated love among delightful scenery. Touch of rape here and there, I thought. A few childbirths. One or two virgins in the snow. The odd symbolic game of chess.'

'Hullo, Liz.'

'Hullo, Adrian.'

'Look, Elizabeth, Liz, you – er – you know, if you've got anything you ought to be doing this evening, don't hesitate to . . .' She looked hurt. She felt that she was boring him. She felt humiliated. How could he have been so clumsy? 'I hope you haven't. I just thought I'd better ask. You haven't, have you?'

She couldn't say that she had something else she'd rather do. He managed to get a drink by the ruse of walking past his favourite pub, saying: 'That looks nice,' and going in. The landlord said: 'Nice to see you back again, sir. How are your friends?' Elizabeth looked at him in surprise, and he felt an absurd panic at the thought that his tiny deception had been discovered. 'Your old porter's retired, you know, old Jim has,' said the landlord. 'It was his gout, poor old chap. Well, sir, and how's the world treating you?' And they realized that the landlord said this to all unknown faces, and the danger was past.

Elizabeth began to mime elaborately, screwing up her face. 'Going to sneeze,' she gasped, hunting for her handkerchief. For what seemed like five minutes she sat there, with her face screwed up, while he idly practised his pronunciation of 'Gesundheit'. Then the spasm passed, she touched each side of her nose ritually with her handkerchief, sniffed and said: 'Sorry. False alarm.' She made it sound as if they had narrowly escaped an earthquake.

They discussed Cambridge, British education, politics, Leicestershire, hunting, Paris, Dundee cake, modern buildings, Vietnam – all the usual subjects that interest lively young minds. Both were passionately anti the American policy in the Vietnam war. It really was amazing that one never met anybody – Robert himself included – who hadn't foreseen the whole tragic course of it years before any of the people involved. They were both anti-hunting. Robert expressed his stubborn and persistent socialism, 'despite everything'. Elizabeth professed disillusion with all parties. Both thought Leicestershire attractive in parts, Paris magnificent but waning, modern buildings with a few exceptions hideous, and Dundee cake overrated.

He named a restaurant that he had heard good reports of – from himself, last time he'd eaten there – and booked a table.

'You don't seem at all like a typical instrument maker,' she said, over her paté.

'What is a typical instrument maker like?'

'I don't really know.'

'Hullo, Liz.'

'Hullo, Ranulf.'

'I'd hate to be exactly like what one would be expected to be like by someone who knew exactly what one was,' he said. 'I hate the idea of businessy businessmen and arty artists and studenty students.'

The sole arrived. Conversation flagged. At a neighbouring table an elderly Cambridge eccentric, or a man playing at being an elderly Cambridge eccentric, a man in a baggy green suit with wide turn-ups, said to his young companion: 'But the imagination is not all-powerful. It is impotent. I have just ordered boiled potatoes. In a few minutes I shall experience the sensation of eating boiled potatoes. If all this, the waiter, the chef and the potatoes existed only in my imagination, I should be able to order boiled potatoes, at one and sixpence, and experience the sensation, in my own mind, of eating Duchesse potatoes, at two shillings. I should have saved a whole sixpence, albeit an imaginary one.' The waiter, who had half heard the conversation, said: 'Sorry, sir, was it Duchesse potatoes?' and the elderly Cambridge eccentric said: 'No, it was not. Nor will it be, alas, in this prosaic world. It was boiled potatoes,' and his companion blushed scarlet, and Robert was filled with the immediate pain that was the absence of Sonia, and the more distant, more evocative pain that was the absence of Frances. Goodness knew where Frances was. Sonia was in Bristol now. Last night had been a bright bubble. Now it had well and truly burst. Would he ever marry Sonia?

'Oh, Lord,' said Elizabeth.

'What?'

'Are there bright red spots under my ears?'

'Er – yes.'

'I'm allergic to fish sometimes.'

Why do you eat it then, you noodle?

'What happens apart from bright red spots under your ears?'

'. . . excuse me.'

She left the room. He finished his sole with diminished enthusiasm. Elizabeth returned, paler. She managed a coffee and insisted, like a policeman, on accompanying him to the station.

'You haven't seen much of Cambridge,' she said.

'Too cold. Those bloody Urals. I must come again, when the tulips are out. Horrible people, the tulips.'

Using someone else's jokes. Failing virility? Ask Schmuck.

Mystery murder sensation search row inquiry murder mystery. He bought a paper.

'This station is unique,' said Elizabeth. 'It's one long platform, and the trains come in to different bits of the same platform.'

93

'Good lord, how extraordinary.'

He entered the train, and leant out of the window.

'Don't wait,' he said, while thinking of the polite formula which would ensure that they parted for ever without dishonour.

'Does this train go to King's Cross?' said a voice.

'Yes, sir.'

'Then we shall not be able, by any stretch of the imagination, to experience the sensation of arriving at Liverpool Street?'

'No, sir. You want the nine forty-two for that.'

'Thank you.'

'You must be freezing,' he said.

'It is a bit. I'm sorry I was sick.'

'You couldn't help it.'

'Thank you for a lovely day.'

'Thank *you*.'

'Hullo, Liz.'

'Hullo, Julian.'

'I'll show you London some time.'

'That'd be nice.'

'Perhaps I'll come down again one weekend soon.'

'Yes.'

'Goodbye, Elizabeth.'

'Goodbye, Robert.'

The train slid off through a cold, inarticulate evening, towards a London denuded of Sonia. He sank back wearily into his seat. The train gathered speed. Good-bye, Julian. Good-bye, Ranulf. Good-bye, Mike and Adrian and Adam. Good-bye, youth.

16 Excellent Opportunities for the Right Man

Marketing Director. This new post is being created to cope with rapid expansion of growing group of British Companies.

The Posts of Assistant Marketing Director and Marketing Area Sales Directors are also available.

'Why are you leaving Cadman and Bentwhistle?'

'Well, I've become rather dissatisfied with the opportunities there. I find them a little bit – er —'

'A bit stick-in-the-mud?'

'Exactly. I'd say they're resistant to new ideas.'

'Would one of the new ideas to which they're resistant be the idea of continuing to employ you?'

'Oh, no. No.'

'Good.'

Is the sack written on my face?

'You live in N.W.5. What's that? Hampstead, is it, or High-gate?'

'Kentish Town.'

'Oh. What do you have there? A house or a flat?'

'A bed-sitting room.'

'I see. And you aren't married.'

'No.'

'Not that it makes any difference. Why not?'

'I haven't met the right person at the right time.'

'Your private life is completely your own affair, of course. Do you drink?'

'Yes, sir.'

'Much?'

'A fair amount.'

'Smoke?'

'Hardly ever.'

'What did you vote at the last election?'

'Labour.'

'Why?'

'I believe we still have a long way to go before we achieve social justice.'

'Are you pleased with the Labour Government?'

'Not very, though I think their deficiencies have been exaggerated.'

'What about their economic policies?'

'I think they leave something to be desired.'

'What?'

'Prosperity.'

Ouch! You fool, Bellamy. You'll put their backs up.

'Would you still vote socialist today?'

'Yes.'

'Do you think this country would have been in such a mess under the Conservatives?'

'It's impossible to say. The opposition in this country always seems to know all the answers, whichever party it is. We may not have the best government in the world, but we have the best opposition.'

Stop trying to be clever, you stupid fool.

'Define a good marketing organization, Mr Bellamy.'

Careful. Don't rush. Think it out. Don't be too clever. Don't be too stupid either. Don't take too long. Don't seem indecisive. Above all, be yourself. I wish I was with Sonia. I love her. A good marketing organization. Make it look as if I'm thinking. I should have married her long ago. A good marketing organization is one which organizes the marketing of goods – of good goods – well. How long have I been silent? Half an hour? Two years?

'A good marketing organization is one which achieves more sales than the product deserves,' said a stranger inside him, much to his surprise.

'How would you go about selling a particular product?'

'By emphasizing honestly and at the same time imaginatively its virtues,' said the stranger inside him.

'Supposing it had no virtues?'

'I'd refuse to sell it,' said the stranger.

Manager required. A manager is required for the Consumer Products Division of a London Company with wide international interests.

The Division is poised to achieve a dynamic breakthrough and the opportunities are limitless for the right man.

'What would you say are your greatest virtues?'

'It's rather difficult.'

'That's why we're asking you.'

'Well, I think I work hard and well, I'm loyal, I have a sense of humour, and – er – it's rather difficult.'

'You say you're loyal. In that case why do you want to leave your present job?'

'I've been loyal for 12 years and I feel it's time to be loyal to someone else.'

I wish I felt poised to achieve a dynamic breakthrough. But I don't. I feel randy.

'What about judgements? And decisions? Do you find it easy to make up your mind and act upon it?'

Frances. Dark and white. The shy but passionate Frances Lanyard. Where are you now? What has happened to you? How are the children? I must make up my mind what to say about making up my mind.

'I try to make my decisions at the last possible moment.'

'What do you mean by that?'

97

What indeed? Quick. Think.

'Well, sir, I believe in finding out as much as one can before making a decision, providing of course one doesn't delay too long. Once a decision is made one should stick to it, except in very exceptional circumstances. But it's hard to generalize. Each decision is a different problem.'

I'm sorely tempted to make a joke. I must resist it. All this is a charade. Yet it's necessary and I know it. Help. Someone has asked me something.

'Pardon?'

'I asked you what your powers of concentration are like.'

'Very good.'

'What sort of car do you have?'

'I don't have a car.'

'Oh. Why is that?'

'I just don't want one.'

Perhaps I don't want one simply because people like these can't understand why anyone shouldn't want one.

'And you aren't married?'

'No.'

I travel light – no car, no wife, one room. I don't expect to live for ever. I'm just passing through. But I will have a wife. And several rooms. Perhaps even a car.

'Marriages can have its disadvantages too, of course. And in any case your private life is your own affair. Some American companies vet the wives and make secret inquiries to find out whether you've any communist connections. A few English companies do it too, now that there's so much American money pouring in. I personally deplore it. What we at the Ulthrippe-Dormington Group are concerned with is simply your ability as a worker. Though of course we do like to know just a little about your private life, so that we can treat you as a human being, an individual. Have you ever had any associations with the communist party?'

.   .   .   .   .

98

Sales Analysis Instructor. A vacancy exists in one of Britain's leading industrial test firms.

We have created more than seventy highly successful tests for measuring the potential capacity and suitability of industrial employees – and sometimes employers, too!

The successful applicant will help train our interviewees and research staff. The opportunities are limitless in this rapidly expanding field.

'You've come out about average. That's much better than most people do. Now those are the tests you'd be teaching other people to use. Do you think you could do that?'

'Yes, I think so.'

'It's important that you should know something about interviewing, obviously, if you intend to teach others how to interview. Have you any experience of interviewing?'

'No.'

'If you were interviewing me, what sort of questions would you ask?'

'Well, I'd say: "If you were interviewing me, what sort of questions would you ask?"'

'Yes, well, I don't think you'd get very far asking questions like that. Now imagine that you're interviewing me. Go on. Interview me.'

'What qualities do you think a successful interviewer needs?'

'The ability to sum people up, to distinguish between truth and lies. The ...'

'Good. Good.' Robert didn't want this job, didn't believe in all these tests. He felt abandoned, irresponsible, happy. 'Well, let's see how this works out in practice,' he said. 'Imagine that you're interviewing me. Go on. Interview me.'

'Yes. Er – what qualities do you think ...'

The interviewer paused and glared at Robert. They stared at each other in silence for some thirty seconds.

'Thank you, Mr Bellamy, for coming to see us,' said the interviewer.

Foreign Sales Technical Correlation Officer. This exciting new post is being created to deal with the rapid increase in scientific communications in the exports division of a far-flung industrial empire.

'What would you say are your greatest faults?'
'It's rather difficult.'
'That's why I'm asking you.'
'I think I'm sometimes rather hasty and over-emotional. I have a quick temper. My sense of humour sometimes gets the better of me. I – er – it's rather difficult.'
'Well, that's a very fair answer.'
'May I put a question to Mr Bellamy?'
'Certainly, Trubshawe.'
'This address of yours, 38 Blessington Road. Kentish Town isn't it?'
'Yes.'
'By an odd coincidence I happen to have had certain dealings with a shop at that very address. It's a kind of a . . . a kind of a chandler's, Sir Henry.'
'A yacht chandler's, you mean?'
'No, Sir Henry, not exactly a yacht chandler's. There's not a lot of yachting up Kentish Town way. More a . . . a general chandler's.'
'A grocer's, you mean?'
'Not exactly a grocer's. A general store. Odds and ends. Little knick-knacks.'
'An antique shop, you mean?'
'Not exactly an antique shop. Just a sort of shop. It sells, you know, useful things.'

'A junk shop?'

'Not exactly. Just a little shop, that's all. I have occasionally picked up some useful things there. You don't have anything to do with that shop, do you, Mr Bellamy?'

'No. I just live above it.'

'What on earth has this to do with it, Trubshawe?'

'Well, nothing, really. It's just that it struck me as being rather an odd place for, you know, someone in this sort of position to live.'

'I hardly think it fatal for a man to live near a shop, Trubshawe. I'm sure some very worthy people have lived near shops. I once did myself. Marvellous sextants they used to sell. I often picked up a sextant there. But I don't think this is getting us anywhere. Not relevant. What is the name of this shop, Mr Bellamy?'

'Well, sir . . .'

'Come on. You've nothing to hide have you?'

'The North London Surgical and Medical Supply Centre.'

'I see. Yes. Any further questions, Trubshawe?'

17 A European Trip

'Do you have a British passport, sir?' said the man.

Of course I do, thought Robert. What do you take me for? You don't think I'd have one of those French passports, do you? Rotten, flimsy things, melt at the first touch of rain.

'Yes,' he said.

For all those who didn't have British passports there were humiliating forms to fill in. Ducks and waders flew away from the train across the saltings. Mist covered the silent, still estuary of the Stour. Even Nature seemed to know that it was Sunday morning. They arrived at Parkeston Quay. The aliens went through their door, the British through theirs.

Robert made straight for the bar and ordered a Heinekens. He was glad to be leaving England and glad to be going by boat. It made it seem more like a human activity and less like a business trip.

The boat began to move. It was a Dutch boat, so you could use British or Dutch money, and the announcements were made in two languages. In the British boats the announcements were in English only, and you had to use British money, and Robert felt ashamed.

The boat shuddered steadily. Robert's glass and bottle rattled, his chair vibrated, his socks fell down. He looked round the sparsely-filled bar. Only his table seemed to be affected. He moved to another table. The shuddering was even worse. Harwich slid past, a ghost town. The bar began to fill. Businessmen, a young girl near to tears, British soldiers, Dutch *au pair* girls, a few out-of-season tourists. Robert began his detective story – he reserved detective stories for his travels – and had another beer. Foghorns boomed. A buoy clanked sullenly. He went on deck and looked out over the stern at the sea foaming away behind the boat like-like-like a sea foaming away behind a boat. It was bitter cold, in the wind of the ship's own making. A Dutchman was photographing the gulls, twisting his body as he followed the flight of the birds. Robert thought of the first time he had made this trip, in 1954. 608 Private Bellamy. XOX Draft. It sounded like a call for help.

The photographer stood beside him.

'It looks like the North Sea,' said Robert.

'But it is the North Sea,' said the Dutchman.

They watched the wake, mesmerized by the churning of the water. Later they lunched together, in the bowels of the ship, on fricandeau of veal. The Dutchman, a travel writer, praised Scotland, the Lake District, Bury St Edmunds, Cambridge, whisky, English breakfasts and kippers. Robert praised Dutch beer, Leiden, Delft, Uitsmeters, Amsterdam, Dutch breakfasts and Vermeer. After lunch they went into the bar. Robert had a Dutch gin and the Dutchman had a Scotch whisky. And as they sat there, juddering together in time with the languid friction of the boat, Robert told his new friend about the first time he'd passed that way.

The first time he'd passed that way.

He was posted to Germany in June, 1954, but Aunt Maud needed an emergency operation, and for a few days it was touch and go. A compassionate officer gave him compassionate leave. When he returned to camp his draft had gone. He spent six weeks in the depot regiment, idle, forgotten, an administrative oversight, an anachronism in uniform. Then, late in August, his posting arrived. He was XOX Draft.

He caught the military train to Parkeston Quay on a glorious summer night. Farmers were combining under floodlights. He had a whole carriage to himself, and thought this odd.

At Parkeston Quay there were three customs officers, one for XOS Draft (The Gloucestershire Regiment), one for YBB

Draft (400 men from the Royal Artillery) and one for XOX Draft (Robert).

He was the first man on board the *Vienna*.

'Draft?' said a corporal at the top of the gangway.

'XOX.'

'B Deck. Berths 1–350.'

Half an hour later the corporal woke him up and said: 'Hey, you, where's the rest of your draft?'

'I'm all there is, corporal.'

'All there is? All there is? I'm indented for 350 men.'

'No, corporal. There's only me.'

'Well, fucking roll on.' The corporal gave him a long, hard look, as if expecting 349 men to come tumbling out of his pyjamas. 'You think you're very clever, don't you? Getting yourself 350 bunks. You think you're very smart. What's your name?'

'Bellamy, corporal. 608 Private Bellamy.'

'You haven't heard the last of this, Bellamy.'

In the huts at the Hook of Holland there were three separate queues for breakfast, one for the Gloucestershires, one for the Royal Artillery, and one for Robert. He managed six cups of coffee from his enormous urn, and four boiled eggs, not liking to disappoint his cooks.

On the troop train he had 44 reserved compartments. Farther up the train they were standing in the corridors.

On his arrival at Munster Hauptbahnhof he was met by a major, a sergeant, three corporals, and twelve trucks.

'Who are you?' said the major.

'Bellamy, sir. XOX Draft, sir.'

'Where's the rest of you?'

'I'm all there is, sir.'

'I was expecting 350 men.'

'No, sir. There must have been a mistake.'

'We've had 16 huts cleared out specially for you, Bellamy. We've had 350 late teas laid on. We've got 350 seats laid out in the lecture room so that Sgt Major Hawkins can lecture you on not getting into trouble with the Fraüleins. Q. Watson has aired 350 mattresses. And now you tell us you're only one man.'

'I'm sorry, sir.'

'So you should be.'

He drew his bedding from a surly Q. Watson. He was given his late tea by a catering corps corporal so livid that he broke Robert's plate with the serving spoon. In the huge, cold lecture room Sgt Major Hawkins glumly advised him to steer clear of the Deutsche bints. He slept alone in an empty hut in an empty wing of an empty block. In the morning he went on parade before the sergeant major, six sergeants and eighteen corporals. He marched past the C.O. Then the C.O. marched past him. Then the C.O. halted, left-turned, and came violently to attention.

'XOX Draft ready for inspection, saaaaaaaaaaaaaaaaaaarrgh,' said the sergeant major.

The C.O. inspected Robert. So did the sergeant major, the six sergeants and the eighteen corporals. Then he went to the C.O.'s office for an interview.

'I was expecting more of you, Bellamy,' said the C.O.

'I know, sir.'

'On Saturday week you were going to do a little exercise against 300 men of the third regiment. Have to cancel it. Wouldn't be fair on you.'

'Thank you, sir.'

'You're a damned nuisance, Bellamy. I think we'll have to move you over with C. Squadron. They turned up two months ago a man short.'

'I think that must have been me, sir.'

'Oh, that was you, was it? Well, you'd better take his place. I mean, take your place. I mean, be yourself. Well, you know what I mean.'

'Yes, sir.'

'Damned nuisance, Bellamy. Damned nuisance.'

'Yes, sir.'

'An amusing incident,' said the Dutchman.

'Embarrassing,' said Robert.

'You felt singular.'

'Exactly. You know, you speak very good English.'

'Only the bare rudiments, I'm afraid.'

Shortly after that the Dutchman fell asleep. The boat shuddered gently on across the North Sea. The British soldiers eyed the Dutch girls round the corner of their lurid paperbacks, dreaming of sweet seductions in the lifeboats, believing that because they were out of sight of land they were also out of the range of all social taboos. The girls waited with amusement for the clumsy advances that would follow after two more beers. Robert thought about Sonia and Frances, and the fact that he still hadn't got a job, despite his interviews. He tried to get into his book. Five times Sir Thomas Edgenutt's body was discovered by mysterious Jane Ibberling in the Gothic summerhouse at Cawston, lovely civilized yet sinister Jacobean Cawston. Five times she gasped 'Oh, my God'. Five times Robert lost the place and began to think again his wintry thoughts.

He went on deck again. Nothing was visible except grey water and mist, a square mile of visibility moving steadily towards Holland. The air was salty and wet. There were five gulls behind the boat.

'Dutch gulls,' said the Dutchman.

'You've woken up.'

'Yes.'

Robert made a big effort to be cheerful. He had never felt depressed at sea before.

'The GPO put a hundred bottles in the sea at Harwich – and none of them was ever seen again,' he said. 'It's a joke about the inefficiency of the postal services.'

'I understood it,' said the Dutchman.

And so they reached the Hook of Holland. Robert said good-bye to the Dutchman, waited until he was seated in the Amsterdam train, and then joined a different carriage. They were friends of the sea, and of the sea alone.

The mist was less thick over the land. Beside the line, almost all the way, were houses and flats, the curtains left undrawn in the Dutch style. Thousands of women handing thousands of cups of coffee to thousands of families, above and below and beside each other, unknown to each other, but known to Robert. The same television programme shining out into the same night again and again, in rows, like a giant animated polyphoto. Perhaps it was the same family again and again as well. This is the future, he thought. Owing to her small size, her large population and her undrawn curtains, Holland presents a grim warning to us all.

Amsterdam. Mist here too, mixed with cigar smoke and the burnt rawness of winter. He tried to shake off the depression. A room. A shower. A meal. Sleep. But no sleep. All Europe in the grip of a spell of intense central heating. The sweat streaming out of the red hairs of thickening, growing puddingy Robert Bellamy. An enormous thirst. Glass after glass of slightly warm hotel water.

Another day. A Dutch breakfast. Wot, no honeycake? Then he noticed that everyone else had honeycake. Once so popular with hotel staff, friend of the underprivileged Robert Bellamy had now become beyond the pale. No honeycake for that red-haired bastard in 307. He won't complain. A small thing, a missing slice of honeycake, in a man's slow journey towards death. But important to Robert just now. Hell, didn't tell Schmuck he wouldn't be coming on Wednesday. Send card to Schmuck. Nice canal scene for Schmucky-Wucky. Ha, the curve of the canal is like a female torso.

He met Mr Van Gend, the agent. Charming as always. Why didn't you stay with us? During the day they visited firms engaged in land reclamation and the steel industry. Robert's technique was usually straightforward, free from jargon, confident. Today he found that he was pressing a little more than usual, trying to prove himself to himself. His mind went blank while he was praising a new gauge to measure deep water currents. He was not quite his usual self in expounding the advantages of a new X-ray diffractometer. His lunchtime *rijstafel* gave him indigestion. Small things, but annoying.

After work they drove to Mr Van Gend's charming house in an inner suburb, where he lived with his delightful wife and children, his beautiful modern furniture, and his exquisite plants. Robert would have loved to spend a quiet evening with the Van Gends, but he had a reputation for gaiety, ever since his first visit, and the Van Gends looked forward keenly to their carouses.

'I lead a quiet life,' said Mr Van Gend, deftly overtaking a tram.

'I lead a quiet life, too.'

'Like hell, I think. Last time we had a great night, Robert. The greatest. But this time, I think I must take my wife. No deer evening for us this time.'

'Stag.'

'Oh, yes. Stag. I hope you understand. I have to take her sometimes.'

'Of course.'

'We have someone for you, of course. A friend of my wife. A charming girl. Intensively cultivated. Very keen on art. You'll like Anna. Her husband was killed by a tram in September.' He swung round another tram with gay aplomb. 'She's still very upset. It will do her good. I hope you don't mind.'

'Not at all. I much prefer being with the women.'

'You do?'

'Yes. And you know how much I like your wife.'

'But this is wonderful. So do I, actually.'

They arrived. Robert taught the children English card games. Anna arrived, dark, subdued, with big limbs, not very tall. He didn't like to look at her too closely, because of the sadness. He felt nervous about Anna. Robert and Mr Van Gend went to the little white house at the end of the road, with the words Café Billiard in huge letters on the side. The women joined them after the baby-sitter had arrived. Drinks were consumed. They took a taxi into the city centre, had a drink on a heated terrace in the Rembrandtsplein, followed by large steaks in a noisy restaurant. Then they went to the Blue Note. Later, after the cabaret, after the dancing, after midnight, they went to the Yellow Windmill. From there they went to the Pink Clog, which specialized in what the guide book called 'typical Gipsy emanations'. Piped Hungarian music, in other words. He danced with Anna. She was drunk, but her heart wasn't in it. He danced with Mrs Van Gend, who bit his ear, amorously and very hard, and said: 'Mrs Van Gogh, not Van Gend.' She repeated this to the others. Anna said that Burne-Jones was a far greater painter than Van Gogh. Mrs Van Gend denied this. Mr Van Gend carefully watered a plant with his drink. Anna burst into tears and said that Robert would be hurt.

'I'm not hurt,' said Robert. 'I think Van Gogh was a better painter than Burne-Jones, too.'

'You're just saying that.'

'I'm not.'

'You hate Van Gogh.'

'I don't.'

Mrs Van Gend sat on the floor, rolled Robert's trousers up to the knees and began kissing his legs.

'Come and have a look at Robert's lovely red hairs,' she said to her husband.

'I don't want to,' said Mr Van Gend.

'Rembrandt was a far better painter than Dante Gabriel Rosetti,' said Robert.

They went home by taxi. The taxi stopped at Anna's.

'Why don't you go and have coffee with Anna?' said Mr Van Gend. 'Come round at eight and we'll drive down.'

Robert and Anna went into the house.

'You don't have any children,' he said.

'No.'

She began to cry.

'I'm sorry,' he said.

'It's not your fault.'

She made a strong pot of coffee, breaking a cup in the process. She tried to show him her book about the Pre-Raphaelites. He put it to one side and unrolled her tights. Her thighs were sturdy and she had big but sexy knees. He kissed her sturdy thighs and her big but sexy knees. He felt utterly tired. He looked at the flesh in front of his eyes, and it was a stranger's flesh. Who was this nice Anna, to be trampled all over by his clumsy boots?

He sat up beside her on the sofa, and kissed her lips, more out of politeness and international goodwill than desire.

'Do you mind if we – er – don't?' she said.

'Not if you really don't want to,' he said, relieved.

She began to cry, to shake. He held her, useless, an intruder. She uttered just the one word, 'Herman'.

'I hoped to be wildly drunk and forget,' she said, after the crying. 'I feel quite sober but dizzy and sick.'

'It never takes you the way you want it to.'

'There's a spare room you can have,' she said.

He kissed her goodnight, and said: 'Oh, Anna, you're all such nice people, and you all speak such good English, and tomorrow I'll be gone.'

She said: 'That's how we seem to you.'

She showed him his room, and gave him the sudden impulsive kiss a girl might give her father. 'You've come too soon. I'm not ready,' she said.

She woke him at seven and gave him a Dutch breakfast. He was utterly exhausted after two and a half hours' sleep, but hadn't the heart not to eat it, the cheese, the cold meat, the rusk, the honeycake. Anna seemed ill at ease.

'Please, Robert, will you do something for me?' she asked.

'If I can.'

'They're worried about me. I want them to think I'm better from Herman. Please could you – give them the idea that —'

'Yes, all right.'

He kissed her good-bye.

'Dear dear Anna,' he said.

At the Van Gends there was just time to teach the children some English swear words. 'Anna gave me breakfast,' he told the pale, fragile Van Gends, accepting a cup of coffee. 'She's – er – very nice. I hope that, you know, my *being there* with her like that, and, you know, the – er – and everything. I mean, it won't upset her my just going off afterwards like this, will it?'

'No. You've done her good. You're what she needed,' said Mrs Van Gend. They were pleased. She looked at him with the sheepishness of one who cannot remember the latter part of the previous evening at all, but has suspicions. 'We did enjoy it,' she said. 'It made a change. You mustn't think we do that every night. We lead a quiet life.'

So they did. He envied them it.

Mr Van Gend drove to Robert's hotel, where he paid his bill and shaved. Then they drove down to the site of the Delta project where the results of trials with a C and B depth analyser were closely studied and a substantial trade agreement was cordially reached. The sun was shining and Robert was in rather better form. They all drove to Rotterdam for an early evening rijstafel. Mr Van Gend waved until the train was out of sight. Robert had indigestion and slept but fitfully in the train.

He changed at Cologne and reached Düsseldorf after midnight. His room was so luxurious it seemed a shame to waste it by falling asleep. He ought to sit and look at it all night.

At eight-thirty he met the agent, Herr Brinkmann, the aggressively well-shaven Herr Brinkmann. Robert's clothes were beginning to look travel-weary, and he was conscious of this. Düsseldorf is shiny. It is elegant. It is the expense account of the Ruhr. On still days, in the winter, a pall of money hangs over the city. It is a symbol of German energy. Some of the modern buildings combine sleekness with good taste in a near-impossible way. Only the names of the architects are ugly. Robert felt ill at ease in Düsseldorf. It was a day of grinding hard work, flogging fluorimeters and diffractometers to some of the big boys in the Ruhr. It isn't easy to beat the Germans on their own ground, and Robert didn't. Probably he couldn't have done so on any occasion, but today he certainly couldn't. His lunch on the Königs Allee was too rich. The central heating was too hot. It was all too difficult. He wanted to go to bed and sleep for sixteen hours.

Herr Brinkmann had a charming house, with a delightful wife and children, beautiful modern furniture, and exquisite plants. Robert would have loved to spend a quiet evening with the Brinkmanns, but he had a reputation for gaiety, ever since his first visit, and Herr Brinkmann looked forward keenly to their carouses. Usually his small, bird-like wife accompanied them. Robert liked this, since she was attractive. But on this occasion she was not included in the programme. Robert vaguely recalled, next morning, an enormous plate of potatoes, a sauce that included crumbed pumpernickel, noise and jokes, Herr Brinkmann making playful remarks to married women as they passed, a little bar with vaguely Parisian overtones, a little bar with vaguely Oriental undertones, sausages and mustard and smoke, endless glasses of beer, and a feeling of growing desolation, which the presence of Anna would have effectively soothed. He remembered strident women, grotesquely painted women, fat women. He remembered deciding, half way through the evening, that in the morning he would go to Munster. He couldn't remember why.

These recollections were made not in his luxurious hotel room but in a broken camp bed in Herr Brinkmann's living room. What on earth did Brinkmann think he was doing, putting him in a torn, rickety camp bed? One foot had gone right through. He couldn't get it out.

Herr Brinkmann's children came in and watched him solemnly. He said 'Guten Morgen' with the gravity one must always use before the very young, and they wished him a Guten Morgen too, and fled. He managed to extricate his foot. Herr Brinkmann came in, looking completely fit.

'You've broken the bed. Never mind,' said Herr Brinkmann. 'I'm sorry about the aunts.'

'What aunts?'

'I explained to you that we have aunts in all the bedrooms.'

'Why am I here and not in my hotel?'

'You insisted. You threatened to hit me unless I accommodated you. You said all hotels were impersonal.'

'Oh, Lord. I'm very sorry.'

'We had a nice evening.'

'Yes.'

'You mustn't think I do that every night. I lead a quiet life.'

He never saw Frau Brinkmann at all, which was a disappointment. He explained that he must leave for Paris early. Herr Brinkmann took him to his hotel, watched him shave and pay his enormous bill, accompanied him to the station, helped him buy a ticket to Paris, and put him on a train he didn't want to catch. He realized that he liked Herr Brinkmann very much, and was sorry he wouldn't ever see him again.

At Cologne he got off and caught a train to Munster. It took him back to Düsseldorf, where he had to change. He was terrified he would see Herr Brinkmann. His next train took him through the Ruhr itself, bursting with dirty vigour and civic enterprise. It took him through the fertile marshalling yards and Gothic water towers of railway Germany. It took him across the rich plain of the Munsterland, dotted with solid farmhouses. He wished he was a solid farmhouse.

At Munster no trucks awaited him. Nothing awaited him. He

booked a berth on the night train to Paris, the Nord Express. He deposited his luggage and went out into the town. He admired the attractive Romanesque cathedral, the rebuilt gabled houses, the Gothic St Lamberti church, the new theatre. It began to come back. Old haunts. Cafés. Even a vague recollection of Geordie Wilkinson's face. Egg and chips at the Toc H. Beers and cokes in a little country inn by the Dortmund-Ems Canal. Mufti. Performances at the opera. *Doctor in the House* six times at the Globe Cinema. He visited his old camp, finding the right street unconsciously. It was on a straight, bleak road. Lines of blue lorries rumbled past. He felt nothing. He peered in. The guard looked at him suspiciously. A lid of heavy cloud was sliding into place across the sky. The city was waiting for the winter to come down from the north.

He had a meal in an old haunt, scrubbed wooden tables, traditional costumes, antiques, bustle. He remembered Geordie Wilkinson throwing up into a warming pan. He remembered not getting to know the Germans at all. But of Robert Bellamy, the young soldier, he remembered nothing. He wondered why he had come.

He seemed to feel the pride and tradition of the country throbbing beneath modern Germany like the engines far below the sun-deck of a luxury liner. He feared these things. Was he right to, or was he merely influenced by past events? He felt unable to answer, inadequate, naïve, tired.

He made his way to the station, caught the Nord Express, let the boat of Germany shudder on across the map to Paris, and awoke with a headache.

He breakfasted on coffee and croissants. Two horseshoes dunked in chicory. A brief walk. That incomparable Paris feeling, of elegance within oneself, lent him for a moment new energy and assurance. In Paris he worked rather better, and even sold some fluorimeters.

He would have loved to spend a quiet evening with the Phillipes, but he had a reputation for gaiety, and M. Phillipe looked forward keenly to their carouses. Robert remembered next morning a great confusion of foods and wines and music, and of M. Phillipe telling him that he mustn't think he always lived like this, he led a very quiet life.

He felt oysterish. Mme Phillipe came in and gave him some coffee. He couldn't understand what she was doing in his hotel. Ah, he wasn't in his hotel. He had insisted on booking out at 3.35 a.m. M. Phillipe was his greatest friend. He had insisted on staying with M. Phillipe. Mme Phillipe had been awakened at 4.5 a.m.

Robert went out to buy a present for Mme Phillipe, and suddenly found himself staring at the only brothel he had ever visited.

The only brothel he had ever visited.

He had pulled off his deal with M. Bernard and his rookery, his first deal. He felt good. He would return to London on the nine o'clock flight. Now was the time to make the European experience complete. Martin had given him the address. His analyst had told Martin that it would do him good. It hadn't.

So he did what he would never have dared to do in Soho. He rang the bell that said: 'Maison D'Amitié (Prop. Mme M. Antoinette).'

The door closed behind him. The roar of the traffic was hushed to a soothing murmur. In front of him was a stone flight of stairs. On the first floor there was another door. He rang the bell. He hoped it wouldn't smell like a brothel.

The door opened. A comfortable, plump, middle-aged woman stood before him.

'Madame Antoinette?'

'Oui.'

There must be some terrible mistake. This wasn't a brothel.

'Je suis Anglais.'

'Ah. Welcome, sir.'

'Thank you.'

'I speak the English. I was three weeks from West Hartle-pools. A friend of a pen. I stay from her family. I learn the English. Did you know this nice town?'

'Paris?'

'West Hartlepools.'

'No.'

Mme Antoinette showed him into the waiting room. There were wall-to-wall carpets, and flowers on the table. On the walls were pictures of sister establishments throughout France. They all looked identical. He gazed at a bedroom in the Maison D'Amitié, Lyons (Prop. H. de Lafayette). He thought, soon there'll be drive-in brothels, called Mothels. There was a suggestions box, which he longed to open, and on the table a visitors' book. Henry Chadwick from Preston had found it 'very comfortable'. Arthur J. Doornsticker from Maine, USA, voted it 'the best yet in five countries', while Spiro E. Bertorelli from New York State thought it good value for money and promised to tell the folks back home. A Swede from Malmo said, if Robert's scanty Swedish was not mistaken, that he had spent the five happiest days of his life there.

'Ah, you read the book.'

'Yes.'

'Afterwards you will sign. Come now. Do not be on the nervous edge. All my girls is clean.'

'I'm sure they are.'

'All decent girls. They like the English. They is not so much demanding. Not like them Germans. Phew!'

Mme Antoinette led him into a back room where three girls were playing cards. They wore green uniforms stamped: 'Maison D'Amitié', with their names – Annette, Claudine and Martine.

Annette was thin, with raw red skin and a dead, sad face. Claudine was plump. She looked jolly and homely. Martine was thin, but not so thin as Annette. Brown hair rather than a brunette. Quite a good figure. Doughy skin. Pastry faced. A face that looked as if it had been very attractive until it had been kneaded slightly out of shape by a jealous sister. The forehead and chin a little too flat, the eyes too close together, the nose slightly squashed. But not an unattractive face. It would have to be Martine. He hoped some people chose Claudine, because she was so jolly, and Annette, because she was so pathetic. How absurd to care about that.

'I think – it's difficult, but I think Martine.'

Mme Antoinette led him to a medium-sized room furnished with a large bed, a green armchair, a hard chair and a small bedside table. On the window-sill there was a geranium in a pot, and the sunshine was streaming through the net curtains and making net patterns across the bed. It was a modest hotel room, without the bible. It didn't smell of a brothel, or of exotic scents. It smelt of heat, and carpet and impermanence. A notice on the wall gave the official tariff.

He didn't feel remotely sexy. He began to undress, slowly. Martine did the same. It was the sort of afternoon on which any self-respecting county team would have reached 163 for 3.

'J'avai oublié mon Français,' he said. 'Je regret.'

She shrugged.

They finished undressing.

Time stood still.

They stared at each other, naked and bored.

He shrugged.

Far below them the traffic rumbled.

He had expected to be embarrassed, now he was embarrassed because he was too bored to be embarrassed.

He said: 'It's no good. Ce n'est pas bon. Sorry. Pardon. Kaput.'

He began to dress. Martine began to dress. She never said a word the whole time. He gave her a large pile of francs.

'You is satisfied?' said Mme Antoinette.

'Yes, thank you. Very nice.'

'We are the modern idea. A chain house. You understand?

We have from fifty-two French towns the house exactly the same with this. You will visit all these others?'

'Perhaps.'

Now he stood staring at this house, with an expensive piece of jewellery which he hadn't wanted to buy, and growing iller by the minute. Perhaps this was the dreaded oyster poisoning, scourge of crustacean lovers the world over. He felt a wave of self-disgust, vague, amorphous, cold.

He gave Mme Phillipe her present, said his good-byes, walked down to the air terminal, caught the bus to Le Bourget, and ordered a *citron pressé* in the bar, hoping the freshness would do him good. It burnt into his stomach like a laser.

On the plane he came out in a heavy sweat and shivered constantly. He tried to concentrate on the clouds, motionless in layers at thirty miles an hour, making speed meaningless by its relativity. He clutched his paper bag. He longed to tell everyone that it wasn't air sickness, but too many oysters.

At Heathrow he at last realized that this wasn't oyster poisoning. It was a simple dose of flu. He took a taxi home, feeling worse with every passing pound note. He was never ill. He prided himself on that. He was cracking up.

There were two letters – two letters in a week. One from Aunt Margaret, the other offering him the betting opportunity of a lifetime. There were also two giant carpet sales. Goodee.

The phone was ringing. Sonia! Wondering where he'd been. 'I'll see if he's in,' he said.

He came downstairs again, unlocked his door, and fetched a pencil and paper.

'He isn't in,' he said. 'Yes ... Yes ... Helsinki a wash-out. Bogelmann done for. Right.'

He took the message upstairs. On the way down he met Dr Strickman.

'There's a message for you,' he said. 'Helsinki a wash-out. Bogelmann done for.'

'Thank you. You don't look well. Go to bed,' said Dr Strickman.

He went to bed. The house seemed sordid. He was shivering uncontrollably.

Nothing will happen to him for a while. He will be in bed for six days. Long enough for us to look at Mr Mendel's pride and joy, and the shy but passionate Frances Lanyard.

18 Mr Mendel's Pride and Joy

Mr Mendel's pride and joy was Number 38, Blessington Road. He owned Numbers 32 and 26 merely to support his family. Number 38 was different. He loved it. He lavished his care upon it.

The ground floor was already occupied, when Robert moved in in 1955, by the trusses and ointments of the sex emporium. On the first floor lived Robert, with Michael at the back and Mrs Crutchley opposite the stairs. Michael did the local insurance collection round, was quiet, pleasant, and appreciative of Robert's jokes. He died of leukaemia in 1959. Mrs Crutchley was a suspicious old woman who had no intention of taking any part in the narrative. Mr Mendel thought her a blot on Number 38. 'I offer her to move to Number 32 or 26. I have a better room, Mrs Crutchley. More warmer altogether, I say. But she won't. I can't turn her out, an old woman. So what do I do?' She died of old age in 1960. Above Robert lived Miss Flodden, the teacher who later began to write bitter letters about tidiness and was rumoured to take baths with Mr Marshall. Above Michael lived Mr O'Reilly, a quiet red-faced Irishman. Above Mrs Crutchley lived Doreen and Brenda, that domesticated duo from Dewsbury, as Robert called them. On the top storey lived Mr and Mrs Tennison. Sometimes Mr Tennison was an actor and Mrs Tennison a typist, and sometimes Mrs Tennison was an actress and Mr Tennison a typist. When they were both acting they became unbearably chirpy and noisy, and when they were both typing they became unbearably depressed and a definite suicide risk.

Mr Mendel's one great fear was that there would be a suicide in one of his houses – but above all in Number 38. 'There's a great deal of it about. Statistically I am due for one,' he would say. He lived in Barnet. Robert saw him every Saturday morning, when he paid the rent. Sometimes Mr Mendel stopped for a coffee.

'You're happy, Robert?'

'Not too bad.'

'That's good. You have some mail today. That's nice. It cheers you up.'

'Yes.'

'Michael is not getting much mail. Hasn't he any friends?'

'Some, I think.'

'Will you do me a favour, Robert?'

'If I can.'

'Keep Michael cheerful.'

'I think he's all right. He expects very little from life.'

'What about the girls?'

'Brenda and Doreen? They're in fine form.'

'You all get on quite well, don't you?'

'Yes, I think we do.'

Mr Mendel pushed his spoon slowly round in his coffee.

'There has been nothing at all between you and the girls?'

'Nothing like that, no. We're just good friends. It's all just rumours, Mr Mendel.'

'It would be nice, though. A romance in Number 38. If ever you want, you know, to bring a girl in . . .' Mr Mendel took a spoonful of coffee. He drank from the spoon when he was embarrassed.

'Thank you,' said Robert.

'And the Tennisons? They are working?'

'I don't see them as much as you do, Mr Mendel.'

'Well, thank you for the coffee. I see you next week. You let me know if anyone is a little down in the dumps, Robert.'

'Yes.'

Sonia came to Number 38 occasionally, and got on well with Doreen and Brenda and Michael. Stephen, on a Northern paper in those days, sometimes stayed on the camp bed. Dick and

Bernard and Martin were regular visitors. They often played poker all night. Robert expected Bernard to find the place a bit beneath him. It was Bernard's role in life, in Robert's eyes, to find places beneath him. But Bernard didn't seem to, although of course he kept that sort of thing to himself.

Martin made it almost a second home. And sometimes he called on Brenda, and stayed the night. He didn't tell Robert, for fear he'd be annoyed, for fear he regarded everyone in Number 38 as his property. In fact Robert knew, because Brenda told him.

One spring Saturday in 1957 Martin called round at ten forty-five. Robert was just having his breakfast. He suspected that Martin had come to see Brenda, but had got no reply.

'Do you really enjoy your work?' Martin asked him.

'Yes, I do. Why?'

'Are you good at it?'

'I think so. I hope so. Why?'

'What were your parents like?'

And Robert had to tell Martin his life story. This was unheard of. Martin never asked one about oneself. Not that he talked much about himself, either. He talked to you as if neither of you really existed, as if only an abstract world of distant ideas had any reality.

'Why all these questions, Martin?' he asked, after about an hour.

'Dr McCabe told me to take more interest in other people,' said Martin.

Martin was with Dr McCabe until 1959, when Dr McCabe had a nervous breakdown.

'I hope you find me interesting,' said Robert.

'Yes, quite,' said Martin.

'What more can I tell you? I'm a schizophrenic paranoiac, I'm slowly changing into a woman – a Lesbian, luckily – and I suffer from acute hydrophobia – that's fear of large hotels. I . . .'

There was a knock on the door.

'Come in.'

It was Mr Mendel.

'Ah, Robert. Oh, you have a friend.'

'This is Mr Mendel, the landlord. Mr Mendel, Martin.'

'Hullo. Robert, it's eleven fifty, and there's no noise from the girls. Are they away?'

'I think Doreen may be, but Brenda's here.'

'I think I smell gas. Perhaps she's done away with herself. Has she been depressed lately?'

'No, I don't . . .' began Martin, before he remembered that Robert didn't know he'd been seeing her.

'I don't think so,' said Robert.

They went upstairs with Mr Mendel.

'Perhaps it's too late already,' said Mr Mendel.

'I expect she's just asleep,' said Robert.

'I feared this. Last Saturday she was pale. I said, cheer up, Brenda.'

They listened outside the door. There was no noise.

'You smell gas?' said Mr Mendel.

Robert and Martin sniffed. Mr Tennison came downstairs, slim and lithe in his jeans and gym shoes, with a string shopping bag. He looked at them in amazement.

'You smell gas, Mr Tennison?' said Mr Mendel.

Mr Tennison sniffed. Robert and Martin sniffed again.

'Something,' said Martin.

'Could be,' said Robert.

'Not very strong,' said Mr Tennison.

They knocked on the door and called out. There was no reply.

'I think we'd better break in,' said Mr Mendel. 'Oh, dear. That this should happen in Number 38. And I only just re-decorated.'

He backed away across the hall, a fast bowler measuring out

his run. He ran towards the door, huge, stooping, ungainly. At the last moment he turned aside.

'She could just be out,' he said. 'What do you think?'

'Who can say?'

'You never know, really.'

'We must try. Every minute is vital,' said Mr Mendel. He measured out his run again, then hesitated. 'I can't break down my own door,' he said. 'Robert, you're a strong boy. You do it, and I charge you no rent this week.'

'I'll do it,' said Mr Tennison.

'It's all right,' said Robert. 'I'll do it.'

He charged at the door. It splintered, but did not break. He charged again, went straight through the door, and collapsed in a heap on a pile of dirty cups and saucers. Coffee slops and butt ends flew in all directions. Brenda and Bernard looked up from Brenda's bed in astonishment, pulling up the tangled bed-clothes instinctively, so that only their heads and feet showed.

'Could we have an explanation?' said Bernard, his calm voice shaking fractionally.

'Mr Mendel thought Brenda was committing suicide.'

'We knock. There's no reply,' said Mr Mendel.

'We were tired,' said Brenda.

'Brenda,' said Martin reproachfully.

'Sorry, love,' said Brenda.

'Everything is all right, after all,' said Mr Mendel.

'We thought we smelt gas,' said Robert.

'There's a leak,' said Brenda. 'I was going to mention it, Mr Mendel.'

'Are you all right?' said Mr Tennison.

'I've hurt my shoulder a bit, that's all,' said Robert.

'You've broken all my cups,' said Brenda.

Robert gave Bernard a cool glance. Bernard blinked like a blinded owl. Mr Mendel looked sadly at the damage.

'Never mind. I will repair it. And you're all right, Brenda. You're happy. You don't do away with yourself. None of you pay any rent this week. You are all such good tenants to me,' he said.

'Why didn't you use your key?' said Brenda.

'What?'

'You've got a key, haven't you?'

Mr Mendel turned white.

'I forgot,' he said. 'It was an emergency. Break the door down, I thought.' He pulled his chain of keys from his pocket and stared at it sadly. 'Funny how you do things. I'm sorry we intrude. You carry on. This afternoon I come back.'

'How can we carry on? There isn't a door,' said Brenda.

The rescue party retired in confusion, Mr Mendel staring at his keys. 'It was because it was an emergency. I thought, what's the quickest way? Break the door down,' he said. 'Funny how you do things.'

Robert felt outraged at seeing Bernard there. He didn't mind about Martin. He liked Brenda, and her morals were her own affair. But Bernard. It didn't fit in at all with his idea of Bernard. It was altogether too hole-and-corner.

All that had been a long time ago. Married now, and respectable, Brenda. Bernard too. And Doreen. Martin disappeared. Mrs Crutchley dead. Michael dead. The Tennisons divorced and married to other actors and typists. Only Miss Flodden remained now.

Mr Mendel was showing his age, stooping more than ever.

'You ever hear from Brenda and Doreen?' he would ask.

'No.'

'It's a shame.' No one had ever married within the fraternity. 'Miss Flodden and Mr Marshall, they take baths together, no?'

'It's rumoured.'

'Maybe one day – who knows? But it's not the same, Robert. Number 38 isn't what it used to be.'

'Nothing remains the same, Mr Mendel.'

'True.'

'Nothing is constant any more. Not even any of us. All human ambition, all human feeling, all human history is just a mayfly in the year of eternity, Mr Mendel. And the existence of this world is merely a second in the history of other worlds.'

'Very true. You're a philosopher, Robert.'

'This Jew goes into an ice-cream shop. In the queue are two Englishmen. The first one says: "An ice cream, please, Mr Cohen." Mr Cohen gives him an ice-cream. The second Englishman says: "An ice-cream, please, Mr Cohen." Mr Cohen gives him an ice-cream. The Jew says: "An ice-cream, please, Mr Cohen." Mr Cohen says: "I don't have no ice-cream." The Jew's angry. He says: "When the two Englishmen want it you have ice-cream. When I, a Jew, want it you don't have no ice-cream. What kind of a Jew are you?" "Have you tasted our ice-cream?" says Mr Cohen.'

'Very good. I can never remember jokes.'

'I didn't remember it. I made it up.'

'You can't have. I've heard it before.'

'Oh. Well, I thought I made it up.'

'Dr Strickman, he gets funny messages, no?'

'Yes.'

'You think he's all right?'

'In what way?'

'You don't think the messages are threats? You don't think they prey on his mind?'

'I don't know. How can one tell?'

'Statistically, a suicide is becoming more and more certain. So far I am lucky. But every day it becomes more likely. You mark my words, Robert, very soon we'll have a suicide in Number 38.'

19 The Shy but Passionate Frances Lanyard

It seemed to Robert afterwards to have been love before first sight. And all because he and Dick, quite by chance, in the late autumn of 1962, met Boris in 'The Just Good Friends' one Saturday evening. Boris, deep-voiced, broad-shouldered, and one-sixth Latvian. Boris was one of those people you meet, by chance, every eighteen months, but never by arrangement, although you enjoy their company. Robert had met him in Madrid, Pisa and Sheffield.

Boris introduced them to Catharine, and the four of them had a drink, and Boris said that he was invited to a rather ghastly party, and he hated parties, but there would be plenty of drink, and they must go too. Two more drinks put them in party mood and it was with quickened pulses that they entered the two rooms in which Donald and Belinda Parkinson were providing liquid, edible and musical refreshment for their wide and varied circle of friends.

Amid such remarks as 'How thrilling. Jeremy, come and meet a real live spy', 'Belgian drivers are the worst in Europe', 'Addis Abbaba is the one interesting place in Africa', 'We love it round here. Kennington's the coming place, you know', 'All Italian drivers believe they're Fangios. About ten per cent of them are' and 'Well, where can I do it if not at a party?' Robert heard two or three really not totally impossible people (how misanthropic one becomes, in self-defence, at parties) discussing a woman called Frances. Remarks overheard included: 'I thought Frances was coming', 'Don't say Fran couldn't make it' and 'How is the Frances bird?' And Frances was of interest to him, before he'd even seen her.

The arrival of the Frances bird in up and coming Kennington coincided with Robert's involvement in a long conversation with Eva, the Parkinsons' *au pair*, whose nose was almost as broken as her English. Robert had just said, to keep the ball rolling: 'I can tell where you come from by your accent. Don't tell me. Rothenburg-ob-der-tauber. Near the bottom of the hill, probably on the right,' and she had said: 'No, Hamburg' and there was someone saying: 'Frances, hullooooowe'. As soon as he had a chance, for he believed in being polite to German *au pairs*, Robert introduced himself.

'Hullo, Fran,' he said.

'I don't know you, do I?' she said.

'It's my misfortune,' he said.

Robert soon found out that she was married, and separated, had four children, lived off the Fulham Road, rarely managed to get out, and was unhappy. He tried to cheer her up with some jokes. She wasn't cheered up. He was drunk. Frances drifted away. Boris began telling him a Latvian story. Behind him someone said: 'But women never tell the truth about their ages. They deceive only to be flattered,' and someone else said: 'The Turks have never decided which side of the road they *are* driving on.' Boris's Latvian story suddenly grew fascinating, but the point depended on one's having listened very carefully to the beginning. Then he was once more with Eva, who had not made a hit with Donald and Belinda Parkinson's wide circle of friends. This time, despite or perhaps because of, his drunkenness, he talked to her quite seriously, and found that she had much to offer. It was therefore after one o'clock when he next spoke to Frances. She was listening to a man who was saying 'The Germans are very undisciplined drivers, surprisingly.'

'Excuse me,' said Robert. 'Do you mind not boring this lady?'

'I beg your pardon?'

'She doesn't get out very often, and she doesn't want to hear about German drivers.'

'Get stuffed.'

'Do you, Frances?'

'You're both drunk.'

'Get away from her. Go on. Shoo.'

'Take your hands off me.'

'You can come outside, if that's the way you want it '

'All right. I will.'

'Stop it. You're both drunk.'

They went out into the garden, and took off their coats. A few of the guests wandered out to have a look. Robert advanced on the motoring bore, and the motoring bore advanced on Robert. They were both drunk, but Robert was the drunker. He got in one good blow, then was sent reeling. Just as he was advancing, dazed but determined, Donald and Belinda Parkinson rushed out with helpers and the two offenders were efficiently pinioned.

'Do you all mind coming inside now?' said Donald. 'We've got the neighbours to think of.'

A taxi was procured for Robert, and he agreed to go on condition that he was given Frances's phone number. He caught a last blurred glimpse of Boris and Catharine looking sadly at him, and Dick talking earnestly to Eva, and Frances looking upset, and then he was off.

The next day he rang her up. She declined his invitation. But after four more calls she agreed, a day was fixed, a baby-sitter arranged, and he took her out to dinner. Her hair was black and thick, her skin very white, her lips large and sensual. She was five-foot-three, fractionally plump, and wore spectacles. He felt sick, and could hardly eat. Nor could she. Juliet was ill. She ought to be at home. What did they talk about? Neither had any idea. Yet they must have talked, just as they must have eaten. He rang her up the next day. How was Juliet? Not too bad. Nothing to worry about. She was sorry she'd spoilt the evening. Apart from that she'd enjoyed it. Far more, to be frank, than she'd expected.

He took her out again the following week. Again they had a long, slow dinner. Again neither felt hungry, it was just an excuse for sitting in a quiet alcove together. Again she didn't relax. 'I'm sorry,' she said. 'I worry about them. Supposing I was run over by a bus. They'd have no one.' He squeezed her hand, then traced the line of her thigh under the table. She removed his hand. He supposed she was not beautiful, with her spectacles and slight white plumpness. Except to him. And he knew he must be very careful. He mustn't say that he loved her. He must clench his teeth and take her home by taxi. He asked her, tentatively, clumsily, how she did for money. Henry sent her some, but erratically. So far it had just proved adequate, and she hadn't had to work, but she never knew when it would come, or where from, or how much it would be. He was a violinist. He was working on the continent. There was, she thought, a woman. She didn't want to talk about it. Divorce? She hadn't faced the subject yet. There were too many meals to cook. Her own frustrated ambitions? She had never found out what they were, but she knew they were there. Writing? Teaching? Painting? She didn't know. She'd never had time to find out. She'd been married at eighteen, straight from boarding school. There ought to be a law against it. He took her home by taxi.

The next week she couldn't come out. Juliet was ill again. She was going through one of those spells. It was probably psychosomatic. Then all the children caught it. A nasty epidemic of the psychosomatics. He offered to come and help. She didn't seem to want that. He thought of turning up and forcing the issue, but decided against it.

At last they managed to fix up another dinner date. It drove him mad, waiting. This was typical, falling in love with a woman with a real live husband and four psychosomatic children. It would end in disaster. She could be his salvation. He mustn't carry on with it. He couldn't wait till Wednesday.

'You're going to Spain to wait till lovely, are you, Bellamy?'

Oh, Frances. Your lovely X 117s.

'Because the agent never thought I'd feel like this about anyone.'

'What?'

'I'll have to go away with her on the 28th.'

'What?'

Suddenly Robert realized that he was in his office at Cadman and Bentwhistle, talking to Tadman-Evans.

'Are you all right, Bellamy?'

'Of course. Why?'

'Well, is that all right?' said Tadman-Evans.

'Sorry. I didn't quite catch what you said. I was in the middle of some calculations.'

'Oh, sorry. I asked if you were going to Spain to demonstrate the X 117s, because the agent wants to know straightaway, as he's going on holiday on the 28th.'

'Oh. Yes, I will. Yes.'

At last six o'clock on Wednesday came. They had a drink. He was overwhelmed with desire.

'I want to make love to you, Frances,' he said.

She closed her eyes.

'All right,' she said.

He took her back to Number 38 by taxi. In the taxi he tried to kiss her.

'Not yet,' she said.

'Why not?'

'I'm shy about kissing in public.'

The driver shut the adjoining window.

'I love you,' he said. And that above all he had not meant to say.

He steered her hurriedly past the window of the North London Surgical and Medical Supply Centre, frightened that a false note might put her off.

She let him take off her stockings, and kiss her legs.

'Lovely legs,' he said. 'You're so lovely.'

'I'm not lovely,' she said.

He tried to undress her. Her hands insinuated that she didn't want him to. She went to the lavatory. He put out the light and began to undress. She returned, dressed only in her coat, and slipped quickly into bed. He hopped in after her. He lifted back the bed-clothes.

'What are you doing?'

'I want to look at you.'

For just a moment, vaguely, in the dim electric firelight, he saw a luxuriant white body, all the more desirable for being so secret. Then she pulled the clothes back.

'I'm cold,' she said.

He kissed her, with a light repetitive frenzy.

'I've taken precautions,' she said.

So she had expected this and wanted it. She was awkward and not very responsive. Perhaps just shy, perhaps thinking of the children. She was slow to be roused. It was hard for him. He liked a quick, fierce rhythm. He had never learnt to be subtle.

At last he entered her and she gave a sigh, it might have been of pleasure or regret. It might have said oh my love or what a fool I am here I go again I ought to have my head examined. The money ran out in the electric meter and the fire went out. He just managed to wait for her but it wasn't relaxed and it wasn't very good for either of them. Afterwards she clung to him and kissed his ears and told him that she loved him. He didn't want this. It hadn't been good, you thought about it for so long and then it wasn't good.

'Was it all right?' she said.

'Fine. Thank you.'

He'd need a fortnight in Spain if he was to do the job properly. There were three separate places he ought to go to.

'Was it all right for you?' he said.

'Yes, thank you.'

Demonstrations at all three places. Let them try it on their own before making up their minds. He must learn Spanish.

'Are you sure it was all right for you?' she said.

'Yes. Of course.'

You couldn't learn much Spanish in a fortnight, but he'd do his best. Not knowing Spanish had been a big drawback last time. And anyway it was such bad manners. A lot of Bellamy money had gone into his education. They had a right to expect immaculate manners.

'You seem disappointed,' she said.

'Nonsense.'

He shouldn't have committed himself.

'I'm not terribly good. I know that,' she said.

Henry Lanyard (violin) was probably a vicious brute, making her hate sex. And she had been thinking of the children.

'You were thinking of the children.'

'Yes. All the time.'

They went out and ate. She was very quiet. He felt flat and uncertain. He felt a nasty attack of jokes coming on. He told several.

'Sorry,' he said. 'I seem to have caught a nasty dose of jokes.'

'There's a lot of it about.'

Suddenly he realized that she was just very very tired. The love-making, coming on top of the children's illnesses, had been too much.

'You're tired, aren't you?' he said.

She admitted it. Now she no longer had to make the effort. Now he no longer had to expect her to say interesting things. Now they could be like married people.

He took her home by taxi. She demurred at the extravagance but he insisted.

'It's the children first every time, darling,' she said in the taxi. 'Not very romantic, but it's got to be.'

'Of course. I understand.'

133

They stopped the taxi in the Fulham Road, and said good-night there.

'If you want to back out, I'll understand,' she said.

'But I don't. I love you, Frances.'

'Ring me tomorrow.'

'I love you. I do.'

'I'll be out shopping some time in the morning, but I'll be in most of the day.'

He didn't sleep at all. In the morning he rang her, and suggested another evening.

'It's difficult,' she said. 'Come here to dinner instead.'

It was a three-storey nineteenth-century house, not large when there are four children.

The youngest child, John, had gone to bed, being only three. He was introduced to the other three, Karen first, dark like her mother.

'Hullo, Karen.'

'I'm seven.'

'Juliet.'

Brown. Pale, like her mother. But thin.

'Hullo, Juliet? How old are you?'

'Ten.'

Barely audible.

'And I'm twelve. I'm Roger. I'm the oldest.'

'Hullo, Roger.'

Unfamiliar features – his father's son, perhaps. Very confident.

He followed Frances into the kitchen.

'When do they go to bed?' he whispered.

'Not yet.'

'I want you.'

She made a face.

'Well, you can't have me, can you?'

'Can't they play upstairs?'

'No. Now leave me to do your cooking. Go and amuse them.'

'Bloody hell.'

He went back to amuse them.

'You've come to dinner with our mummy, haven't you?' said Karen.

'That's right.'

'She's a good cook.'

'That's lucky for me, then, isn't it?'

'Yes.'

'Don't mind Karen,' said Roger. 'She's only seven.'

'Well, you were seven once,' said Karen.

'Never said I wasn't.'

'It's not my fault I'm seven.'

'He never said it was,' said Robert.

'Well, why did he say it, then?'

Why, indeed?

'What a lot of nice toys you've got. My word.'

'John's only three anyway,' said Karen scornfully. 'That's why he's asleep.'

And Juliet watched.

'Do you play Monopoly?' said Roger.

'I must admit that I'm not entirely without experience of it,' said Robert.

'You can be the boat,' said Roger.

'I didn't say I was going to play.'

'You are, though, aren't you?'

'We'll see.'

'Grown-ups always say that.'

He tried a smile on Juliet. She smiled back, then turned away. I'm hooked, he thought. I'll play Monopoly. Bloody hell.

'It doesn't really matter what you are, as long as Karen's the iron,' said Roger. 'She has to be the iron, or she cries.'

'I don't.'

'Don't waste time arguing, or it'll be bed-time,' said Robert.

'It isn't our bed-time for ages,' said Roger.

'Oh.'

'Come on.'

'O.K. You sort the money out and I'll tell your mum.'

He went into the kitchen and said: 'I'm just having a quiet game of Monopoly. Is that all right?'

'Of course. Why shouldn't it be?'

'No reason. You look lovely when you're crying. When we're married we must have onions every day.'

She mouthed a kiss.

'Henry did,' she said. 'He had to, so that I had an excuse for being in tears when he got home.'

'Why did it all go wrong?'

'Because I gave him onions every day.'

He stuck out his tongue, then wiggled it amorously.

'No, seriously, why?'

'Onions. And don't ask any more questions.'

'We're ready,' said Roger, bursting in.

'O.K.'

'Why are you crying, Mummy? Have you heard from Daddy again?'

'No, dear. It's just the onions.'

'Oh.'

He took his place at the gaming table.

'What do you want to be, Juliet?' he said.

'I don't mind.'

'I don't mind what I am as long as it isn't the iron,' said Karen.

'You're just saying that,' said Roger.

'You're just saying that,' said Karen.

'Copycat,' said Roger.

'Copycat,' said Karen.

'Stop it,' said Juliet. That was better. She had been moved to speech.

'I shan't play if you argue,' said Robert.

'Karen doesn't play properly anyway,' said Roger.

'I do.'

'I mean it,' said Robert.

The game began. Embarrassing good fortune attended the early moves of Robert Bellamy Esq. He began not to buy things in order not to win too easily.

'You know you play stupidly,' said Roger.

'I'm out of practice,' said Robert. 'Past my best. Over the hill.'

Now Roger began to win easily. He played like a property developer. Karen and Juliet had appalling luck. Karen accepted her bad luck philosophically. Juliet clearly ascribed hers to the impossibility of life.

Gradually the luck of the girls began to improve. Juliet's stations began to prove a wise investment after all, and Roger's constant landing on Karen's electricity company was a source of amusement for all.

Frances came in and said: 'Bed-time, Karen.'

'Oh, can't she just finish the game?' said Robert.

Frances gave him a cool look.

'We've almost finished.'

'All right.'

Nice popular game-continuer Bellamy R. and his new friends found their game turning into a marathon. Luckily Juliet's luck ran out, Roger said: 'Juliet's going to cry,' and there was an excuse for ending the game. Juliet cried. They were all sent to bed.

'I haven't done anything,' said Karen. 'Why have I got to go to bed?'

The children retired to bed.

'Want a sherry?'

'Thanks.'

She made the children their cocoa, then laid the table.

'Don't blame me if it's all over-cooked,' she said.

It wasn't.

'A very nice meal,' he said.

'Terribly simple. I couldn't face any more.'

He did the washing up.

'I like the kids,' he said.

'So I noticed.'

Coffee was made and sampled. On the sideboard stood a head and shoulders portrait of a man.

'So that's Henry Lanyard (violin).'

'Yes.'

'He looks quite nice.'

'He's human.'

'That looks nice, too.'

'What?'

'Your legs.'

'They're human, too.'

'You've got what every girl needs. Human legs.'

He ran his hands up her human legs and felt for the top of her stockings, while she listened for the children on the stairs.

'Not yet. I'll see if they're asleep,' she said.

He looked again at Henry Lanyard (violin). Perhaps a touch of cruelty, when you looked hard. The mouth. The chin. Yes, an ugly customer. The case of the venomous violinist.

The door opened.

'O.K.,' she whispered.

She led the way to her bedroom. Carefully they undressed and hopped into bed. She felt cold. He began to warm her up.

She stiffened.

'What?'

'Sh'sh.'

After a minute or two of silence she whispered: 'Sorry. I thought it was Juliet. She goes to the lavatory.'

'Don't we all?'

After that it was no good. Eventually he got dressed.

'Sorry,' she whispered.

'It's O.K.,' he whispered.

He crept out of the house and got a taxi home. Next day he rang her and asked her round to dinner on Wednesday. It was better at his place. She rang on Wednesday to announce a flu epidemic among the baby-sitters of the Fulham Road. He went round there instead, joining an enormous crowd. Chelsea were playing Manchester United in an evening match. He felt absurd, tearing himself away from this irresistible stream down Frances's quiet street. Several fans followed, thinking he knew a short cut. Chelsea had a gate of 62,473. Frances had a gate of one. He played Monopoly. Just as Roger won a great cheer burst out. Chelsea had scored. After dinner they made love. This time it was all right but just after it was over Juliet went to the lavatory. They wondered if they had woken her, if she had heard anything, if she would be able to make any sense out of what she had heard. He crept out of the house after giving her long enough to get to sleep.

And then he went to Spain. He was there for a fortnight, driving long distances through strange arid landscapes, and he hadn't even learnt the Spanish for 'I'm sorry. I don't speak Spanish', and as the hired car jolted he thought erotically of Frances, and smiled at the driver, and watched the vultures and buzzards and eagles all circling patiently up there, waiting for the end of Franco's government. Had he really fallen in love before they ever met, or did it just seem like that afterwards? He wrote to Frances, long letters, it was breaking his heart that he saw all this alone, without her. He sold several metals analysers without really trying. He bought souvenirs for them all and when he arrived back he rang her from London Airport and could hardly speak for all the feeling welling up inside him. And then he was there, walking down her little street in the snow. He arrived at Karen's bed-time and gave everyone their little presents, except of course for John, who was asleep, and even Juliet had a go with her castanets, and he felt he had come home. After the children had gone to bed Frances said: 'You shouldn't have brought things for the children. It'll make them wonder what your role is,' and he said: 'They aren't as Machiavellian as you think.'

'But it's such a worry. Every little nuance worries me. I can't cope, Robert.'

He told her that she was coping very well, but she obviously didn't believe it.

'They need a father,' she said.

'I wish they could have me,' he said.

They touched each other a great deal during dinner. And then they went to bed, and Frances was just the same, still not really relaxed, and reaching the higher slopes just as it was slowly dying with him, but dying with affection and love and a sense of great great goodness. Juliet went to the lavatory twice during the night. From time to time he slept but Frances listened for Juliet and for John being disturbed. At six o'clock Robert crept stiffly out on to a cold, snowed-up world, feeling like a criminal making his great hoofprints in the snow, and no buses, and a long long wait for the tube at Fulham Broadway.

That Sunday he came to tea and they played Monopoly and this time he lost easily despite trying hard and was secretly rather annoyed. And he said: 'The snow's deep outside. It's reached two feet,' and Roger said: 'Come off it. It never,' and he said: 'It has. My two feet,' and Juliet actually laughed, and he felt warm and lovable and then he went home and on Tuesday evening Frances found a baby-sitter and came to dinner and Robert cooked a palatable meal and they made love and it wasn't terribly good but they didn't mind, and then they ate the palatable meal, somewhat overcooked by now, and drank a bottle of excellent claret, and he took her home by taxi which they stopped in the Fulham Road, and he wished that he could find an acceptable way of offering her some money to get extras for the children. He watched the small area of white leg between her boots and her coat and tried to trace the fleshy amplitudes that lay beneath the shapeless winter garments.

She turned the corner without waving, and he stood for a moment, shaking with excitement on this knife-edge of possession and loss, at the place where pain and pleasure meet.

That was the last time he ever saw her. She rang on Thursday from a public call box to say that Henry had turned up unexpectedly and she didn't know what would happen now. Obviously he mustn't get in touch with her. She would write as soon as she could, as soon as she had something to say.

'No. Don't ring off,' he said.

'I must get back.'

'Please. Frances, please.'

'I must. Bye bye, darling.'

A kiss, followed by a click. He waited in agony until Tuesday morning, his life suspended. That night he didn't sleep until six-thirty. He woke up at nine. He would be terribly late for work. And there was the letter lying outside his door, and there was Mr Mendel.

'What a surprise,' said Mr Mendel.

'I'm late.'

'There's a letter for you.'

'Ah. Thank you.'

'From a girl, I hope.'

'Yes.'

'Good. Good.'

He forced himself to walk to the station. Then he read his letter, waiting for the train.

Darling Robert,

I don't trust myself to speak to you on the phone. Henry arrived back without any warning, typical of him. I hardly knew whether to laugh or cry, but the children were in no such difficulty. Since then I have tried to fight against what I know to be inevitable, as I'm sure you do too in your heart of hearts. Hence my delay, which must have been awful for you. Believe me, I have gone through hell. I have become an old woman in four days, trying to be normal with Henry, and trying to find a way of arguing myself into giving him up in favour of you. But there is no way, Robert dear. For eight hours each night I have pretended to be asleep, while thinking thinking thinking. And each day I have had to simulate pleasure at Henry's return. I didn't know I had the strength. Only the children enable me to go on.

I am such a physical mother. I carry my children inside me always. And for their sake, Robert dear, I must try and make a go of it with Henry. He is still their beloved Daddy. I think we can do it. He is very well-meaning really and although you would never believe it, it was as much my fault as his. I never expected this, truly, or I would not have started with you. I'm amazed to find that he has missed me so much. I still love him, I think, though not as deeply as I love you. I don't think that's a contradiction, is it?

Well, that's it. What more can I say? The children have told Henry about 'the nice man' and are expecting you to come again. No doubt he realizes what has been going on and sees through my attempts to conceal my feelings. And yet perhaps he doesn't. He has that curious blindness that seems to go with extreme sensitivity. In any case, I shall never tell him. You are too valuable to me to form any part of my life with Henry. You are my secret.

Do not write to this house. If ever you want to write to me, write c/o Miss Jenny Craythorne, the Old Mill House, Lower Cleverton, Dorset. She is an old friend and will see that I get the letter without Henry seeing it.

I could say a lot more but there's no point.

With love and thanks

Your loving Frances.

A week later Robert wrote back:

Dear Frances,

I have written several letters and thrown them all away. I love you very much but it has not had time to bite too deeply into me and I shall quickly recover. I am very busy at work just now, and that helps.

I wish you all the best, the children too. I do wish I could see you all again.

I shall take up either long-distance running or missionary work. It's too early to say which yet.

I think I must have left a knee at your house. If you find it, could you send it on. It has sentimental value.

I'll try not to write again but I'd like to hear how it all goes and how the children are doing. Really I would. *Please* write. And of course if things should change again, by any chance, don't be shy about getting in touch. If I felt that you would be it would make it very hard for me not to try and find out what is happening.

Don't worry. I'll be all right. I won't hang around the Fulham Road in despair, to catch a glimpse of you. It means I won't be able to go to Stamford Bridge, but it never was my favourite ground!

As you can see, I'm better already. Thank you, darling, for going to that party.

    All my love
        Robert
P.S. I've found the knee. It was half way up my leg. Can't think how it got there.

Shortly after Frances he saw Sonia. He had been neglecting her but she had not complained. They met in a pub. He told Sonia all about his relationship with Frances, all about his love

143

for her. Sonia began to sob. She shook helplessly. He said: 'Stop it. Sonia darling. Please.' So now he knew without words that she had loved him hopelessly for years, and had accepted the tormenting terms of their relationship because those were the only terms she thought she could get. All the customers looked at them, because after all you read such terrible things in the papers. He couldn't bear to have them all looking at him as if he was a monster, so he bundled Sonia out into the street and took her back to Bayswater by cab.

She made coffee. The smallest routine activities have a calming effect.

'Have you been miserable all the time?' he asked.

'Yes.'

'But you can't have been. I mean, I'd have noticed. Surely I'd have noticed?'

'I tried not to show you.'

'You must have been happy sometimes.'

'No. I've had pleasures, but I've not been happy.'

'Poor Sonia. But how the hell could I not have noticed?'

'I don't know.'

'I'm not a brute, am I? Tell me I'm not a complete brute.'

'You're not a complete brute.'

'Thank you. Oh, darling, I'm sorry.'

She gave him her famous coffee and said: 'I'm sorry too. I'm sorry to bring this on you just now. It's been bad enough for you without this.'

'Oh, God, that doesn't matter.'

'I suppose I must have thought you were incapable of anything more. I'm upset to find you can feel more deeply for someone else.'

He wanted to say that from now on everything would be different.

'This'll make a difference, you know,' she said. 'It'll be that bit harder for us to go on at all.'

Perhaps they should stop. Either that or marry. He couldn't

144

marry, not now. Not yet. Not after Frances. Perhaps he ought to stop seeing her. But could he do it? Why didn't she do it? Surely it would be better for her, in the long run?

They went to 'The Just Good Friends' and had a rather subdued meal. It was no use doing anything irrevocable in this emotional atmosphere.

'You were upset because I was crying in public,' said Sonia, as she listlessly nibbled a piece of bean curd.

'I know. Awful. But people were staring at me so horribly. I suppose I'm very selfish, aren't I?'

'You're just human.'

'I'm always the central character. It's the Robert Bellamy story. I wish to remain eponymous. There you are. A joke especially for you, because you're in publishing. No trouble is too great. Individual jokes tailored for your every occasion. Want a joke that will corpse a delegation of Yugoslavian drapers? Ring Intergag, the passport to international hysterics. Oh, Sonia, I'm sorry about all this.'

Things were more difficult after that. The sequence of events was, first, an attempt by Robert, heroic but doomed, to fall in love with Sonia. Following the failure of this, an agreement not to meet. Inevitably, after a few months, a chance meeting. A joint resolution to meet from time to time, on a purely platonic basis. An occasion, after a party, when the platonic rules were broken. The whole thing starting up again. Robert once more on the verge of proposing the moment his flu was gone.

20 The Farewell Party

We haven't missed anything. He's been lying there, listening to the radio, all the programmes getting jumbled up in his feverish head. Gwen has met an old friend of Jenny's, who has found Walter Gabriel's missing bedsocks in the boot of a car belonging to Ludwig Schmidt (baritone), who broadcasts by kind permission of Sheffield Wednesday, who this afternoon paid £80,000 for Henry Lanyard (violin). Damn damn damn. So the man was still going strong.

It's Thursday evening now. He must go to work tomorrow, his last day. There's so much to be done. And he mustn't miss his own farewell party. He must get up and try his legs. Can those heavy lifeless things really be his legs? Mr Mendel has been very good, bringing him food which he hasn't wanted. He must try and eat a decent meal tonight. He struggles to the Blessington Café. He struggles back to bed. He thinks about Henry Lanyard. Try and sleep. Get ten hours tonight. Not tired, though. Phone ringing. What time? Ten twenty. It'll be for Strickman. No, because he thinks it's for Strickman it won't be. Hurry. Cold in hall. Pick up phone before it stops ringing. Then hastily tie up dressing-gown. 'Hullo . . . I'll see.' Legs so heavy. Have to be dragged every inch of the way. 'He isn't in. . . Just a moment.' So heavy. Pencil. Paper. Bloody man. 'Right . . . Yes . . . They've got Mussenheim. Istanbul too dangerous. Right.' Up the stairs again. No strength. Down again. Sink into bed. No sleep. That bugger Lanyard played quite well. Very sorry for self. Light on. Read book. File on Puchner. Jenny in bed with Herring. Bland found dead in Kurfürstendamm. Can't concentrate. Close book. Lights off. Lie back. Sleep.

No sleep. Jenny in bed with Puchner. Herring found dead in Riga. Sleep at last. Jenny in bed with Henry Lanyard. Frances found dead in Kurfürstendamm. Frances in bed with Henry Lanyard. Henry Lanyard beating Sonia with a violin. Seven forty. A cold morning. Switch on all three bars of fire. Upstairs slowly to have bath. Muffled laughter and splashes in bathroom. So it's true. Blast and damn. Dress quickly. No clean socks. Domestic chaos due to trip abroad, illness and lack of wife.

Have cup of tea. Go out. Catch train. Don't feel very strong. Get off Highbury and Islington. Bacon sandwich in workmen's café. Buy new socks. Arrive Cadman and Bentwhistle. 'Morning, girls. Yes, thank you. 'Morning, Julie. Yes, thank you. Go into toilet (executive!). 'Morning, Sir John. Yes, thank you. Hope I'll see you tonight at the pub. Little farewell party. Oh, the usual crowd. Enter cubicle. Change socks. Flush old socks, push them down with brush.

Work hard, feeling tired. Successor to be Neaves. Nice lad. But insular. Get Julie to ring round about farewell party. Write to Portuguese chap. Write up Europe trip. Long analysis to Stockholm, write boffin's report on deficiency of R203. Would like to tell Sir John what's wrong with department but he wouldn't be interested. Lunch with Neaves. Neaves chooses English food. To typing pool. So stuffy. No strength in legs. Sit down. Mrs Roberts very concerned. Shouldn't work so hard. What do they care? Chorus of yes, that's right. See you all for drink five thirty well hope to can't stay long though Friday evening bad night good film odeon dance boy friend not much notice what about you Mrs Roberts well I don't usually indulge but just one little one see you all five thirty without fail without fail without Tadman-Evans finish two letters exhausted finish report I think there is little doubt that the 276RB represents as good value for money as five past five nearly finished just time do this other ends have to be left loose hell didn't want to have to leave loose ends hell hell hell no strength you've rung everyone Julie good see you five thirty well can't stay long such short notice boy friend.

Promptly at unbarring of doors Robert Bellamy entered the

saloon bar of the Moorish public convenience, seated his tired frame on the bar stool thoughtfully provided for just such an eventuality, and ordered a pint of bitter.

The girls from the typing pool came in en masse, shrieking with laughter. He bought them each the drink of their choice, dubonnet where it was dubonnet, gin where it was gin. Not all the girls found it easy to make up their minds. Mrs Roberts plumped for gin and orange. Shyly Mrs Roberts presented him with a cigar box from the girls, accompanied by a list of subscribers. The friendly comments ranged from 'Good luck – Rosie' to, anonymously: 'Get stuck in there'. One or two of the girls clapped. He was touched. Julie arrived with Perrin and Neaves and Wallis and most of 'Europe', though some including Tadman-Evans had prior engagements. One or two people from other departments filtered in, including Rice and Barker, two of the science boys with whom Robert had struck up an acquaintance, and Jimmy Lane, the official C and B sponger, whose arrival was gratifyingly greeted with cries of 'Trust old Jimmy' and 'Smell a drink a mile away'. Jimmy Lane grinned, profoundly flattered by all this attention. Sir John arrived, cast his wet blanket on the proceedings, and plumped for a whisky. Robert to his own disgust instinctively ordered him a double. The landlord muttered that it wasn't a private room. Robert shepherded everyone into a corner. Sir John bought everyone a double whisky, regardless of what they wanted, grimaced to humorous effect as he paid, and said: 'Don't know how I make ends meet these days.' Sir John left, one or two others left, several girls poured their whiskies into other people's glasses, and left to meet their boy friends. Someone offered Mrs Roberts another gin. She wasn't sure whether she ought to. She did. Rumour had it that Jimmy Lane was about to buy a drink. Rumour proved an unreliable informant. Wallis told Neaves a dirty joke. Neaves went home. Janet went home. By six twenty-five it was already clear that it wasn't going to be one of those memorable farewell nights that passed into Cadman and Bentwhistle history. Someone bought Mrs Roberts an orange. There were seven double whiskies left untouched. Robert and Jimmy Lane and Perkins had one each. Robert tried to buy everyone more drinks, to keep them there, but this had the opposite effect. They fled at the prospect of utter debauchery. By six forty only Robert, Mrs Roberts, Jimmy Lane, Wallis and Rosie remained. Jimmy Lane finished his last double whisky dubonnet and tonic and staggered homewards. Everyone agreed that he was disgusting.

Wallis was eyeing Rosie lecherously.

'Well, I must be off,' he said. 'Are you coming, Rosie?'

'No, Rosie's staying here with us, aren't you?' said Robert.

'Well, actually I really must be going,' said Rosie. 'I promised Maureen.'

'Let her make up her own mind,' said Wallis.

'I am. It's you who're not,' said Robert.

'Sorry, but I must go,' said Rosie. 'See you Monday, Mrs Roberts. Bye bye, Mr Bellamy. Thanks for the drinks. And good luck with your next job.' Robert didn't reply. 'Oh, charming. Thanks very much.' They departed. Robert hurried to the door, and shouted: 'Bye, Rosie,' but she didn't hear.

'Are you sure this is just orange?' said Mrs Roberts.

'I don't know,' said Robert.

On all sides the tables were piled with empty, half-full and full glasses. Several bore traces of lipstick. There was cigarette ash everywhere. He felt ill.

'Are you all right?' said Mrs Roberts.

'It's the after-effects of the flu.'

'You need something solid,' said Mrs Roberts, and she led him to the Italian Café. They sat in the tall waiter's half, and had minestrone soup and escalope milanaise with spaghetti.

'It's a lovely place, Italy,' said Mrs Roberts. 'We always went there, when Mr Roberts was alive. He never took to the food, but I couldn't get enough of it. This is nice, isn't it?'

'Quite good.'

'We stayed at Viareggio the first year, and we took a day trip to Livorno. Then of all the coincidences we met Mr and Mrs Trellis on the beach, they lived in Streatham then, though they've moved since, to Yorkshire, I think, or was it Lancashire, and they said they were going on a day trip the next day to Leghorn. Where the chickens come from. Or was it Derbyshire? Anyway, we thought we'd go with them, they're a nice couple. Well, of course Livorno turned out to be the same place as Leghorn. One's the Italian for it and the other's the English. Mr Roberts was furious but I couldn't help seeing the funny side of it. Anyway we went to the same café because we knew it and of course I said Here we are again, and I explained why. I mean anyone could make that mistake. It's nothing to be ashamed of. But Mr Roberts was furious. Why do you have to go and tell them, he said. You make us look ridiculous. It's you, I said, making us look ridiculous, arguing. But there it is, you see, that's men all over. Always worried about making a fool of themselves. I mean, take you tonight. You were worried, because everyone was going. You thought it was your fault. But it was just because they didn't have the notice.'

'Have some more wine.'

'Thank you. I won't say no. They say Italian wine doesn't travel, but this is all right.'

'It doesn't travel, because it doesn't start. They keep the best stuff for themselves.'

Mrs Roberts suddenly shouted: 'Bella Italia' and began to sing popular Neapolitan ditties. Robert tried to pay.

'No, this is on me,' said Mrs Roberts.

'No. It's my party.'

'I insist.'

He let her pay. Then he helped her into a taxi and gave the driver a pound note, which she didn't see.

She leant out of the window.

'It wasn't your fault they all went home,' she said. 'They didn't have the notice, you see.'

2I Sonia

Next day Robert got up very late and he didn't feel very well and Mr Mendel was worried.

'You take a good rest,' he said.

'Yes.'

'You don't have any letters this morning.'

'No.'

'You have very few letters all week.'

'I know.'

'Never mind. It's not everything.'

'No. Oh, by the way, Mr Mendel, they do bath together.'

'You're sure?'

'Absolutely.'

'You see them?'

'No. I just heard them.'

'Still, that's good news. You don't think they know each other before they come to Number 38?'

'No.'

'Thank you, Robert. You're a good boy.'

Robert made himself a pot of coffee, put the fire full on, opened the window, put a wet flannel on his forehead, poured out a cup of coffee, and thought about Sonia. He couldn't go on like this. He must get engaged to her.

He went out into the corridor, with his sixpence. Mrs Palmer was coming downstairs.

'Asphyxia,' she said.

'I'm sorry.'

'The Great Asphyxia. That was the name of the woman I was telling you about. I remembered afterwards. You know, the lion-tamer. She fell ill, and had to have her appendix out, and I went on at short notice and stood in for her.'

'Oh. Asphyxia. Yes. Nice to see you again, Mrs Palmer.'

He began to dial. Mrs Palmer shuffled off downstairs. He heard Sonia's French tones ringing. Then he heard her voice.

'Hullo.'

'Sonia?'

'Yes.'

'It's me. Robert.'

'Oh. Oh, hullo.'

'You don't sound very pleased.'

'It's impossible to sound pleased enough to please you, Robert.'

'You are pleased to hear from me, aren't you?'

'Of course.'

'How are you?'

'Fine.'

'Can I see you?'

'Of course.'

'When?'

'Well, I don't know, er—'

'Today?'

'It's a little difficult. The thing is, Robert . . . well, I could manage an hour or so. I'll come and see you.'

'I could come and see you, if you'd rather.'

'No, I'll come. I'll be there about three.'

'Fine. I'll look forward to it.'

'I must rush now, Robert. Good-bye.'

''Bye.'

It had been absurdly short and basic. Something was wrong. She sounded unhappy. Poor Sonia. One of life's losers. Everybody's second best. Always the blushing mistress, never the bride. Well, all that would soon be changing, he hoped. Surely she wouldn't turn him down? Surely it would work out all right? It would be like that wonderful evening long ago. That evening fascinated Dr Schmuck. Robert had got stuck on it. It had done him a permanent injury. Like a nice trauma, said Dr

Schmuck. Something delectable in the woodshed, Robert had commented.

He ran his hands over the shape of Sonia's body, and smiled.

He made the bed. He tidied up the room, sweeping, dusting. He sat down, exhausted. Just before she was due he put on a pot of coffee. He stood at the window, trying to catch a glimpse of her, but the roof of the sex emporium hid everything except a tiny stretch of pavement on the far side of the road. A heavy drizzle was falling. She'd be cold and wet. He stared at the fire, as if exhorting it to do its best, and put his next shilling in, to encourage it. There was her knock. An erotic shock passed through his body. He opened the door. How tall she still was. He barely had to bend to kiss her delicate lips. They tasted of rain.

'Sonia,' he said.

She looked serious. Something *was* wrong.

'What's wrong?'

'Nothing.'

'It's good to see you again, Sonia.'

She smiled nervously.

'Give me your wet things.'

She gave him her wet things.

'It's a dreadful day,' he said.

'Awful.'

'Coffee?'

'Please.'

'You look well.'

'I feel it.'

'I've been ill. Flu.'

'Oh, dear. You're all right now, are you?'

'Just about. Two spoons?'

'Please. Robert?'

'Yes.'

'I've got something to tell you.' He felt a small earthquake. 'I'm going to be married.'

'Really?'

'Yes. Don't sound so surprised.'

'No, well, it's not that. I mean, er – well, great. That's wonderful news. Congratulations. Is it anyone I know?'

'Well, yes, it is, actually.' She sighed. 'It's Dick.'

'Good God!'

'Yes.'

'Good God. Well.'

'Well what?'

'I don't know. Not well, then.'

'What do you mean?'

'Nothing.'

'Aren't you pleased?'

'Delirious.'

'What about that coffee?'

'Oh, yes.'

He didn't want her to see that his hand was shaking. She didn't want him to see that hers was.

'I just can't get over it, that's all,' he said.

She smiled, relieved.

'You must come and stay with us often, Robert.'

'Oh, great. Thanks. I'll love that. Dick can probably unearth some gawky female cousin from South Africa or somewhere and we can all play whist. Just what I wanted.'

'Robert!'

'Well, what do you expect me to be? Pleased?' He paused, for effect. 'I was just going to ask you to marry me.'

She didn't believe him. Damn it, it didn't sound believable.

'You don't believe me, do you?'

'I don't know.'

'I don't blame you. But it's true, Sonia. I swear it is.'

She put out one of her long arms to touch him where he sat on the Finnish sofa. Sonia had chosen a hard chair. He held his hand in hers. A pigeon was cooing away complacently on the roof outside. Damn it, why hadn't he come straight out with it? It would have been too late, but she'd at least have known.

'Oh, well, never mind,' he said. 'Good old Dick.'

'You aren't too upset?'

'How do you know what I am? Why the hell shouldn't I be upset? I am upset. Of course I am. Typical Robert, isn't it? I finally make up my mind just as you're off getting engaged.' He banged his head with his hand.

'Don't you . . .'

'Don't I what?'

'No. There's no point.'

'Well, you'll have to tell me now you've begun. Do you think I can't face the truth about myself? I'm not quite as pathetic as that, am I? Well, come on. I'm waiting. Don't I what?'

'All right. Well, it's not important. I was just going to say, you know, aren't you rather too inclined to see things as typical Robert?'

'It's what I told Schmuck. Love-hate narcissism. I'm my own worst enemy.'

'Perhaps . . .'

'Perhaps what?'

'No.'

'Perhaps what?'

'This time I'm not going to say.'

'Marvellous, isn't it?'

'Oh, Robert.'

'You expected me to be upset, though, didn't you? You were nervous.'

'More about Dick than anything.'

'Yes. That is hard. Why Dick, of all people? You never even liked him.'

'No, well. That's life, as they say.'

'No, but why? And when?'

'He rang me up the day after that party. He was coming

down to Bristol on a case. We went out. There was no case. It was all quite quick. Can I have some more coffee?'

'Of course.'

He was almost enjoying this. Funny. The main thing was that she was here, that they were involved and intense in this conversation.

'Sonia?'

'Yes.'

'Stay a little while. Don't go till I ask you to.'

'Well, I . . . well, all right. Within reason. Coffee.'

'Oh, yes.'

He went into the little kitchenette and poured out the coffee.

'Not up to your standard, I'm afraid,' he called out.

'Not bad, though.'

He brought her the coffee. Their hands weren't shaking now. He'd like to make love, as a parting. Did that prove he didn't love her?

'When did you get engaged?'

'Wednesday week.'

'You haven't rung me.'

'We were going to.'

'When?'

'I don't know.'

'I think you might have told me, Sonia. That hurts. You're my friends.'

'We *were* going to. I suppose we funked it.'

'Funked the angry scene with hot-tempered ageing juvenile Robert Bellamy, the famous Kentish Town pugilist. Robert Bellamy throwing things. Black eyes all round. I don't blame you.'

'Robert!'

'Don't keep going "Robert". There's nothing more infuriating than having your damned name called out every five minutes.'

There was another silence. He was trying to sort out his

156

emotions. He stood up, went into the kitchenette, keeping Sonia on tenterhooks, keeping her ignorant as to his mood. He returned with a bottle of Glenfiddich malt whisky, and two glasses.

'Have a drink,' he said. 'To the success of your marriage.'

'That's very nice of you.'

He poured the drinks.

'To you and Dick.'

'Thanks. I'm touched.'

'You must be, to marry him.'

'M'm. Nice whisky.'

'Mercurial old Robert. Defeated lover wishes happy couple good luck. I bear no grudge, he avers.'

'Do you really not?'

'I don't know yet, quite honestly. Seriously, though, Sonia, why Dick?'

'God knows.'

'That I doubt.'

'I just found I liked him. Perhaps even loved. Perhaps I'm just grateful for being asked. For being taken down off the shelf.'

'I could have done that.'

'To dust me, once a week. You've never loved me, Robert. Believe me, I'm flattered at the lengths you went to to try and kid us both that you did.'

'You'd better have all your books back.'

'You can keep them, if you want to.'

'Bitter mementoes. Perhaps I'll become a Trappist monk. Britain's most bad-tempered Trappist monk. Don't raise your finger at me. That was a joke. I meant, don't raise your voice at me, but Trappist monks can't talk. Get it? But you do raise fingers at people so it didn't work. Even my jokes don't work these days.'

'Why, what else doesn't work?'

'Me. I've been sacked.'

'Sacked?'

'Sacked. Not the right type at all for Cadman and Bent-whistle. Becoming an alcoholic. Can't get another job. Suddenly it isn't Robert Bellamy.'

'I'm sorry you were sacked. What happened?'

'I used the non-executive bog and drew a rude picture of the exports manager on the wall.'

'You can be dead crude, you.' Sonia's humorous Yorkshire accent was wildly inaccurate. She was probably the world's worst at accents. Coffee, alpha plus. Accents, gamma minus. 'Honestly, though, what can you expect?'

'I only wanted to introduce the human touch.'

'I know.'

'You don't bloody know. Sorry. Have another whisky.'

'Thanks. You know you drink too fast.'

'Who cares?'

'I do.'

'Bollocks. Cheers.'

'Cheers.'

'There's no need to look at me like that. I know I'm nervy. It's been a bit of a blow.'

'What did you mean about not being able to get other jobs?'

'I've had four interviews. No good. I live in one room in Kentish Town without a wife or a car. They can't quite make me out.'

'Isn't that a good thing?'

'Not when you've just been turned down for job after job.'

'I suppose not. It's funny, isn't it? Funny peculiar, I mean. I loved you for ages, until I gave up hope and forced myself not to.'

'It's ironic. Isn't life ironic? Isn't life incredibly ironic?' She didn't answer. 'I didn't mean that. I was being ironic. Life isn't ironic at all. Merely senseless. A senseless, vindictive bloody farce. I hate it.'

'Robert, you don't.'

Silence fell. He had been expending nervous energy prodigally. He was tired. He didn't want all this drink, nice though it was.

'You're right,' he said. 'I do drink too fast.'

'This is new.'

'I know. I'm going to see to it. After tonight. You must allow me to get drunk tonight.'

'All right.'

'After tonight, a new start.'

He went to the window and looked out over the wet sex emporium roof.

'I ought to leave this dump.'

Sonia said nothing.

'What do you think?' he said.

'It's up to you.'

'I know it is, but what do you think?'

'I think you've been here long enough.'

'Yes. It's played out. I'll move.'

Silence again.

'You'd better go now,' he said.

They seemed to have been talking for days, but it was well under an hour. He finished his drink and then made a pot of tea, and listened to the football. He didn't care any more. Once he had cared. He had been a Spurs fan. Part of the great mass of ordinary lovable football fans, his atonement for going to a rugger school, his apology for being born into a privileged class. But he couldn't talk to people about the game, didn't know enough. Nor did they, but the two levels of ignorance never quite met. Soothing, though, listening to the excitement. And still a touch of spiteful satisfaction when Arsenal lost.

He rang Bernard.

'I'll fetch him,' said Jean.

'How are you?'

'Fine. He's upstairs.'

'How are the kids?'

159

'Fine. I'll just get him.'

'Hullo, Bernard,' he said. 'How are you?'

'Fine.'

'I just wondered if you were doing anything tonight.'

'Well, I am really. Why?'

'Well, I felt like a drink. Sonia's marrying Dick.'

'Good Lord. Well, I'm sorry. I mean . . . well, you know what I mean.'

'I feel fed up.'

'I can't make it this weekend, Robert. Things are difficult. Perhaps Monday.'

'What do you think friendship's for?'

'I'm sorry, Robert. I can't make it.'

'You're a complacent bastard, aren't you?'

He slammed the phone down, stared at it malevolently, picked it up and slammed it down again. He rang Stephen. Out. He slammed the phone down again.

Spurs lost. Arsenal won. The voice droned on. Sonia United 1, Sonia Bromwich Albion 2. Sonia Town 1, Sonia and Sonia Athletic 0.

The phone rang. Sonia. I've been thinking. It's you I . . . no, stop that. No stupid fantasy. It'll be for Brinkmann I mean Strickman anyway. Ruppenschmidt has exploded. Abandon S. America.

'Hullo.'

'Oh, hullo, Robert. Bernard here.'

'Oh, hullo, Bernard. Sorry I, you know . . .'

'That's all right. Sorry, I, you know, had to be like that. I'm just ringing to say I'm not really complacent. It's just that things really are difficult. I can't explain, but I really honestly just can't come.'

'O.K. I believe you.'

'Ring me on Monday about half-past five.'

'O.K. Bye, Bernard.'

He got ready to go to the pub. Would he actually have gone

through with it if Sonia had still been available? He was beginning to doubt it now.

Sorry, body, he thought. You've picked a right one here. Who'd choose to be my liver or kidneys? Sorry, chaps. I get you on your feet again after the flu and then I'm shoving the booze down you again. But if you'll just bear with me for tonight – I've had a disappointment, you see – everything'll be different from now on. If we all pull together we'll get through this thing all right. I'll get my old spirit back. O.K., chaps? Good. You play ball with me and I'll play ball with you.

The man-machine moves its leg forward. It is walking. It is in Kentish Town. It buys both classifieds, *Standard* and *News*. It enters the Blessington Arms. It orders the usual, please, guv. It does not work when it says guv, especially since guv cannot remember what its usual is. It drinks. Its satisfaction ratio dial whirs. The absurd man-machine glances at the football papers. Oh so lucky Arsenal scrape home. Hurst header rocks timid Tottenham. This is now a man-machine which knows that oh so lucky Arsenal have scraped home and that a Hurst header has rocked timid Tottenham. You wouldn't know, to look at it.

The man-machine talks to a confectioner-machine. The confectioner-machine tells the man-machine all about East Africa. The man-machine does not listen. The man-machine lets the sounds of the pub wash harmlessly over it, and gets steadily drunk.

22 Kentish Town Miniatures

On the phone.

'It's Robert here.'

'Oh, hullo. I'll fetch him.'

'How are you?'

'Fine. He's upstairs.'

'How are the kids?'

'Fine. I'll fetch him.'

'Hullo, Robert.'

'Hullo, Bernard.'

'Look, I can't make it tonight, Robert, but I'll see you for the Christmas drink as usual. When is it?'

'I suppose Thursday. Usual place.'

'Fine. How are you?'

'Not too bad.'

'Fine.'

'Hullo, Dick. Robert here.'

'Oh, hullo.'

'Congratulations.'

'Thanks.'

'Surprise, surprise.'

'Yes . . . I hope you – you know – aren't . . .'

'Oh, no. No.'

'Good.'

'We're having the usual pre-Christmas drinks on Thursday. Can you come?'

'Yes. Fine. I may be a bit late arriving, but fine.'

'Bernard and Stephen are coming.'

'Oh good. I saw Bernard the other day, with his wife. Phew!'

'What do you mean, phew?'

'She's a beautiful woman.'

'Jean?'

'Yes. I'd always imagined her as rather dowdy.'

'How did they seem?'

'Oh, we didn't talk. They didn't see me. They disappeared into some club. I was waiting for – er —'

'For Sonia. That's her name, Dick. Sonia.'

'Hullo, Stephen, Robert here.'

'Oh, hullo.'

'We're having our drinks on Thursday. Can you come? Bring a few of the others?'

'Well, I'll be working, but I'll be able to pop along.'

'How's – er —'

'Gertrud. She isn't. It's off.'

'Oh, I'm sorry.'

'She's got some other bloke.'

'Oh, dear. Well, I'm sorry.'

'It's a bit of a bastard. Shaken me up a bit, actually.'

'Poor old Stephen.'

'See you Thursday, anyway. Should be fun.'

At the escritoire.

Dear sir, I am writing to apply . . .

Dear sir, I am writing to apply . . .

Dear sir, I am writing to apply . . .

. . . qualifications you need . . . twelve years' experience . . . wide experience of every aspect of modern marketing techniques . . . very keen to branch out into a new field after several years dealing with Europe . . . have several years' experience of dealing with almost every European country and feel that my abilities would therefore be . . . has long been my ambition to work in chemicals . . . keen to continue working in Europe . . . particularly interested in aluminium . . . great experience of . . . fascinated by plastics . . . completely familiar with . . . every facet of . . . in all its aspects . . . modern . . . sophisticated . . . sophisticated modern . . . techniques . . . technical revolution . . . technological . . . dynamic technocratic . . . dynamic modern . . . expanding modern technological . . . particularly keen . . . particularly interested . . . particularly suitable . . .

At the grocer's.

'Small tin of tomato soup, please, Peter.'

'Not at work today, Mr Bellamy.'

'No. Not today. And two oranges.'

'Nasty today.'

'Yes. Very. Half a pound of butter. Doesn't look as if we've got much chance against the West Indies.'

'I don't know. We often seem to do very well out there.'

'That's true. And a small white.'

'I mean, the touring team has an advantage in team spirit, doesn't it, being together like that?'

'That's true. And half a dozen eggs. Yes, we'll probably beat them hollow.'

'Not with that Sobers. Never get him out.'

'That's true. That's the lot for today.'

'Eight and a penny.'

'I can do it exactly.'

'Oh, ta. Oops, I'll pick it up for you.'

'Thanks. 'Bye, Peter.'

'Good-bye, Mr Bellamy.'

In the café.

He is not used to lunching at the Blessington Café. Evenings, yes. Lunches, no. At lunchtime on a wet weekday it is crowded, umbrella-sodden, rivulets of rainwater on the tiled floor, wet raincoats smelling of drying on the hooks over the radiator. There is a special all-in Christmas dinner, but Robert doesn't have this. He chooses from the list of dishes of the day, indifferently typed, riddled with misprints. He plumps for steak and kodney pudding. Three people sit at his table, dripping. The two waitresses have a jolly word for everyone, all the men make suggestions to them, it is one of those cafés where the suggestions are always fresher than the vegetables. Behind him a small boy asks his mum if they are going to use their luncheon vultures. Robert has imagined himself as rather a high peak in the life of the Blessington Café. In the evenings there are lonely old men, given to prolonged bursts of sneezing, and spitting into their handkerchiefs. Now, at lunchtime, he feels that he is one of the lonely old men. He can think of nothing suitable to say to his waitress, as she brings his steak and kodney pudding.

Suddenly a great burst of laughter rends the air. It is, thinks Robert, the typical loud raucous laughter of a race which cannot carry off high spirits in style. The Italians do these things much better. Robert looks at the handsome young Italian who works the coffee machine, icebox and till, expecting the Italian's face to register his disapproval of the false note in the laughter. But the Italian smiles broadly at the festive group. I'm the one with the false note, thinks Robert. Come on, you man of the world you, he urges himself, what's eating you, why are all these tiny things so important? He orders apple rumble to follow. He begins to sweat. It is hot and damp. His pudding arrives. He has a frightening feeling that the food isn't going into his mouth properly but sploshing all over his face. His skin prickles with sweat as if he was a pincushion. It streams down his face. The other people are crowding in, leaving no room, no room to use his fork properly, all moving their jaws, turning the chef's careful preparations to mush. It's revolting. He pushes his plate away. The café is the inside of a drying steaming raincoat. He must leave. He will say, bet you'd rather be in Naples than in Kentish Town today, but he decides not to say this, because he knows the handsome Italian is happier in Kentish Town, where he can earn a living. Past others at his table awkwardly apologetic crumbling all leg and armish walks he the till towards to handsome pay the Italian. Oh, leave a note and don't wait for change. Must get out, out, out, out.

In the pub.
   'Evening, John.'
   'Evening, sir.'
   'Pint of bitter, please.'
   'You like it in a jug, don't you?'
   'No, a glass.'
   'Oh, yes.'
A glass is the one without handles. A jug has handles. Robert thinks that to like it in a jug is an affectation, so he makes a point of having it in a glass.

At the workmen's café.
   'Bacon sarnie, please.'
   'Rose. One bacon sandwich.'

   In the library.
   'What the hell's wrong with this place? You haven't got a single book by Dostoievsky.'
   'They're out, sir.'
   'What, has the populace round here suddenly gone Dostoievsky mad?'
   'It's just one of those things, sir.'
   'It isn't just one of those things, is it? It's bloody inefficiency.'
   'Now, listen. There's no need to speak to me like that.'
   'You just haven't ordered enough, have you? That's the truth, isn't it? You think we're all too stupid for Dostoievsky round here. Incompetence. I can't stand incompetence. Well,

166

you can have my ticket. You can stuff it. That's the last time I'm coming to this library.'

On the telephone.
  'What do you want for Christmas, Aunt Margaret?'
  'You get me what you like, dear.'
  'I want to get you something you want.'
  'I don't want anything.'
  'I must get you something.'
  'You get me what you like, dear.'

23 An Important Session with Dr Schmuck

By Wednesday evening, when it was time to see Dr Schmuck
again, Robert was really at a low ebb. Three days of unemploy-
ment in Kentish Town had made him feel superfluous to the
requirements of the universe. He'd had two more interviews for
jobs, with no success. He had not yet summoned up the energy
to do his Christmas shopping. I will, he said to himself, I
will give him up. I can't afford him now that I'm out of work.
And it isn't doing me any good.

It's ironic, he thought. I'm going to give him up just when I
really am in a state which justifies my going to him. I've been
toying with this analysis. I've never allowed myself to become
deeply committed. I went out of self-indulgence. I stayed out of
fondness for Dr Schmuck. If I stay on now it will get really
serious, and I'm not prepared to let it get really serious.

He rang the bell. He entered. He sat down. He knew that
because he was here for the purpose of talking it would be easy
to talk. The room was warm and spacious. It was all so com-
forting, like the drugs whose use Dr Schmuck so fastidiously
avoided.

'How did Europe go?' said Dr Schmuck.

'Very well. A little hectic, but otherwise very well.'

'Good. You got some good orders?'

'Not bad. I - I did a bit of nostalgic returning, too. I went
back to my old army camp in Munster. And I went to the street
in Paris where I visited the brothel.'

'You seem to be starting to analyse yourself.'

A cue. Miss that, and you will never speak out. Come on.
Quick. Come on, words. What's keeping you?

'I've come to tell you that I'm giving up the analysis, Dr Schmuck,' he said.

Dr Schmuck took this news calmly, not believing it.

'Why?' he said.

'I can't afford it, now I'm out of a job.'

'You can owe me until you get another job. I have faith in you.'

'It isn't just the money.'

Dr Schmuck picked his nose thoughtfully.

'This is encouraging,' he said. 'It means we are reaching a critical point.'

'Yes. The point where I get up and go.'

'What are the other reasons, apart from the money?'

'Well, I – I don't want to hurt your feelings.'

'My feelings! You aren't paying to think of my feelings.'

'All right, then. I just don't feel it's doing me any good.'

'But these are early days, Robert.'

'Early days! I've been coming for three years. And I'm getting worse, not better.'

'Then this is hardly an appropriate moment to leave.'

'But you're supposed to make your patients better. You can't make them worse and then use that as an excuse for keeping them. That's criminal.'

'This is very encouraging.'

'I could kill you sometimes.'

'Nonsense. You are incapable of real violence. That is why you indulge in petty violence so often.'

'Is that supposed to be clever?'

'No. Simply true. And I'll tell you something else which is true, Robert. You are in a state. You are not in a good frame of mind. I think this is why you want to leave – because you are afraid of becoming too involved in this.'

'That's true, actually. That's very perceptive of you.'

'I'm paid to be perceptive.'

Dr Schmuck walked over to the window, drew back the

heavy, brown, drooping curtains and looked out at the lights of London perceptively. Robert often wondered whether his movements were deliberate or instinctive. Perhaps he had a woman's instincts. He gave out a vague impression of being homosexual, but this might be a professional pose adopted to deal with this particular case.

'You've seen Sonia,' said Dr Schmuck.

'That's got nothing to do with it.'

'On the contrary . . .'

'Listen a minute. I admit I've seen Sonia. She's getting married to Dick.'

'Ah.'

'You see. You register satisfaction, because it helps to explain. You ought to be sorry.'

'No. It's not my job to take your point of view against the rest of the world. You need help, not sympathy.'

'And I'm not getting it, Dr Schmuck. I'm getting worse. Twist it around as you will, that is a very good reason for leaving you. Listen. There's one very simple basic thing about me, which I've never told you, but I'd have thought it was pretty obvious. I don't like being called Robert. I want to be called Bob. I long for people to call me Bob, but they don't. Something in me prevents them. You could have worked wonders by calling me Bob, but you didn't even see that.'

A ghost of a smile flashed across Dr Schmuck's face like a barn owl flying through a farmyard into a dark barn at dusk. 'I've refrained from doing so, Robert. We have to approach this the hard way. We can't take short cuts.'

'Because you want to go on for ever, getting my easy money. You're nothing but a charlatan. A clever charlatan.'

'I've always hoped you would find it in you to insult me.'

'Hoped my arse. There, I've said arse. The inhibitions are breaking down. Bum. Knickers. Menstruation. Prick, Hooray.'

Dr Schmuck's smile came out and settled on a gatepost. He

was enjoying this enormously. He was convinced that it was part of the game.

'No, Dr Schmuck. It's all over.' He stood up. 'This isn't part of the game.'

'Sit down,' fired Dr Schmuck so sharply that Robert sat down instantly. But the moment he realized why he had sat down he stood up again. 'Listen, Robert. I can't force you to stay, in the end. You know that. So sit down for a moment, and let's talk. Right?'

'All right.'

Robert sat down again.

'I'm a human being, Robert, despite appearances, and although I'm not paid to do so, I like you. I don't want you to make a hasty decision. I don't think you're in a fit condition to make this decision. You are indulging in two of the greatest vices of this age – self-pity and violence. In your case, self-violence.'

'I've been watching too many Westerns.'

'I mean it, Robert. I'm serious. You are being very destructive to yourself.'

'In other words, as my mother told me without charging four pounds an hour, I'm my own worst enemy.'

'Perhaps your trouble is that you are also your own best friend.'

'Paradoxes. Do you know what paradoxes are, Dr Schmuck?'

'No. What are they?'

'Statements of the obvious.'

'How paradoxical. Aren't you playing a game now?'

'I want to leave, Dr Schmuck.'

'All right. But first give me, clearly and carefully, your reasons.'

'I've given them. (a) You're too expensive. A man has to be a big success before he can afford to have his failure analysed by you. Now that by your terms I need you, I can't afford you. (b) I've no confidence in you any more. (c) It's not doing me any good at all. All right? Convincing?'

'We'll take them one by one. First, money. I could cut the rate to, say £3.'

'It won't make any difference.'

'£2.'

'No.'

'I can't go any lower without seeming to need you as much as you need me.'

'But you do, Dr Schmuck. Far more.'

'No. But you need to feel that I need you.'

'Please. Let's just have a business discussion. No analysis. Otherwise I'll go. All right?'

'You leave me no choice. Now, Robert, let's take your second reason, that you have no confidence in me. It's my name, isn't it?'

'What?'

'Schmuck. It's like a parody of a psychiatrist's name.'

'Well, yes, it is, but that's got nothing to do with it.'

'This has happened before. It's not the first time. Don't think I don't know the kind of remarks people make. One of my clients once suggested I ought to take a good honest British name. Why should British names be honest? He suggested John Thomas. Infantile sexuality. But why should I change? What's in a name? Besides, we Schmucks have a great deal of family feeling. There have been Schmucks in the herring fishing industry in Schleswig-Holstein since 1500. So, Schmuck it remains. I am not ashamed of being a Schmuck.'

'It's got nothing to do with your name.'

'Then why, if not the name, the lack of confidence?'

'Simply because of the third reason. Why should I have confidence if it's not doing any good?'

'Because I can't do you any good unless you have confidence.'

'Well, then, since I don't have confidence, I must go.'

There was a silence. Dr Schmuck's right eye twitched violently. A reflex action after death. A cuckoo clock struck the half hour. Dr Schmuck suddenly looked nearer sixty than forty-five. It was over. Robert stood up.

Dr Schmuck came to the door.

'I still believe I can help you. I would be delighted if you came back,' he said.

'We'll see.'

'If not, then perhaps you will call as a friend. Come to tea, or for a drink. I sometimes give little parties. I will invite you.'

'Thank you. We've been more than half the session. I must pay you for today.'

'Nonsense. It was only because of my insistence that you stayed. You can't pay.'

For all I know I may be his only patient, thought Robert.

'Well, thank you.'

'Do call, Robert, to see me, with no obligation.'

'We couldn't just talk as friends now. A professional relationship corrupts.'

'It would be nice, anyway, if you would call and let me know how you are getting on.'

'Well, perhaps I will.'

They shook hands. Dr Schmuck held Robert's hand, and stroked it very gently, so gently that afterwards it was impossible to be absolutely certain that he had done so.

'Good-bye, Dr Schmuck,' said Robert.

'Good-bye, Bob,' said Dr Schmuck.

24 The Pre-Christmas Booze-up

Almost opening time. Five sixteen. Feel better when he'd had a drink. Often felt like this nowadays round about opening time. Dry in the mouth. Tense in all his nerves. Each tooth sharply defined in his mouth.

He went for a cup of tea in a gloomy little snack bar, run by a middle-aged Italian couple. Two old men drinking tea, one noisily, the other twitching his nose with each sip. The tea acrid, been standing in the pot for hours having regular doses of water. The Italian woman acrid also, been standing in the café having regular doses of tea. A fat and surly woman, not a bit like Tuscany. Two sprigs of holly. It made you want to cry. And Christmas pudding added specially to the tiny menu. Christmas pudding bolognese.

It was a traditional thing, meeting in the Magnet and Two Stoats before Christmas. It was Robert's equivalent of an annual 'at home'. Mr Robert Bellamy will be 'at pub' on Thursday, December 21st, five-thirty to eleven. They had had some jolly times. Friends, work-mates, fellow residents at Number 38, sometimes there had been upwards of twenty people there. Lately the numbers had fallen off, due to marriages, deaths, and changing circumstances. Last year there had been eight. He knew that the others were losing their enthusiasm for it and he wished that he'd had the sense to suggest its discontinuance himself.

He paid for his cup of stewed water. Sixpence.

'Grazie,' he said.

'Thank you, sir.'

The old cow didn't even have the decency to say 'prego'.

'I spoke to you in Italian,' he said. 'Can't you even return a simple courtesy?'

She looked at him in astonishment. The two old men didn't even look up. And she *was* returning his courtesy, really, by speaking to him in English.

He went across to the pub. Not the Magnet and Two Stoats. He mustn't be the first to arrive.

If he had to wait for service he'd get angry. He was all knotted up inside. He hadn't chosen to be all knotted up inside. He was full of foreign bodies. Where did the self reside? What came out from inside oneself was so often unwelcome and unaccountable that the self must be in the skin. Robert was a thin skin stretched over a sick society.

He did have to wait for service. He forced himself to be patient, to demonstrate to himself his control over what was inside him. One could deliberately think. One could make oneself think a certain thing. But one couldn't deliberately feel. One was at the mercy of one's feelings. He felt angry. He thought calm. Thought won, but at a cost. At last he was served.

The first pint. He looked at it with admiration. It glowed. It was good stuff. It slid down his throat. It had been a bad day. Another interview, but still no job. The interviewers could smell his failure. A man with a woman who looked rather like Frances. Not so nice, though. Harder. Wonder what she's doing. I've never shared a Christmas with children. I wonder how Juliet's getting on. Poor Juliet. The meek shall not inherit this earth. I could have had several years as their father. I'm ageing now. Hair thinning. Sometimes after I've been to the lavatory I go back in a few minutes later and I can smell it in the air, a faint tang of my own old age. Old men smell ashen. It must be on my breath, too, just beginning. Not now, though. Beer on my breath now. Have another one quickly. No, better not. Compromise. A half.

He walked towards the Magnet and Two Stoats. The rain had cleared away. It was a hard, starry, pre-Christmas night, ideal for wise men, not so good for Robert Bellamy.

He was the first. There was no one there, just a great crowd of strangers.

Then Bernard arrived.

'You're late.'

'Sorry.'

He bought Bernard a drink.

'Merry Christmas.'

'Merry Christmas.'

The pub was grotesquely over-decorated with great balls of coloured paper. Bernard looked tired.

'So old Dick's marrying Sonia. Well, well,' said Bernard.

'Yes. Oh, God, I don't know. I heard about it the very day I was going to propose to her. Would you believe it?'

No, Bernard wouldn't believe it. Nobody would believe it, including himself.

Bernard bought a round.

'Where the hell is everybody?'

'I don't know.'

'Christ almighty, what the hell's wrong with them?'

'You're shouting, Robert.'

'Who cares?'

'I do.'

'This isn't Pinner, you know, Bernard.'

'Perhaps I'd better go,' said Bernard.

'I'm sorry.'

'I can't stay very long, anyway.'

'Oh, God. It's Christmas. You always stay.'

'It's Jean, Robert. She's expecting me. It's carbonnade of beef.'

'It's always bloody carbonnade of beef. Carbonnade of beef comes but three hundred and sixty-five times a year. You have it deliberately, don't you? Get away from your nasty boozy rough friends, back to Pinner.'

Some knotted nit deep-knit inside him was pouring this stuff out. Bernard just stood there, blinking, moving his face towards

Robert. His large blue chin, twice nicked while shaving, filled Robert's field of vision.

'I am not doing it deliberately,' he said, grinding his words out evenly, calmly but viciously. 'It's Jean who does it deliberately. It's my bloody awful wife, and her bloody awful stinking foul Belgian beef.'

There was a silence.

'I'm sorry,' said Robert.

'Can you hold my glass while I light my pipe?'

'Right.'

The lighting of Bernard's pipe could take upwards of ten minutes. Robert wondered how he got on with his pipe at home. Someone spilt a pint down his left leg.

'Not much room.'

'No. It seems to get worse every year.'

Bernard fiddled infuriatingly with his pipe, calmly, intently.

'So I shall go fairly soon,' said Bernard. 'I shall go because I want things to be as easy as possible over Christmas. For the children.'

You always feel guilty if parents mention their children before you have.

'How are the kids?'

'Fine.'

At last the pipe drew. As he bought the next pint Robert said: 'Excuse me' and some tit at the bar said: 'Why, what have you done?'

He gave Bernard his drink.

What words would fill the silence that lay between them? A joke? He had intended to say, at some stage of the evening, that a criminal is someone who hasn't been wanted enough as a child but is wanted too much as an adult. It had seemed brilliant. Now it seemed very familiar. Sometimes every possible combination of words seemed familiar.

Someone spilt a pint down his right leg.

'Been to any football recently?' he asked.

'Not for years.'

'Hullo.'

'Oh, hullo, Stephen.'

'Where's everyone?'

'I don't know.'

Bernard bought a round of drinks.

'Merry Christmas.'

'Merry Christmas.'

'Merry Christmas.'

There was a brief, unfestive pause. Then Bernard said: 'Well, how's Fleet Street?' at exactly the same moment as Stephen said: 'Well, how's British education?'

'Not too bad,' said Robert, for them both.

'Pretty depressing time for you, Bernard,' said Stephen.

'What?' said Bernard, blinking.

'Fulham.'

'Oh. Yes.'

'Relegation, I reckon, this year.'

'Yes.'

'Isn't Alastair coming?' said Robert.

'He can't make it. It's a pretty busy night. I'll have to rush myself, I'm afraid.'

Stephen shrank back about half an inch, instinctively, from the expected storm. But there wouldn't be any storm. He would demonstrate his control.

'I heard a good one about the breathalyser,' said Stephen. 'The police ask this motorist to give a breath test. I can't, he says. Why not, they say. I've got a collapsed lung, he says. So they take him to the station and ask for a blood sample. I can't, he says. Why not, they say. Haemophilia. Well, will you give us a urine test, then? I can't, he says. Why not? Prostate gland, he says. Well, will you walk along that white line, they say. I can't, he says. Why not, they say. I'm pissed, he says.'

They laughed. Robert hoped that it wasn't going to turn into a joke session. It was so embarrassing when you didn't find them funny.

'By the way,' he said. 'Dick's getting married.'

'No! Who's the lucky bird? One of his usual gungepots?'

'Sonia.'

'What, your Sonia?'

'Yes.'

'Bloody hell.'

Poor old Robert. Say it. Well, think it, then. And look it. Poor old Robert.

'Talking about lucky girls,' said Bernard. 'I understand you've got a rather luscious little girl up your sleeve.'

'It's off,' said Stephen.

'Oh, I'm sorry.'

'So am I. There's another bloke. She's gone off with one of her bloody customers. One of those damned smoothies that hang around the El Hambra, I expect. Same again, is it?'

Beneath his stubble Bernard could be seen to be blushing heavily.

'Thanks.'

'Thanks.'

At the bar Stephen said: 'Excuse me' and the tit said: 'Why, what have you done?'

Stephen handed the beers above the heads of the crowd to Robert and Bernard.

'Merry Christmas.'

'Merry Christmas.'

'Merry Christmas.'

'A criminal is a person who's not been wanted enough as a child and is wanted too much as an adult.'

'Hullo.'

'Oh, hullo, Dick.'

'Sorry I'm late. Hullo, Bernard.'

'What are you having?'

'It's my round.'

'Oh. Well, a pint of bitter please.'

'Crowded in here, isn't it?'

'Yes, it seems worse than ever.'

'Where is everybody?'

'Who?'

'Well, I don't know. Everybody. Ah, thanks.'

'Merry Christmas.'

'Merry Christmas.'

'Merry Christmas.'

'Merry Christmas.'

'Rather a depressing time for you, Bernard.'

'What?'

'Fulham.'

'Oh, yes. By the way, Dick, congratulations. And to - er – er.'

'Sonia,' said Robert. 'Her name's Sonia. You don't have to be tactful and not mention her.'

'Robert!'

'Well!'

'What's got into everybody? By the way, talking about marriage, what about old Bernard? You've been hiding your light under a bushel,' said Dick.

'What do you mean?'

'Your wife. I saw you with her the other day. You didn't see me.'

Bernard blinked. A slow flush suffused his cheeks. He mouthed warning signals to Dick.

'Swedish, is she? She looks it.'

Jean was small, brown-haired, unmistakably not Swedish. Bernard's friendship with Dick had been dead before Bernard's marriage, to which Dick had not been invited. Bernard had invited three people, Jean forty-eight. Robert had been best man.

Robert shook his head at Dick, trying to get him to change the subject. Dick merely looked puzzled, as did Stephen.

'Got it,' said Dick. 'I knew I'd seen her somewhere before. She serves at the El Hambra.'

Bernard's slow flush deepened. Stephen looked from one face to another. Robert tried to look nonchalant.

'You,' said Stephen. 'You bastard.'

'Well, how was I to know?' said Bernard.

'I suppose she doesn't even know you're married,' said Stephen.

Bernard didn't reply.

'Poor old Fulham,' said Dick.

'You've said that already,' said Robert.

'Let's have another bloody drink,' said Stephen, his Yorkshire accent broadening instinctively.

'I'll help you,' said Robert.

'Excuse me,' said Stephen.

'Why, what have you done?' said the tit.

'Shut your mouth, or I'll ram this glass up your arse,' said Stephen.

'Did I say something wrong?' said Dick.

'No. No,' said Bernard.

Robert and Stephen struggled back with the drinks.

'Merry Christmas.'

'Merry Christmas.'

'Merry Christmas.'

'Merry Christmas.'

'I heard rather a good joke today,' said Dick. 'I don't usually tell jokes but this one's so good. The police ask this motorist to give a breath test, you see . . .'

'Well, I must be off,' said Bernard four jokes later. 'Bye bye everyone. Merry Christmas.'

'Merry Christmas.'

'Merry Christmas.'

'Merry Christmas.'

'I'd better go too,' said Stephen.

'Oh, bloody hell, this is pathetic,' said Robert.

'I can't help it. I've got a job to do.'

'All right. There's no need to shout.'

'Well, you get so bloody clinging. You're like a bloody octopus.'

'Do you have to swear so much?'

'I'm off. Bye bye. Merry Christmas.'

'Merry Christmas.'

'Merry Christmas.'

'I put my foot in it,' said Dick.

'You weren't to know.'

'I suppose not. Robert, I'm frightfully sorry if this business with Sonia has upset you.'

'I'm all right.'

'It would upset us very much if it came between us. It won't, will it?'

'I can't say, can I?'

'Anyway, we very much want you to be best man.'

'I can just see that.'

'Well, why not?'

'Consolation prize.'

'Well, we're both very fond of you and we both agree that it'll make our wedding day much happier if you'll agree.'

'Is that the end of the joint communiqué?'

'Yes.'

'Good. Well, I shall have to consider it very fully. These are difficult matters which will have to be gone into very carefully. I don't wish to say anything at this stage which might prejudice the issue. Where the hell is everybody?'

'Who?'

'There used to be enormous numbers of people.'

'Times change.'

'Have another one.'

'Thanks.'

Robert struggled to the bar through a crowd of drunken office workers. Here and there stood a regular drinker, glaring at these once a year people. The bar was awash. He didn't want any more to drink, but bought himself another pint.

He managed to get back to Dick with the drinks.

'How's the law?' he asked.

'All right.'

'You'll be famous one day. You'll be known for your short, pithy speeches. The only judge whose sentences all run concurrently.'

'Very good. Is that the time? I must be off.'

'Bloody hell, not you too.'

'I'm afraid so.'

'What a great night. Off you go, then. Run home to Sonia.'

'No. I wouldn't leave for that. I've got an important case tomorrow. I've got some work to do tonight.'

'You're a busy man. I understand. You're all busy. I'm the only one who's not busy. No work at all. No friends. Can't get anyone to stay with me even on the pre-Christmas booze-up.'

'Oh, Robert. It isn't that.'

'Yes, it is. That's what it is. Well, go then, if you're going.'

'Go back home, Robert. You've had enough.'

'I might get into trouble on my own, might I? I'm not safe on my own?'

'Well, you aren't in the best of moods, are you?'

'You needn't worry about me. Not that I flatter myself that you would anyway. Of course I'll go back home. What have I got to stay out for?'

'Well, I'll be off, then.'

'You be off, yes.'

'Merry Christmas, Robert.'

'Merry Christmas.'

25 A Brush with the Law

Robert pleaded not guilty, less because he believed in his innocence than because he had not the faintest recollection of what had happened.

He felt terrible. He felt incapable of opening his eyes, let alone conducting his own defence. Someone had hired out the top half of his head to stage a ten-pin bowling competition.

Sgt Platt prosecuted. The first witness was PC Plunkitt.

'I was proceeding in a northerly direction up Laxton Street when I saw the accused staggering in a southerly direction towards me,' said PC Plunkitt. 'He was clearly inebriated, and he made some remarks.'

'Are those the remarks written on the two sheets of paper which I submit as Exhibit A and Exhibit B?'

'That is correct.'

The two sheets of paper were shown to the magistrate.

'Can I see them?' said Robert.

He saw them. He groaned inwardly.

'What did you do then?' said Sgt Platt.

'I apprised him of my identity.'

'What was his reaction to that?'

'He said,' and here the constable consulted his notebook: '"Piss off. You are no more a police constable than my backside."'

'The accused's backside is of course not a police constable?'

'That is correct.'

'What happened then?'

'I said "I am 271 PC Plunkitt and here is my warrant."'

'What was his reply?'

'He said: "Pull the other one. You are trying to deceive me. You must take me for some sort of a mug."'

I don't talk like that, thought Robert.

'I said to him: "I must ask you to come with me" and he replied: "Are you making a proposition?" I said: "You are drunk and disorderly and I am taking you into custody."'

'And what did he say to that?'

'He said: "Oh." I said: "Come along then" and he said: "You are making a big mistake. Obviously you do not know who I am. I am one of the three wise men. I am looking for my myrrh." I replied, endeavouring to humour him: "Yes. I understand. We will find it for you. Now I must ask you to accompany me to the station."'

'Did he?'

'No, sergeant. He said: "I have left my frankincense at Belsize Park Tube Station." I replied: "Yes. I understand. We will fetch it for you. Now I must ask you to accompany me to the station." He then hit me, catching me with a good right-hander, causing severe bruising of the left cheek.'

'Is that the same bruising that the court can see on your cheek today?'

'That is correct.'

'What did you do then?'

'I grabbed his arms and pinioned them, taking care not to give rise to allegations of police brutality. I said: "Now will you come with me?" and he replied: "Yes. You're a fair cop. Hey, that's a good one, isn't it? Get it?" or words to that effect.'

'What happened then?'

'I let go and he collapsed in a north-easterly direction. He ended up in the gutter. His right ear was seven feet two inches from the door of the All-Night Mini-Chop House and his left foot was 218 yards north-west of the junction with Cox Road.'

'Is that the one-way street eastwards linking up with Russet Street?' interpolated the magistrate.

'That is correct. It runs from Russet Street to Granny Smith Avenue. It was made one-way in 1965.'

'That was at the time of the Quorl Roundabout Scheme, was it?' said the sergeant.

'Yes, sergeant. Twelve streets were made one-way at that time.'

'And what happened then?'

'I blew my whistle. PC Burnside came to my assistance and we carried the accused to the station where he was formally revived and charged.'

Robert put no questions. The next witness was PC Burnside.

'You interviewed the accused after he had been revived?' said Sgt Platt.

'Yes, sergeant. I asked him for his name and address. He replied: "I am Jesus Christ. Take me out and I will walk on the Serpentine."'

'What did you say?'

'I said: "I have reason to believe that you are giving me a false name." He replied: "You are right. I will come clean. My real name is Fergus Tuck. I live in Peckham and am a chartered taxidermist. I have been working too hard. It has been a bit of a rush, what with Christmas and everybody wanting polecats. I haven't had a single drink. I was visiting my fancy woman in Muswell Hill. Can't a bloke have any fun these days?"'

'What did you do next?'

'I said: "Come on, there's a good fellow. You know you're being a bit of a chump" or words to that effect. I said that the contents of his wallet gave me reason to believe that he was Robert Bellamy, of 38, Blessington Road, Kentish Town, and he replied: "You believe what you like. I am saying nothing."'

Robert asked no questions. The final witness was the police doctor, Dr Partridge.

Dr Partridge said that Robert's speech had been blurred, his breath had smelt strongly of drink, and when asked to walk along a white line he said: 'I can't. Haemophilia.' Samples showed that he had drunk the equivalent of fourteen pints of beer and three whiskies, or eleven pints and five double tia marias, or two bottles of hock, three small ciders and an orange curaçao. His trousers had had the equivalent of two pints of beer.

'Did the accused say anything else to you?' said Sgt Platt.

'Yes,' said Dr Partridge. 'He said: "You are a bastard. You are all bastards. This country is finished. I am a friend of the chief constable. I will have you struck off the register."'

Robert asked no questions and offered no defence. He was fined £2 for being drunk and disorderly, £5 for using obscene language and £25 for assaulting a police officer.

26 A Dip into the Mail Bag

Elm Cottage
Clevely Juxta Mopwell
30-1-49

Dear Robert,

Thank you for your nice long letter. I'm sure you will settle down at school better soon. I don't like dead rats, either.

The cottage is beginning to take shape but it will be a very long job. It will be quite a surprise for you to see how it has changed when you come home for Easter.

It has been raining here today, but now the sun is out and everything is shining brightly. I wish I had the words to describe it to you properly. I am thinking of my dear boy and wishing he was here with his mummy. But there it is. We can't have what we want all the time in life.

About Saturday week. You must realize, dear, how difficult it would be for me to get there without Randolph's car. You are right. I must learn to drive. I promise. But in the meantime I can hardly come by train or bus, the services are literally *impossible*, so I'm afraid you will have to put up with Randolph. He is not my chauffeur, so I can hardly dump him in some sordid café for the afternoon. I do beg of you to try to like Randolph. He means well and is very fond of you, and his 'know-how' is essential to the success of my work. Maybe he does look a bit like Hitler, but you must learn not to judge from appearances. And never never mention that to him. I'm sorry all the boys sang a song about him after our visit last term. This time we will meet you at the gate. He will not get out of the car, and I will persuade him not to go into the town at all.

Anyway, I promise you that at half term I will stay for the

weekend and Randolph will not be there. He will drive me down and then go on to see his friends the Brindles at Pungley. You remember Jessica and Cerise Brindle. Sammy threw Jessica into the pond at Hackles and you always used to fight with Cerise.

I am looking forward to Saturday week. Keep on working hard. You are a good boy and I am proud of you.

With all my love
Mummy

Pungley Manor
Pungley
Aug 9. 1951.

Dear Robert,

Very many thanks indeed for your long letter. I found it flattering, in large part gratifying, yet in the final resort disturbing. May I put my reasons for this to you now?

Incidentally, the cause of my slight delay in replying is that I am staying here with my very good friends the Brindles for a few days. Indeed a most happy event has occurred. I have asked for the hand of young Jessica Brindle, who was twenty-one the ninth Sunday after Trinity, and I have been accepted. At the age of forty-one I felt that wedlock had passed me by, so you can imagine my delight. God works in a . . . etc etc. You will be seeing Jessica at the 'Coll' after our marriage next January.

All that is perhaps not entirely irrelevant to your letter. I am of course delighted to hear that you regard my confirmation classes as the high spot of your life at the 'Coll'. But are you not going a little too far? You say that only God is making life meaningful for you. Fair enough. It is God who makes life meaningful. But it is not just life in chapel, it is every aspect of life that God illuminates.

So my answer must be this. No, I am not prepared at this

moment to give you advice on how to take up a monastic life. You are far too young.

I think you have come to God in a most encouraging way, and I hate to seem to be trying to dampen your enthusiasm. But are you quite certain that this is what you want to do? You are at an impressionable age. You must be quite, quite certain before taking so momentous a step. These may seem harsh words, Robert, but I must put them to you. Many people embrace the church because they are afraid of life. It is too much for them. These people do not have a vocation. The person with a vocation has tasted life and is not satisfied with it. It is too little for him. For instance, you say you want celibacy. Now I certainly do not want celibacy. I want Jessica. And yet I do not believe myself to be an entirely Unchristian person. I do not want to go too deeply into this, but it is my view that one should not become a monk because one wants celibacy. That is dangerous. One should accept the glorious sacrifice of celibacy because one wishes to become a monk. Also, your remarks to me last term about self-abuse lead me to believe that you are not ready for a decision on that score just yet.

You describe me as being the most inspiring and wonderful man you have ever met. Thank you, Robert, but I wish you could see me as I do. I am aware that I have an appearance of great holiness, even saintliness. It is unfortunate. It creates upon impressionable youth an effect altogether too startling. I have even toyed with the idea of plastic surgery – though Jessica, I hasten to add, likes me as I am! But you would not think so much of me if you had seen me, as I did, yielding to a childish temptation last Michaelmas term, and emerging from the Common Room with six chocolate digestive biscuits concealed in an envelope in my jacket pocket. You must learn not to judge from appearances. The force of this adage came home to me only yesterday when I encountered, in the village, a forlorn individual who has been hanging around Jessica and making a positive nuisance of himself, sending all sorts of expensive gifts and presuming on the basis of some slight acquaintance that she will fall madly in love with him. The poor fellow bears a marked resemblance to the late Adolf Hitler, and comes in for more than his share of sarcastic local comment. I spoke to him and found him deeply sympathetic, highly sensitive, and very unhappy. I explained to him that nuptials were impending, and he simply said: 'I see. I'm terribly sorry. I don't take *The Times*, you see' and left the village on the next bus. We had all underestimated his worth just as surely as you have overestimated mine.

Well, Robert, these are straight words, and I hope you will do some straight thinking. It is a high and a special calling that you are considering. Wait a while, until we can be certain that your motives are as high and special as they must be.

I hope that you will have a very pleasant summer holidays. Write again if you still feel disturbed. I shall be here until the 17th.

> Your very dear friend
> Holy C

> 26 Cemetery Road
> Putney
> 12-4-55

Dear Robert,

Your national service is now almost five-sixths over and you are looking forward to your release from your obligations towards the defence of those of us at home. It has been an experience which has caused you to endure many hardships and humiliations, yet it has also had its pleasant side. It has afforded you the opportunity to travel, and to meet people from a station in life more modest than your own.

It has afforded, too, in between its disciplines, moments of harmless joy, such as no young person should be denied.

Of course I am not upset that you are not coming home to see me on your final leave. You wish to see more of the scenery of Germany, and that is entirely natural. I must warn you to be extremely careful not to fall into the Rhine. These continental rivers are exceedingly treacherous. Try to interest yourself as much as possible in the natural beauty of the country, and be extremely chary of engaging your interest in its art. All art is dangerous for a young man, and German art particularly so. The insidious excesses of the rococo and the baroque provide a kind of spiritual temptation against which one has to be constantly vigilant.

While we are on the subject of Germany I must mention the only event which has occurred to ripple the even surface of my daily life during the past week. I was quietly reading a book last Tuesday afternoon, when there came a knock on the door. I have few callers, and was not expecting anyone. Imagine my surprise to find on my doorstep a shabbily dressed person whom at first I took to be a tinker, but who claimed to be an old friend of your mother's. He was a disreputable looking character bearing a distinct resemblance to that appalling Hitler who invaded the Sudetenland and brought so much misery upon your mother. He said that he had fallen on evil days and asked if I could offer him any money. His story was clearly a fabrication and I was extremely frightened, but I told him with a politeness that was doubtless wasted on him that my circumstances, although adequate, allow of extremely little margin in the event of emergencies. He pleaded with me, so I told him that this was a Christian house, and I was not having such slanders upon your dear, unfortunate mother, and I shut the door on him. I confess I am a little worried in case he returns. Is it quite certain that Hitler died in the bunker?

Well, that is all my news. I am keeping remarkably well, and your cheery letters are a high spot in my life.

Your affectionate Aunt
Margaret

Spinney Cottage
Hartingsford Magna
July 11, 1964

My dear boy,

Another line from your old Aunt Maud, who is growing a wee bit older all the time. Once again I was most happy to get such a long and newsy letter from you. Otherwise I only learn about the outside world through the newspapers.

The new film by Jean-Luc Godard is similar to his others – fragmentary, perhaps a little infuriating, but stimulating. Housing in the Maidenhead area is extremely expensive. The exact intentions of the Chinese are hard to fathom, but I daresay you understand these things better than we do in the country. There are no sinologists in Hartingsford.

Is Iris Murdoch becoming attached to a smaller and smaller world, a gothic cage of her own no doubt brilliant imagination? Much as I no longer have any desire to leave Hartingsford, so authors often have no desire to leave their own minds. Something of the sort happened to Samuel Beckett, the great Irish pessimist, who rolled his sad world round and round until it crumbled into pieces. And James Joyce, another great Irish exile, descended into a private world which rendered his last book barely comprehensible. Is Iris Murdoch Irish too? I daresay I am 'wide of the mark', never having read any books by these authors, but I would be interested to hear your opinion. I have raised the subject in the village once or twice, but to little effect. We are not a cultured society.

Will Eric Russell make his two thousand runs? He seems

to be 'on form'. The pound is steadier this month. Do you ever meet Mary Quant? Her designs are all the rage, although of course we don't see them here. The village dresses very conventionally.

I must once again refuse your kind offer of a visit to London. I am out of touch and wish to remain so. I am lucky here. I have plenty to interest me. I welcome each new month, each new season, each tiny change in the fields and gardens. I am an old countrywoman. I look out on the big world and I think 'mad, mad, mad'. One day I believe you will do the same, for I have faith in you.

Nothing happens here. Ben is up for rape again next Thursday, and will get two years if The Faggot is on the bench. Mrs Loope has run away with Mr Bendicott and Mrs Bendicott is looking after all five children. Blounce's daughter is marrying a West Indian. Good for her. These young people have spirit. The Peck is suing the council over the pylons, but will lose.

Oh yes, one tit-bit for you. At last the Farradales are getting poor Timothy off their hands. He's marrying the elder Brindle girl, Jessica. Didn't you know the Brindles once? Jessica has had some bad luck. She's been engaged three times without getting to the altar. The first one was some poor man who unfortunately looked like the Kaiser, so that fell through. Then there was a Popish priest, but her parents caught him stealing a packet of chocolate digestive biscuits, and society is so intolerant of the sins of the flesh in men of the cloth. And then finally she was engaged to an architecture critic who specialized in the baroque, but he fell into the river Neckar and was drowned. Let us hope she has better luck this time.

Well, look after yourself, and come down when you can.

Your soft and foolish Aunt

Maud

27 A Traditional Christmas

After the court case Robert had a bath. As he washed himself lazily he looked forward to Christmas at Charlscombe. His Aunt Margaret Christmases were better now that they went to Charlscombe. At Charlscombe he would be able to relax. No one would expect him to be amusing. He loved Christmas – children, holly, snow, Christmas cards flapping colourfully in the draught of a huge log fire. Over Christmas his disintegration would be halted.

Tommy Madeley had gone to Australia when he was eight, but he always retained, beneath his harsh new accent, a fondness for the old place, the land of his ancestors. He had, they often said, chalk in his bones. He laughed at this. But it was in England, on his very first visit, that he met and married Aunt Margaret's younger sister Hetty. They had four children – Warren, now thirty-four, Doug (thirty), Ben (twenty-seven) and Judy (twenty-four). When all the Wiltshire Madeleys died the old farm went to Tommy. It was the happiest day of his life. Judy came too. Ben came on a visit in 1961, met an English girl in a train, and stayed. Warren came over in 1966, to try and forget his divorce.

Exile had made the Madeleys passionately English. They believed in local customs, local recipes, local sayings, home-brewed wines, village fêtes, harvest festivals, inter-village home-made jam competitions and traditional Christmases. Just what I need in my present state, thought Robert. Solidarity. Though I look solid enough, he thought, looking at himself in the mirror thoughtfully provided by Mr Mendel. His skin reddened by the heat. Quite heavy, developing a pot. Hair beginning to recede rather fast. He dressed wearily, still with a headache. As soon as he put on his clothes he felt steamy and wanted another bath.

He spent the afternoon going round the shops, despairing of ever making up his mind what to buy for presents.

He bought nothing, but came away with a few ideas. And then on an impulse he returned for the first time to Frances's street.

He didn't knock, since there would be no way of explaining his presence. He hovered at the end of the street, like a man crazed, like people he had sometimes seen, mad people, and he had wondered what it felt like to be inside them, and now here he was, not mad but at this moment surely unbalanced, and it felt quite normal.

He tried not to look suspicious. He was tired, having not so much slept as been unconscious in the police cell.

The door of Frances's house opened. His heart stopped. A band of pain shot across his chest, and up his arm. A stranger emerged. Thinking as quickly as his condition permitted, he went up to the stranger and inquired after a fictitious family.

'Excuse me,' he said. 'I'm looking for the Benhams. I think they live at number 23.'

'They can't do. I live at number 23. Name of Grigg.'

'Oh. Well, perhaps they've moved. Have you been there long?'

'Two years. The people who had it before, it wasn't Benson. What was it now? Halyard. People named Halyard. Or was it Lanyard? I know it was something to do with rope. So it couldn't have been Benson, I mean, that's nothing to do with rope, is it?'

'No. Well, I'm sorry to have bothered you.'

'No bother. Merry Christmas.'

'Merry Christmas.'

Robert walked past two pubs, two victories. Couldn't have a drink tonight, not after that humiliation in court. Must fight the dryness, dryness in the throat.

He packed and watched television and drank nine cups of tea. He went to bed at ten-thirty but slept badly, he was over-tired.

At eight-thirty he was in the shops. For Aunt Margaret, gloves. For Aunt Hetty, something pewter, anything pewter. Ring Aunt Margaret. Pick her up at twelve. Catch one ten. Ring Charlscombe. Arrange to be met. Little Hugh would like a big, red fire engine with bells. No, one of these modern educational toys. No, forget education at Christmas. A big, red fire engine with bells. Uncle Tommy, oh God, I don't know, drifting from department to department, why do they have to make toy fire engines so big? For no reason at all buy Uncle Tommy a tin of assorted biscuits. For Warren, something small or I'll never carry it all. Why do they have to make tins of assorted biscuits so big? Modern novel for Warren, do him good. Nothing for Ben and Mrs Ben because oh you shouldn't have not when you're giving to Hugh. Oh well, perhaps just a packet of brieflets as a gesture. What nice handbags. Rather expensive, but Judy's quite pretty. Why am I clanging? Oh, fire engine bells. Time flying. Am late. Ring Aunt Margaret. Pick her up at two and catch three twelve. Ring Charlscombe. They've left, to do last minute shopping and have lunch. They always lunch at the George. Aunt Hetty will send message.

Pick up Aunt Margaret at two nineteen. Rush to Waterloo, should have booked seats, Aunt Margaret must have non-smoker. Porter. Manage to find two seats in hostile non-smoker which resents moving up to make room, although these trains are designed for four a side. Trip. Fall over fire engine. Clang. Drop biscuits. Probably broken. Can't find any change. Aunt Margaret tips porter humiliatingly meanly, her mind in the 1930s. Train late starting.

The train starts, with a jolt. Clang. Three people begin smoking. Aunt Margaret indicates with her eye-brows that it is Robert's duty, in return for her share in his upbringing, to say to these people: 'Excuse me. This is a non-smoker'. He says, feeling a terrible spoil-sport: 'Excuse me, this is a non-smoker.'

The three passengers repair angrily to a corridor so cluttered with Robert's presents that they have to stand on one leg, like commuting flamingoes. One of them trips as the train jolts. Clang. An educational toy would have been far more suitable. I mean, what can you *do* with a red fire engine? That handbag is too old for Judy. Clang. Woking. 'Mary Spurgeon used to live in Woking.' Who the hell is Mary Spurgeon? Clang. Off again. Who in their right senses buys a tin of assorted biscuits for a farmer? Clang. 'Our vicar's sister lives in Basingstoke.' Clang. Those biscuits must be broken now. And Robert has suddenly remembered something. He hates Christmas. What on earth could have made him think he liked it? 'Tickets, please,' 'Do you remember when Arnold Wilkins lost his ticket?' Angry middle-class smokers astride fire engines and broken biscuits as a nondescript dusk falls over a bleak housing estate, and nondescript curtains are drawn in front of 166 semi-detached fairy-lit Christmas trees. We're there.

Warren and Judy hadn't got the message, but pretended not to have minded their two-hour wait. Robert felt thoroughly guilty. It really would be rather nice if he and Judy could have an innocent happy romance, leading to marriage, children and big red fire engines. That was what he wanted, deep down, he felt.

It took Warren half an hour to drive to Charlscombe, a village so isolated that it had twice been voted the best-kept secret in Wiltshire. The farmhouse was a large building with two projecting wings. One wing was timbered, the other of red brick. The weary travellers were refreshed by a cup of tea and a slice of Ginger Lard Cake. Ginger Lard Cake is a local speciality, a cross between a very strong ginger parkin, a very fat lardy cake and a very hard rock cake. It has almost died out nowadays, and is sold only in one shop, whose proprietor is related to a dentist. There was so much pewter around that Robert felt certain that his present would be a fiasco. He wanted to go to sleep. Aunt Margaret was talking to

Aunt Hetty about the journey, in minute detail. He must say something.

'Who's coming for Christmas?' he asked.

'Nobody much,' said Aunt Hetty.

He was glad.

'Except us. Just Tommy and Warren and Judy, and Ben and the family.' Ben and Mrs Ben had a small son, Hugh, soon to be the recipient of a big red fire engine, with bells. 'And Warren's fiancée.'

'What? I didn't know. You didn't tell me, Warren. Congratulations.'

Warren mumbled shyly through his Ginger Lard Cake. He was thin, nervous, battered.

'He's marrying the elder Brindle girl, Jessica, from over at Pungley. Didn't you know the Brindles?'

'Vaguely.'

'Everyone knows the Brindles,' said Judy, giving Robert a charming, secretly conniving smile.

'And Jessica's sister, Cerise, and her husband. He's a doctor. Their parents have gone over to Canada for the winter. They've got relatives out there. So we thought we ought to invite them all. They're very nice. It'll be fun for you to see them again. And Judy's fiancé.'

'What?'

'Didn't you tell him, Judy?'

'He didn't ask.'

A fine time to tell him. That handbag had cost a small fortune.

'Well, congratulations. Who is he?'

'He's a writer,' said Judy.

'But very nice,' said Aunt Hetty. 'Keen on the countryside. Anti, though, which raises problems.'

The Madeleys were staunch supporters of the Penmorden. Cherfont and Charlscombe Hunt.

'And the Cherfont aunts.'

These were Aunt Emily and Aunt Edith.

'And the Penmorden uncles.'

These were Uncle George and Uncle Frank.

'We're planning a double wedding,' said Judy. 'You must come.'

Her smile must have been secretly mocking, not conniving.

'Hullo, hullo, hullo,' said Tommy Madeley, poking his weather-beaten face round the door. 'Welcome to Charlscombe.'

The evening meal was a jolly affair. The darkness of the countryside turned the house into a blazing pool of comfort. Robert felt almost relaxed. He slept quite well that night.

Sunday, December 24 dawned grey and threatening. Robert's relaxed mood had gone. After the traditional local breakfast dish, bacon hash, a mixture of pounded finnan haddock, minced bacon, haricot beans and squashed prunes, Robert walked the two miles to 'Woomera', Ben's attractive sixteenth-century cottage. As he entered he tripped over a large sharp object. Clang. He looked back at a big red fire engine, with bells.

'Dangerous old thing,' said Ben. 'They shouldn't make toys with sharp edges.'

Mrs Ben applied the Dettol and Elastoplast with deft efficiency.

'You know me, don't you?' said Robert to little Hugh. 'I'm Uncle Robert.'

Hugh burst into tears.

'I wonder what nice toy Uncle Robert's brought you this year,' said Mrs Ben, but Hugh was not to be consoled, and was put to bed. He was, it was explained, over-excited.

'Coffee?' said Mrs Ben.

'Yes, please.'

'You look tired, Robert.'

'I am a bit.'

They were looking at him in a strange way. They had noticed. His chaotic state was plain for all to see, it seemed.

'I've made a blunder,' he said. 'I've brought Hugh a fire engine just like that one.'

'Never mind. They'll change it at Crampton's,' said Ben.

'We've changed one there already,' said Mrs Ben.

'It's a very good toy. That's why it's so popular,' said Ben.

Humouring him. Over-excited, indeed. I frighten the boy. I must go outside. I can't breathe.

He made his excuses, leaving them to discuss his state of health.

The writer arrived. Robert and the writer prepared sprouts together, and the writer clearly thought him a dull chap, compared to sprouts. The writer said what pleasure it gave him to handle vegetables. They were so, somehow, natural. So full of goodness.

'You may as well finish them all yourself, then,' said Robert.

In the afternoon he went for a walk. It was raining, spears of rain on a high wind. This was an isolated windswept landscape, overlooked by a great crouching hump of downland, scarred with chalk, topped by a cold circle of trees. Robert walked fast, aggressively, doing battle with the elements, obsessively. On his way home he met the writer.

'Hullo,' he said.

'Hullo,' said the writer, backing away slightly, as if Robert was a horse of uncertain temper. He looked so miserable that he had clearly only gone out in order to impress the Madeleys.

'It's wonderful,' said the writer. 'The house. Judy. All this. Everything.'

It seemed a somewhat spare description. What sort of a writer was this? Why didn't he talk about the stooping sheep-sheared, chalk-ribbed, wind-licked, dung-dry Druid-dead bone-bleached backbone of old England?

'It's all so . . .' The writer searched for the *mot juste*. . . .
'Rural.'

'Yes.'

'It's perfection. Sheer perfection.'

'You haven't tasted bacon hash yet.'

A car swept past, practically demolishing them.

'Road-hog,' said the writer.

They walked back and were introduced to the road-hog, his small, tubby wife Cerise, and Jessica, angular, awkward and nervously gushing, like an inefficient water pump. Robert tried to find his Cerise in this Cerise, but time and habit and perhaps the distortions of memory had wiped her off the map. He was disappointed. That distant young Cerise seemed to be a whole person, revealed in her tiny uniqueness. This larger person was a clothed vagueness. She remembered Robert and indeed her recollection of events tallied largely with his. There was, it seemed, a historical truth to their childhood. Was she remembering the tiny person who was Robert, whom he could not remember at all, never having had a clear view. Recollection was like finding one's position on a map. One deduced, from the way in which certain things had looked, what sort of a person the looker, oneself, had been. It was certainly remarkably unsettling, when one was tired and nervous, to think that perhaps this woman, every aspect of whose clothing and make-up and hair style spoke of an unspecified doctor's wife rather than of Cerise, was looking at oneself – her secret childhood passion? – and was thinking, as with polite courage she attacked a piece of Ginger Lard Cake, how drab and vague and disappointing the adult version had become. It was even possible to imagine that this woman had been brought here deliberately to taunt him at this critical time, and to wonder whether this double engagement was not also part of a sinister attack on his morale. And he had to share a double bed with Warren, and he couldn't sleep, but lay frozen in one position, aching, longing to move, afraid of waking Warren. He was like a child, kept awake by excitement, only in his case it was dread. He couldn't bear the thought of all the goodwill. It was going to be so depressing.

Christmas day dawned, and he still felt that vague childish

disappointment that it was a dawn as grey and gradual as any other. He washed, had oh, perhaps his five thousand five hundredth shave, and went downstairs for this thirty-third Christmas. For Aunt Margaret it was still of religious significance. He ate his bacon hash, which the writer clearly loved. The doctor expounded on its health-giving life-span-extending properties. Uncle Tommy made unveiled allusion to its aphrodisiac powers. It made Robert constipated.

After breakfast the ordeal by gift began. Three huge laundry baskets contained the tastefully wrapped presents. A diary was just what Robert wanted. A sweater two sizes too large was just what he needed. He couldn't imagine how anyone could have guessed how much he felt the lack of a sweater three sizes too small. How did they know he liked narrow, dark, knitted ties? A second diary would be invaluable if he lost the first one. Only the other day he had lamented that he had no ashtray shaped like a phoenix. An enormous pink kipper tie would go equally well with a sweater three sizes too small or a sweater two sizes too large. Oh, how useful. It so happened that he had mislaid his – well, he couldn't be sure what it was – but he had mislaid his shallow concave object with a long bit sticking up. There was a space in the first diary for listing all his presents. He wrote: 'Two diaries. Shallow concave object with long bit sticking up . . .'

Although his own gifts couldn't be worse than the ones he'd received, Robert felt nervous about them. Aunt Margaret's gloves were exactly as expected. Everyone gave Aunt Hetty pewter. Warren said: 'Stone the crows. How original. A book,' and soon discovered that page 167 was worth reading. Judy's handbag was both too old and far too expensive. It made her silently embarrassed and the writer silently livid. Jessica found page 167 revolting. Uncle Tommy was very polite about his big red fire engine. It was just what he wanted. Robert explained the mistake. Uncle Tommy looked at page 167 and made a loud, fruity noise. It was discovered that the sprout-loving writer had written page 167. Aunt Hetty and helpers prepared dinner. Ben and Mrs Ben and Hugh arrived, and Hugh screamed. He was over-excited. Ben thought that a tin of biscuits was a very original present for a small boy, they hadn't realized Robert had been joking about the fire engine. Robert explained the mistake and Ben insisted on driving back, taking the fire engine and fetching the biscuits. Mrs Ben thanked him for the brieflets but said he shouldn't have. The Cherfont aunts arrived. Drinks were served. Robert had to hold back because of Aunt Margaret. The Penmorden uncles arrived. Uncle George, who had managed a linseed oil factory in his palmier days, chatted about linseed oil. Ben returned and explained that some of the biscuits were broken, but not by them, and Robert presented them to Uncle Tommy. The little mistake was explained to the new arrivals, and much innocent mirth was aroused. Passing Aunt Margaret in the corridor Robert smiled – cheerfully, he hoped. She said: 'Never mind. Circulate. Do your duty.'

Lunch was eaten. Robert had to eat a second helping of Christmas pudding, because the first helping meant a girl friend and the second helping a wife. The Madeleys were dab hands at unearthing local sayings. Probably there had been little else to do in Australia.

During the afternoon nuts were consumed – six nuts before three, riches for me. Conversation washed over him. He dreamt bloatedly of Sonia, of Frances, of other women who might have been right for him, if things had gone otherwise. A receptionist at a hotel in Nantes, to whom he had spoken at most ten words. Anna of Amsterdam. A girl travelling with her mother on the Bergen to Oslo train. A glorious proud face whose glance was amazingly met and held in the Sistine Chapel, when he was with Sonia. How typical of him, feeling the wrong thing at the wrong time, to have looked at that girl and ignored the Sistine Chapel, and then, a year later, to have postponed an important meeting with Pontino in order to go and feast on the chapel. Far away, someone was speaking to him.

'Sorry?'

'I knew your Aunt Maud,' said Jessica.

'Oh. Yes. A very nice woman.'

'Yes. Yes. She was. A frightfully nice woman. Yes. Frightfully.' She lowered her voice to a moderate shout. 'I was going to marry a chap down there. Yes. But it fell through.'

He longed to ask why.

'Frank's asleep,' said Aunt Edith.

Cerise was the next to have a word for Robert.

'You know an old school friend of mine. Jean Tibberley,' she said.

Tibberley? Tibberley?

'Oh, Jean. Yes.'

'A very clever girl. Very witty.' Really? 'I wish you'd tell that husband of hers off.'

'Bernard?'

'Yes. The selfish brute. He's killing Jean.'

'Come on, dear. That doesn't sound a very Christmassy conversation,' said the doctor.

'What about a walk?' said Judy.

'Good idea,' said the writer. 'I love walking.'

Uncle George was the next to have a word for Robert.

'Much linseed oil about in London?' he said.

'Not much,' said Robert.

'Margaret's off,' said Aunt Emily.

'Oh, look,' said Aunt Hetty. 'What a beautiful twigfinch.'

'What the devil's a twigfinch?' said Aunt Edith.

'It's the local name for a bullfinch,' said Aunt Hetty.

'I've never heard of it, and I've lived here all me life,' said Aunt Edith.

'Where is it? I've never seen a bullfinch,' said the writer.

'Over there, on the weeble,' said Aunt Hetty

'Tommy's off,' said Aunt Emily.

'Weeble?' said the writer.

'It's the local name for a potting shed,' said Aunt Hetty.

'Never heard of it,' said Aunt Edith.

'I can't see it,' said the writer.

'It's gone now,' said Aunt Hetty.

'Emily's off,' said Uncle Frank.

'I'm not,' said Emily.

'I thought you were asleep, Frank,' said Aunt Hetty.

'Was,' said Uncle Frank. 'Woke up. Chatter. Women prattling.'

'Always the same,' said Uncle Tommy.

'I thought you were asleep,' said Aunt Hetty.

'I don't suppose the young people care much about linseed oil,' said Uncle George.

'Not a lot,' said Robert.

'What about that walk?' said Judy.

'Good idea,' said the writer. 'Nothing like a good walk.'

'Emily's off now,' said Aunt Edith.

'What about you, Jessica?' said Judy.

'I'd love to. M'm. Yes, it's rather a nice afternoon. Yes. Are you coming, Warren?'

'Nope.'

'Oh, come on.'

'Nope.'

'I thought you might want to be with me,' said Jessica.

'I would be with you, if you didn't go out,' said Warren.

'I'll go to sleep if I stay in. I always do after a heavy meal. Not that I mean the meal was heavy. It was just so nice that I ate too much. Yes.'

'Must walk after a heavy meal,' said the doctor. 'Enormous number of sudden deaths caused by too sedentary a life.'

'Really, Austin. How unchristmassy,' said Cerise.

'George's off,' said Edith.

'Going to get my dirty book,' said Warren.

'It's not dirty,' said Judy.

'Isn't it? Spending a week stark naked in a mountain hut with a kinky sheila, living off sprouts.'

206

'Not sheila. Bird,' said Ben. Australianisms were banned.

'There are good plot reasons for it,' said the writer. 'Their clothes have all been stolen. They are forced back on to nature, and they discover happiness.'

'Bring my biscuits, Warren,' said Uncle Tommy.

'You don't want any more to eat,' said Aunt Hetty.

'We must have a biscuit. Robert gave me them,' said Uncle Tommy.

'There's a circus on the telly,' said Aunt Hetty.

'Damned nonsense. Humiliating to animals,' said Aunt Edith.

'Hear hear,' said the writer.

'Hunting dignifies an animal. Circuses humiliate it,' said Aunt Edith.

'I want the circus,' said Hugh.

'No, dear. It's time for your rest,' said Mrs Ben.

'Sorry,' said Aunt Hetty. 'My fault.'

'Are these the biscuits?' said Warren. 'They're all broken.'

'That's right.'

'Are you coming or aren't you?' said Judy.

'Can't wait,' said the writer.

'Come on, then. Coming, Jessica?'

'They want to be alone,' said Warren.

'Do you?'

'Of course not,' said Judy. 'Do we, darling?'

'Er – no.'

'They're just saying that,' said Warren.

'Are you?'

'Of course not. Are we, darling?'

'Er – no.'

'Well, if you're sure.'

'Come on.'

'I mean, are you really absolutely sure? I mean, I want to, but, you know, if I'm not welcome, no, I mean, if you want to be alone . . .'

'Come on. What about you, Cerise?'

'No, I won't. What about you, Austin?'

But Austin was asleep. The three walkers departed.

'Biscuit?' said Uncle Tommy.

Robert closed his eyes. He didn't want to witness the failure of his biscuits.

'No, thanks.'

'No, thanks.'

'No, thanks.'

'Robert's off.'

'Yes.'

'Those are my biscuits.'

'No, dear. That was a mistake.'

'They're my biscuits.'

'No, dear. Uncle Robert gave you the fire engine.'

'I've got a fire engine.'

'Well, we'll change it.'

'I don't want to change it.'

'He can have the biscuits. I don't really want them.'

'No. He's got to learn.'

'Give him a biscuit.'

'Have a biscuit, dear.'

'Don't want one. They're broken.'

'Hetty's off.'

'Yes. Tired. She does too much.'

'I don't.'

'I thought you were off.'

'Just dozing.'

'I want the circus.'

'Let him have the circus, then everyone can sleep.'

A tide of snoring rose and fell over the silent English countryside. It was Christmas afternoon.

'Do you think he's all right?'

'Who?'

'Robert. He's not ill, is he?'

'Why?'

'He seems very tired.'

'He seems nervy.'

'He's working too hard, I expect.'

'He's not been very sociable.'

'He's moody. Quick-tempered.'

'It's the red hair.'

'He was very off-hand when I spoke to him about linseed oil.'

'Fancy giving me a dirty book.'

'Not dirty, Warren. Modern.'

'Fancy muddling up those presents, at his age.'

'Probably got woman trouble.'

'You don't think he's – you know – one of those?'

'Stop it,' said Robert, without opening his eyes. 'For God's sake stop it.'

There was a long silence. He went red, he who hadn't blushed for fourteen years. How could he go on now that they knew that he had heard, now that he knew what they thought and they knew that he knew? Why hadn't he been able to keep quiet?

He stood up and walked out of the room, trying to catch nobody's eye, trying to retain as much dignity as he could. He tripped over his tin of biscuits and went flying. He fumbled for the door and at last managed to get out. He could just imagine what they would say once he was gone.

He met Mrs Ben in the corridor. She applied the Dettol and Elastoplast with deft efficiency. He was shaking.

'They shouldn't make biscuit tins with sharp edges,' he said. His voice sounded peculiar. Mrs Ben looked at him sharply.

He went up to his room. He must stop shaking. With a great effort of physical control he managed this.

How dare they talk about him like that. How dare he be like that, for them to talk about. They were returning to London tomorrow afternoon. He must stick it out. He wanted a drink.

A drink. A drink. He drank two glasses of water. There was a knock.

'Come in.'

It was Uncle Tommy.

'Are you all right?'

'I'm all right.'

'Are you sure?'

'Yes. I'm all right.'

'We're – we're very sorry, Robert.'

'That's all right.'

'It was just an – er – an idle word. You know.'

'Yes, I know.'

'I don't want to seem inquisitive, Robert, but . . .'

'It's nothing. I'm a bit tired. That's all.'

'Well, I'm sorry, Robert. Are you sure that you'll, you know, be all right?'

'Oh yes, I'll be all right. You won't mention this again, will you? I don't want Aunt Margaret to know.'

'Of course not. Well, if you're really sure you'll be all right . . .'

'I'll be all right.'

That at least was lucky – lucky that out of a sense of duty Aunt Margaret had over-eaten and had therefore, untypically, slept.

The worst moment was when he rejoined that great replete gathering. Tactfully they hadn't yet put the lights on, and the deep twilight protected him. The writer and the two girls returned, the writer waxing ineloquent in his enthusiasm for the countryside. Robert joined in the pulling of crackers, the eating of Christmas cake, the spinning of trenchers, the upping of Jenkins, the performing of charades, in a near-coma of repletion and weariness. In the morning they ate bacon hash and went to the meet, and in the afternoon they saw two twig-finches and a smeldthrush, and Robert and Aunt Margaret caught the six seventeen back to London. And no one knew that he was out of work, and Aunt Margaret knew nothing about any of it, and every nerve end in his body was frayed seemingly beyond repair.

He went to bed for a few hours and then caught the 6.47 a.m. from Waterloo. He had two appointments for interviews that day, and four more on the Thursday and Friday, but he had decided to miss the Wednesday ones. This was more important.

He went to the address that Frances had given him – Miss Jenny Craythorne, the Old Mill House, Lower Cleverdon, Dorset. It took a three-and-a-half-hour train journey, an hour's bus ride, a five-mile walk in the rain, and half-an-hour's research, to ascertain that the Old Mill House had been demolished for road-widening, and that Miss Jenny Craythorne had moved, the forwarding address had been to a London poste restante, but then that was typical of Miss Craythorne, who had been pleasant enough, and had caused no offence, but had always believed in keeping herself to herself.

28 More Interviews

Thursday morning.

Britkwik Ltd.

The sort of name that gives no clue as to the product. And there was no mention of the product in the advertisement.

Lorries. Bright yellow. All it says on them is Britkwik Ltd. Filled with cartons. Perhaps they make cartons.

Anonymous dusty sheds, haphazardly arranged. A smell of anonymous dusty sheds.

Ushered into waiting room, then straight into office. Must give a good impression, judicious admixture of honesty and deception.

Still don't know what the hell they make.

'What we need here at Britkwik is enthusiasm. Do you feel you could sell our product with enthusiasm?'

'Yes, sir. I do.'

'Good. What qualities would you emphasize if you were conducting our sales campaign?'

'Well, I suppose its–er–er high quality. Its–er strength. And reliability.'

'What about its appearance?'

'Well I'd say it was er very functional and yet-er elegant.'

'I see. How would you describe its taste?'

'Well-er I'd say it had a-er taste that was both-er simple and also sophisticated.'

'We make paper handkerchiefs, Mr Bellamy.'

Thursday afternoon.

The British Tabulated Filings Corporation.

One or two drinks at lunchtime. Unwise, but needed these days. A sense of hopelessness and irresponsibility, coupled with a profound lack of ambition where the tabulating of filings – or was it the filing of tabulations – was concerned.

A vast place, with a central building large enough to house the Concorde. Great sliding doors. It must have been used for something else before the BTFC took it over.

Outside, an arterial road. On either side of the arterial road, factories, light industries. Beyond the factories, gasworks and marshalling yards. No sign of human habitation.

Robert had decided on a different tactic. A desperate tactic. Total honesty. He was like a football team which doesn't try, not because it doesn't want to win but because it knows that however hard it tries it will lose, and it seeks a kind of refuge in seeming to accept defeat willingly, and it finds there is no refuge there.

'What do you know about tabulated filings?'
'Nothing. I'm not even sure what they are.'
'I see. Then why did you apply for the job?'
'I'm applying for every job that sounds remotely suitable.'
'Why did you leave your previous job?'
'I was sacked.'
'Why?'
'I used the non-executive toilet, and I drew a caricature of the Exports Manager on the wall.'
'Thank you very much, Mr Bellamy, for coming to see us.'

Friday morning.
Mercury Electronics Ltd.
A kind of squashed and elongated Gaumont Cinema. Mysterious buzzings from behind locked doors. A flash of blue light. A smell of canteen.

Nervous. Today caring very deeply, very anxious, desperate for work. Try total dishonesty this time, since total honesty was such a fiasco. Tell them exactly what they want to hear.

'Why do you want to join us?'

'Because I think you're just the kind of company on which this country's future depends. The world of electronics is expanding rapidly. Britain has always played a leading role in electronics, and I want to help her to continue to do so.'

'I see. What particular qualities do you think you can bring to this work?'

'I work hard. I'm imaginative and far-seeing but also good at details. I can both accept and delegate responsibility.'

'You haven't any experience of electronics, have you?'

'Not professionally, no. But they've always interested me. Even as a small boy I loved electricity. Not for me the delights of engine spotting and stamp collecting. It was just electricity, electricity, electricity, morning, noon and night.'

Friday afternoon.

The McMurdoch-Strong Group of Companies.

Luxury. Deep carpets. Sepulchral hush. Elegant tables.

He'd had a drink or two at lunchtime. Nothing much, just to bolster the spirits after the failure of the morning, after watching their faces growing glazed with boredom and disbelief.

He'd tried a veal and ham pie but hadn't been able to get it down. Too dry. He couldn't eat things these days, couldn't get them down.

'This way please, Mr Bellamy.'

'Thank you. Oh, sorry.'

'It doesn't matter. They're plastic.'

'Oh, good.'

'Sit down, Mr Bellamy. This is Mr Forrest, and this is Mr Watson.'

'Nice to meet you, Mr Forrest, Mr Watson.'

'Have you been drinking?'

'Only one or two. Listen, I'll tell you what Mr Forrest wants to know, and Mr Watson.'

'We're wasting our time. Now come on, Mr Bellamy.'

'You want to know what's wrong with British industry. Well, I'll tell you.'

'Now come on. We don't want to have to fetch the police.'

'Mr Forrest and Mr Watson, that's what's wrong with British industry. People like you, and all your bloody silly questions, and plastic flowers, that's what's wrong with British industry. All right, I'm going. I know when I'm not wanted. You don't . . .'

'Mind the door.'

'You don't want me because you think I'm no good. And you're right.'

'Mind the step.'

'I'm useless. Absolutely useless. I am probably the most useless person you have ever interviewed.'

29 A Happy New Year

Robert had a couple of drinks at home in order to raise his spirits sufficiently to enable him to face the prospect of going to the pub. This was a really low ebb, uncovering uncharted wrecks, but no treasure.

He could not have said at what stage he decided to put an end to it all, or exactly when it occurred to him that he couldn't face a new year. No one can ever record the exact moment at which he catches a disease.

Now he went to the Blessington Arms. The idea of a slow pallid pint revolted him. Wine spoke of irrelevant things like culture and good taste. Whisky was what he wanted, a cultured drink too, but also fiery. The moment its fire was withdrawn he began to shiver.

After one drink he left the Blessington Arms, for fear he would have to talk to someone he knew. He wanted anonymity, and chose a great dark vault of a pub, with Victorian fittings dimly visible through the gloom.

We only have the one death. It is up to us to make it a good one. It satisfied him, aesthetically, that he should die on this night of senseless human optimism, this tawdry New Year's Eve. At midnight. As they linked arms and sang. That would be very satisfactory.

He had resolved, during the days following Christmas, not to ring anybody up, but to wait for them, to test them. Only Dick had rung on Thursday. Dick wanted him to go for dinner, to sit there with him and Sonia. Well, said he wanted. He wasn't inviting him so as to gloat, to taunt him with Sonia, Dick wasn't like that, not a nasty person. No, he was doing it because they were worried, they were treating him as a little child, giving him a nice dinner to cheer him up, taking him as a guest for better for worse, for richer for poorer till the end of the evening did them part. What was so unbearable was that they didn't want to see him any more, he was an embarrassment, but because they were nice people they would continue to see him. He couldn't bear that. So he said, I notice you don't invite me on New Year's Eve. A good thrust. Well, they couldn't, there was something arranged. Robert knew how it was. And Robert made what at the time seemed rather a telling riposte, but it didn't seem so effective in retrospect. Oh yes, I know how it is, he said. So anyway then he said, with an accuracy that must have hurt – not that he wanted to hurt, but was forced to – 'You think you can buy your conscience off with one lousy meal.' That one hit home. And then he rang off. Well, he didn't feel bitter against them, it was just the way things were.

He hadn't rung Bernard. He felt guilty about that. He felt shocked by what Cerise had said. He felt guilty about Jean, about accepting Bernard's view of Jean so completely. At some other time perhaps he might have tried to make amends. But not now. It was beyond him now.

Push the glass forward. Have it refilled. Pay two and seven. No need for the human voice. Automata.

He went over to a table and sat down. He was tired. All the morning he had walked through London, walking on and on, anything to keep going, to be part of the crowds on the pavements, perhaps even to meet someone he knew. And he had. A familiar face. Polly. Polly, of the purple paintings, from one crowded evening of a distant past. 'It's Polly' he had said. She hadn't recognized him, had sought in her memory and perhaps vaguely remembered. He had seen all this, seen her thinking what a down and out he looked, longing to get away, but too polite. Married to a rich man, catholic, six children including triplets. Fat, fertile, sexy. Elegant. Beautifully groomed, that was the phrase. He asked her about her paintings. 'Oh, I don't do them any more,' she said. 'But they were so important to you,' he said. She looked at him almost pityingly and said: 'They were just one of those things'. He was appalled at the distance between them. 'How are your grisly family?' he said. 'What on earth do you mean?' she said. 'What do you know about my family?' He felt the blood rising to his cheeks. 'Come and have a coffee,' he said, and it sounded utterly absurd, the moment he'd said it. 'Thank you,' she said politely but coolly, 'but I'm meeting my husband.' And off she went. And he walked on, on and on.

A middle-aged man in a long grey raincoat was sitting opposite him, making abstruse calculations – calculations are always abstruse – on a tiny piece of paper. Robert asked him if he would mind keeping his place, and the man indicated, in the soft tones of Erin, that such a task would not be unwelcome to him, and that he was confident of his ability to carry it out satisfactorily. Nor was his good opinion of himself unfounded, for when Robert returned with his whisky the seat was still vacant.

'Thank you,' said Robert.

'You're welcome,' said the Irishman.

Windows. Seen through the windows, lights. A flickering fire seen through a window from the top of a bus. Ferns beautifully arranged in the window of a tiny Danish house. Sunlight over a Suffolk estuary. The smell of cigars and baking bread in a little Amsterdam street. A tall girl with corn-coloured hair blowing a hooter on a canal narrow boat two fields away. A train seen from a road. A road seen from a train. Other people's lives. And superimposed upon them, an imposition, a cavernous smoky pub, a middle-aged Irishman, and you.

'Will you give me the pleasure of buying you a drink?' said the Irishman.

'Well – er —'

'Good. Good.'

The Irishman went to the bar. Robert had suddenly reached a kind of peace, an equatorial state of mind, where time passed unbelievably slowly, and his mind had been made up.

The Irishman gave him his drink. His mouth was thin and downturned, an exile's mouth, but sensitive and kind. His eyes were bloodshot and wistful, an exile's eyes, but gentle and humorous. He spoke.

'You are in trouble,' he said. 'That's why I have bought you a drink. I have a nose for it. Yes. Ah, that's better. You're an educated man.'

'Reasonably.'

'Education. I never had the disadvantage of that. I've had to find my own way through the labyrinth. It is, is it not, a labyrinth? Do you take my meaning? Do you agree?'

'Yes. Yes, I do.'

'Yes. A labyrinth. That's what it is. There's no two ways about it. But education, that raises expectations which cannot be fulfilled. You are an Englishman?'

'Yes.'

'A terrible burden, for a sensitive man like yourself. Nobody likes the overdog. As a young man what I felt for the English was a kind of admiration tempered by blind hatred. You can understand that?'

'I can. Absolutely.'

'They'd kept us down, you see. In our place. Infra dig in the ribs. And so England is riddled with guilt. Every young Englishman is born guilty. Now that's a terrible thing. Original sin, yes, all right, I've time for that one, but original guilt, there you have me, I won't stand for it. I am damned, but it's not my fault. I am damned, but I'm damned if I'll let it worry me. Do these thoughts not coincide in some way with your mood?'

'Yes. They do.'

'Politically, now, how do you stand? Somewhat communistical, I would say, in an ideological sense rather than a political one. Am I right?'

'Yes, you are. You're absolutely right. Amazing.'

'I make it my business to be.'

'In my opinion . . .'

'Opinions. I've no use for them. They're a waste of time.'

'Will you have another drink?'

'Thank you. I will.'

In two and a half hours I will kill myself, thought Robert, as he bought the drinks.

'Ah, thank you. Your good health.'

'And yours.'

'You ask me about my calculations. I will tell you. Yes. Well, it's a kind of an exercise, to soothe the mind. I take a large number, in this case: two seven six nine one one eight four three seven one two three four five six seven eight nine eight seven six five four three two one one two two three three four four five five six six seven seven eight eight nine nine eight eight seven seven six six five five four four three three two two one one three five eight one two three seven eight. And then I divide it by two, again and again and again. Why do I do it? Because it's there. So much for Sir Edmund Hillary. What does my pattern suggest? All is arbitrary. All is meaningless. Any pattern we create is trapped within the chaos around us. That accords with your mood?'

'In a way.'

'I will tell you this. For all to be meaningless would itself be a meaning. A man can be a passionate believer in atheism. In Ireland it might take great faith. Personally, it's not for me. I'm a religious man. I believe in God. I don't go to church. I got brassed off with that. It didn't coincide with my feelings. But I believe. Now to me God is symbolized, for no reason whatever, by the figure nought. Do you take the meaning of my pattern now?'

'Yes.'

This is a one-sided conversation, thought Robert.

'I will tell you a story. One day I caught the midnight train from Dublin to Cork.'

'That's a bloody lie,' said a second Irishman.

'Why is that a bloody lie? What do you know about it?' said the first Irishman.

'There is no midnight train to Cork, and you know it.'

'I do not.'

'The midnight train is to Limerick. It was to Limerick you went. Admit it now. You're a liar.'

Robert slipped out unnoticed, and set off for home. The gaping hole in the road opposite, where demolition had taken place, was a hole in his head. The people gaping at the gaping hole were his own futility. A chimney cowl was a vulture, turning to get a better look at its intended dinner. A luncheon vulture. Lonely men were potential assassins. He felt hungry, but didn't fancy a meal in a café, the self-condemned man's last breakfast at ten o'clock at night.

He climbed the stairs to his room and went into the little kitchenette. There was the stove. That was where it would happen. He got out his bottle of whisky, poured himself a glass, added a similar quantity of water, and began to drink slowly, to keep himself at this same level of intoxication. He made himself two sandwiches of red Cheshire cheese. Then he sat down in front of the television and switched it on.

He got out his writing pad and began to write.

Dear Aunt Margaret,

By the time you receive this letter I shall be dead. Please don't let it upset you. It's best this way. I have become an embarrassment to everyone. And please don't think that this is something which any action on your part could have avoided.

You still have your faith. I do not, but you cannot claim a monopoly on theories of damnation. This world is damned by its own stupidity. It is a secular and therefore temporal damnation, but none the less terrible for that.

I haven't made a will and believe you are my next of kin.

There isn't a lot of money as I have given most of it away, but I calculate that I have about £986 15 7d. I would like you to give the money away since I know you would not like to keep it yourself. Could you give £10 to each of the girls in the third-floor typing pool at Cadman and Bentwhistle, £100 to a middle-aged Irishman, name unknown, who drinks in the Pike and Osprey, Kentish Town (saloon bar) and can be recognized by his habit of making abstruse calculations on tiny pieces of paper, £100 to Jean Howes, nee Tibberley, of 27, The Driveway, Pinner, and £300 to an elderly beggar whom I saw in Soho Square on Friday, and whom I presume regularly frequents the Soho area. He bears a distinct resemblance to Hitler and called at your house once. I hope you will accede to my requests, strange though they are, for two reasons – because they further the cause of social justice, and because my mother would have wished it.

I calculate that the residue will be sufficient to pay for my funeral expenses, and any unpaid bills which may turn up.

I hope you are well and will continue so for many years.

 With love
  Robert

He poured another glass of whisky and watched the television for a few moments. Then he took another sheet of paper and wrote:

Dear Bernard,
 Cheer up. There is always someone worse off than you.
 Love
  Robert

Then he wrote a third letter:

Dear Dick and Sonia,

Please do not feel guilty. There are many reasons for this and you are not to blame. I am to blame for being what I am.

The television is building to its great climax. They are showing us all the celebrities who are present at the New Year Party, the idea being that we shall all be filled with delight at being able to share, vicariously, their glamour. This obscene activity is a fitting background to my last moments on earth.

I have enjoyed much of my life and in the past I was capable of giving pleasure. I can do so no longer. I have become a burden upon my family, my friends, my acquaintances, the state, everybody. The modern world has no place for burdens. It worships success and I suppose that is a justifiable philosophy, provided the essential corollary is followed – that those who are not successful are eliminated. One day our technological society will achieve that. In the meantime, it is up to us failures to do it ourselves.

I wish you every happiness and thank you both for many rewarding moments of friendship.

For auld lang syne
    Robert

He poured himself another whisky, and then wrote a fourth letter.

Dear Sir John Barker,

By the time your secretary decides that there is no point in subjecting you to this letter, I shall be dead. Remember only this. Work is a very important part of human life, and if men wish to retain any degree of sanity in any kind of a social system then work must be enjoyable. People need to enjoy themselves, and to be useful to other people. All workers are human and must be treated as such.

I remain, but not for long,
    Yours faithfully
      Robert Bellamy

His next letter was to Mr Mendel.

Dear Mr Mendel,

By the time you receive this letter I shall be dead, and at last you will be free of your statistical worry. You should have several years' freedom from further risk. You will find a month's rent in advance beside these letters, which I would like you to post.

Thank you for being such a good landlord,
      Robert Bellamy.

The Archbishop of Canterbury was now speaking. Robert wished he could share his beliefs.

Dear Archbishop of Canterbury,

I saw your appearance on television and as I was committing suicide at the time I felt that I just must write to you. What you say about human life is so true, but I cannot agree when you say that there is a God. The following paradoxical thought occurs to me. If there was no purpose whatever behind life, but everyone was like you, there would be no problem.

    Yours sincerely
      Robert Bellamy.

Big Ben began to strike. Robert went into the kitchenette and turned on the gas. Then he went back to see the television. There it was – the balloons, everything. Another false dawn, in all its full horror.

He went back into the kitchenette.

30 Consequences

Bernard said: 'I failed him, just as I've failed you.'
Jean said: 'It's been my failure as well.'
Bernard said: 'We must make a new start.'

Frances said: 'Good Lord. Robert's dead.'
Henry said: 'Who's Robert?'
Frances said: 'No one you know. Just an old friend.'
Henry said: 'Darling, what's wrong?'
Frances said: 'Nothing. It's nothing.'

The undertaker said: 'That'll be £49–19–11d.'

Dick said: 'It's no use blaming ourselves.'
Sonia said: 'But we are partly to blame.'
Dick said: 'We'll frame those photos of him.'
Sonia said: 'And keep them, for ever, on the sideboard.'

The pathologist said: 'He was a well-nourished man, five-foot eleven, and weighing 12 stone 11 pounds. Death was due to carbon monoxide poisoning.'

Sir John Barker said: 'He didn't die in vain. There are going to be some changes around here. In future there'll be just one canteen for everyone. And a club for all ranks. It'll be called the Bellamy Room. I want you to run it, Tadman-Evans.'

.   .   .   .   .

Mr Mendel said: 'At last I can relax. He was always a thoughtful tenant.'

Mr Randolph Clegg said: 'Bless you, lady. God bless you.'

Martin said: 'He needed me, and I let him down. Help me, Dr Schmuck. Take me back.'
Dr Wilson said: 'The name is now Wilson. I can't help you, Martin. I couldn't help him. I'm useless.'
Martin said: 'We're in the same boat. Perhaps we can help each other, Dr Sch – Wilson.'
Dr Wilson said: 'We can try.'

Stephen said: 'Should we look again at our traditional way of seeing in the New Year? We take it all for granted, the balloons, the linked arms, the frenzied gaiety. But one man did not take it all for granted. For him there were no balloons. No arms were linked with his this New Year's Eve.'

Doreen said: 'That's our Robert.'
Her husband said: 'Who?'
Doreen said: 'This feller that killed himself.'
Her husband said: 'You never told me about him.'
Doreen said: 'It was before I knew you, love, and he was just a friend. Poor Robert. It's put me right off my tea, has that. Amos?'
Her husband said: 'Yes?'
Doreen said: 'He must have been lonely. It's a terrible thing, loneliness. Let's not go down the club tonight, eh? Let's go and see your mum.'
Her husband said: 'Bloody hell.'

The world said: 'Life must go on.'

3 I New Year Resolution

It doesn't seem right that he should die just yet. It seems unnecessarily harsh, just as it would be irresponsible to give him the idea that from now on everything will be better, and he will be a new man.

Let's say the gas ran out in his meter.

Robert has created an air of perversity around him, and he has a knack of turning his humiliations into triumphs merely by relating them. It seems only just therefore to give him the chance of turning this moment of despair and bathos into a Robert Bellamy incident – the time I tried to kill myself and the gas ran out in the meter – and to give him a piece of good luck at the time when he seems to desire it least.

There is the question of will-power, too. How much did Robert really have a will to die? He knew that the money was low in the meter. He could have made certain of death, simply by putting in another shilling. He didn't, because this little chink of hope was attractive to him. He was placing a bet with fate, at extremely long odds, but he knew, looking back over his own past form, that the going suited him, and that he had a chance.

I know this because I was there, scratching around in his head. No wonder he thought they were staging a ten-pin bowling contest there. Well, from now on I'm going to let him keep his thoughts to himself. A fat lot of good I've done him.

He opens the windows and takes a deep breath of London air. He goes to the lavatory and is sick. He goes out into the street and walks up and down. He returns to his room, reads through the letters he has written without registering any decipherable emotion, and tears them up. He picks up the bottle of whisky, almost half full still, and pours himself a stiff drink. I watch objectively.

He takes the bottle and goes into the kitchenette. It looks as if he is going to throw the remainder of its contents down the sink. A banal sentimental image suggestive of new starts, sudden accesses of courage, an end to all despair. I cannot remain objective. He begins to pour. I am about to lean out and restrain him, when he grabs a tumbler and holds it under the stream of whisky. Then it dawns on him that he need not pour the whisky at all, now that he is not pouring it away. He puts the bottle on the draining board and carefully pours the whisky back into it from the glass. I'm ashamed I didn't trust him more fully.

At two seventeen he finishes his drink and goes out into the hall, taking with him a range of articles sufficient to let us safely deduce that he is going to have a bath. At two fifty-four he returns. By two fifty-nine, after a series of events too banal to mention, he is in bed. At three eight, three fifteen, three twenty-seven and three thirty-one he turns over. By three thirty-six he is asleep.

He sleeps until eleven fifty-two. By one eight, after further events unworthy of relation, he is ready to go out. I follow him. At one forty-seven he enters a nondescript café and has – I sit at the next table – minestrone soup and ravioli. I have the same. I think I can deduce, without lapsing from my objectivity, that he does not enjoy his meal.

He then walks to the main post office at Trafalgar Square, and makes some inquiries. I don't hear what they are because I have been held up at a pedestrian crossing.

I see him go into a phone booth. He appears to be unable to get through to the number of his choice.

I follow him to Soho. We go along Old Compton Street, up Dean Street, down Frith Street and up Greek Street. In Greek Street he hands a sum of money to a busker whose efforts to entertain the passers-by can only be described as perfunctory. I note a distinct resemblance to Hitler. I suppose Hitler really did die in the bunker?

In the evening he calls, to my surprise, an Amsterdam number. There is no reply. He goes to the Blessington Café, then makes another call. Again there is no reply. He goes to the Blessington Arms and stays fifty-two minutes. He makes another call, and again there is no reply.

He goes to bed. He gets up. There is intermittent drizzle. He is subdued. He buys provisions and cooks a frugal lunch. He reads *The Times* and sends off some more applications for jobs. He makes two more calls to Amsterdam, without achieving contact. I only hope the whole book hasn't been as boring as this.

At six twenty-three he rings again, and seems to have trouble, for he invokes the help of the operator. After a frustrating wait he says: 'Fine. Yes, I'll be in,' and rings off.

At six thirty-four the phone rings. He leaps towards it, comically anxious.

'Hullo . . . I'll see.' He goes upstairs. I lay out his pencil and paper on the table, to save time. We must get to 'The End' soon. He comes downstairs. 'He's not in . . . Yes. Just a moment. I'll get a pencil.' He suits the action to the word. 'Right . . . Many happy returns. Love from all at number fifty-seven. Right.' He takes the message upstairs.

At six forty-four the phone rings again. Again he answers with comic eagerness.

'Hullo . . . Oh, hullo, Bernard . . . Oh, God . . . I'm sure you are. How's Jean feeling? . . . I don't see why . . . It seems a perfectly sensible question to me . . . I'm not taking anyone's side . . . I don't know the facts, do I? . . . Well, you can . . . Of course you can. I've got a camp bed . . . As long as you like . . . of course not . . . of course . . . of course not . . . of course . . . of course not . . . of course . . . of course not . . of course . . . of course not . . . Well, the thing is, I must stay in. The operator's getting an important number for me. At least, she's supposed to be . . . Well, whenever you like . . . O K., I'll see you later . . . Bye.'

He rings off. Dr Strickman comes upstairs.

'There's a message for you,' says Robert. 'Many happy returns. Love from all at number fifty-seven.'

Dr Strickman faints. Robert gets a glass of water and throws it over him. Dr Strickman recovers. Robert gives him some whisky and escorts him to his room.

At seven two the phone rings again. Robert puts down the sherry, which I forgot to mention he has poured out, and leaps out into the hall, just beating Miss Flodden to the phone.

'Hullo . . . Anna? . . . Hullo, Anna.' I suspected this. It's absurd. We hardly know her. Half of me, the literary half, is worried because an absurdly happy ending is on the cards. The other half, the human half, says 'Hooray'. 'Yes. I expect you are. How are you, Anna? . . . Good. You've not got yourself engaged to some squash-playing Dutchman, have you? . . . Well, no reason, I just thought you might have. Get on with it! 'Look, Anna, the thing is, I'd like to see you again . . . Well, I like you. I enjoyed seeing you.' I don't even have any clear memory of what she looked like. She wasn't supposed to be so important. Does he, I wonder. 'I know, but . . . this weekend . . . I know, but you see I've got to come to Europe and . . . Paris. So you see it won't be much out of my way . . . No, one of the best ways from London to Paris is via Amsterdam.' Why didn't he say Düsseldorf? He isn't safe to be out without an author. 'I'll come over on Friday. I'll let you know the time of arrival later . . . Yes . . . Yes . . . Well, see you on Friday . . . What? You've been sick? . . . Oh, Sickert. Oh, really. Very good . . . Well, anyway, I'll see you on Friday, Anna . . . Bye.'

He pours some more sherry, and puts an unopened tin into a saucepan of water.

He makes a telephone call.

'Hullo, Dick. Robert here . . . Fine. How are you? . . . Good. Look, I just wanted to say I'm sorry I was shirty and will you two come out to dinner with me some time? ... Good. Well, what about tomorrow? ... Thursday, then. Good ... Well, I thought "The Just Good Friends". I'll order Menu A ... Fine ... Well, a pub, I should think. What about The Intrepid Pigeon? ... O.K., six thirty. Bye, Dick. Love to the Sondle-Bundle.'

He paces up and down nervously. I fill in the time with a few speculations. Supposing I was having one of those postscripts which so unfairly tell you all the things you oughtn't to want to know, but do, what would it say? Robert married Anna and they had five children, and Van Gend was best man? Robert married Anna and on their honeymoon he fell into the Tagus? Robert's relationship with Anna turned out to be as indecisive as that with Sonia? Robert and Anna went to see two Ingmar Bergman films and found they had nothing in common and never saw each other again? Robert got a splendid job and lived happily ever after? Robert made a second, and this time successful, suicide attempt six months later? I don't know enough about Anna to predict with any confidence. I'm not sure that I know enough about Robert. I'm not sure that one can know enough to predict a person's future.

Back in his present, Robert is now removing his tin from the saucepan. He opens it. It squirts over his shirt. He empties the contents on to a plate. They do not look alluring. He does not look allured.

He sits on the Finnish sofa and begins to eat.

He switches on the television. A pin-point of light grows into an announcer. The announcer says: 'There now follows a party political broadcast on behalf of the Labour party. This broadcast is also being shown on BBC 2 and ITV.'

Dick's father appears. He has managed to make himself look thoroughly drab. As he speaks Robert eats his supper and presses his remote control switch repeatedly with his foot, sending Dick's father back and forth from one channel to another.

'Living in the jet . . . breakthrough. We must give a lead . . . challenge of statistical . . . end dark ages . . . purposive expansion . . . progress in last ten years than in the previous thousand . . . relevant to the age of automation . . . this dynamic age . . . excitement . . . of jet . . . build a new world together.'

OBSTACLES *to* YOUNG LOVE
DAVID NOBBS

'Three mighty obstacles threaten the burgeoning love of childhood sweethearts Timothy Pickering and Naomi Walls. They are Steven Venables, a dead curlew and God.'

1978: Two lovers perch precariously on the cusp of adulthood. Timothy's life ambition is to take on his father's taxidermy business; while Naomi dreams of a career on stage.

Across the decades their lives continue to interweave, and occasionally cross — bound by the pull of intoxicating first love. But will their destinies ultimately unite them?

Nobbs's rare comic talent delivers a memorable and moving, a tale of love won and love lost. You will never look at the art of taxidermy in the same way again.

'Thank goodness for David Nobbs! He carries on the comic tradition of P G Wodehouse with this marvellous new book...' Joanne Harris